Oxfordshire Education Committee
Curriculum Development

The Heritage of Literature Series

SECTION B NO. 94

THE GUN

THE GUN

C. S. FORESTER

with Introduction and Notes by
D. J. TAYLOR, M.A.

Illustrated with line drawings

LONGMANS

LONGMANS, GREEN AND CO LTD
48 Grosvenor Street, London W1
*Associated companies, branches and representatives
throughout the world*

First published 1933 by The Bodley Head Ltd
This edition © Longmans, Green & Co Ltd 1964
*This edition first published by Longmans, Green &
Co Ltd in association with The Bodley Head Ltd
1964
Second Impression 1964
Third Impression 1965
Fourth Impression 1966*

PRINTED IN GREAT BRITAIN BY
RICHARD CLAY (*The Chaucer Press*) LTD,
BUNGAY, SUFFOLK

CONTENTS

INTRODUCTION
1. *The Napoleonic Wars*   vii
2. *The Gun*   xiii
3. *On Guns and Projectiles*   xxv

THE GUN   1

BOOK LIST FOR FURTHER READING   221

NOTES   223

QUESTIONS   251

ILLUSTRATIONS

A drawing of The Gun is on page vi, and where necessary the Notes (pages 223-249) are accompanied by explanatory drawings.

A map is given facing page 1.

v

muzzle

chase

trunnion

cap squares

vent or touch hole

cascable

elevation scale

elevation wedge

elevation screw

trail eye

INTRODUCTION

1—*The Napoleonic Wars*

Although the British people felt a good deal of sympathy for the early stages of the French revolution, the Reign of Terror, the execution of the king and queen, the spreading influence of the French refugee nobles, the misgivings of landowners and manufacturers, and the declared intention of the new French leaders to spread their republican principles abroad, all persuaded the British government to join in 1793 with Prussia, Spain and Austria in their war against the French Republic. But the coalition was so divided in its purpose that it served only to bring the rival French factions more closely together. So France grew in power and in 1795 Prussia and Spain made peace. In 1796 Bonaparte was given the command of the French armies in Italy and after a series of brilliant victories Austria was glad to make peace.

Britain, with command of the seas to guard her shores, alone fought on. In 1798 Bonaparte led a strong expedition to Egypt but Nelson found the French fleet and transports in Aboukir Bay and destroyed them, leaving the French stranded. With this encouragement a second coalition was formed of Russia, Austria and Britain. But a French army under Masséna beat a combined Russian and Austrian force at Zurich and in 1799, Napoleon, who had returned from Egypt without his army and who had made himself the

First Consul by a military coup d'état, led a fresh army over the Alps to win a decisive victory over the Austrians. The British were alarmed at what the coalition had cost them in gold and disrupted trade, and peace was made with France through the Treaty of Amiens in March 1802.

But by 1803 it was clear that neither side intended to honour the terms of the treaty. Britain feared the large army quartered in the Low Countries and felt a growing threat to her commercial interests. Thus the greatest European land power, France, faced the might of the most experienced sea power, Britain. But it was difficult for either to inflict any serious blow upon the other. By 1804, Napoleon had crowned himself Emperor of the French and had built up a great army, magnificently organized and superbly led. To subdue Britain, he considered direct invasion and a strict economic blockade which would bring an industrial slump and economic ruin upon her. Invasion barges were built, the troops were exercised and plans were made for the French fleets, blockaded in their ports of Brest and Toulon, to break free and assemble in the channel to escort the invading force. Admiral Nelson pursued the Toulon fleet to the West Indies and after it had taken refuge in Cadiz harbour, where it joined a Spanish fleet, he was able to bring them both to battle and defeat at Cape Trafalgar in October 1805. The French could no longer challenge Britain at sea. But Napoleon had already turned back to his European problems and stepped up the economic blockade. Austria, who had joined Russia and Britain in a third coalition in 1805, was defeated by Napoleon at Ulm and a few months later the Emperor defeated a combined Russian and Austrian force at Austerlitz. Prussia had belatedly joined the coalition but in 1806 was knocked out in a lightning campaign at Jena, from which Napoleon pushed rapidly on to close the Baltic ports. At last it seemed possible for him to close all the European ports to British goods and from Berlin he issued decrees which forbade all trade with Britain. Napoleon could now survey a defeated Europe. He gave kingdoms to his brothers, provinces to his marshals: he re-organized the constitution, the laws and the whole social structure of his realms.

Only Britain remained. In September 1807 British troops attacked Copenhagen, seized the Danish fleet and made off with it to prevent it falling into the hands of Napoleon. The Emperor was furious and in December declared that all ports in Europe, neutral or not, should be closed to British ships. But for many years, Portugal, with her long sea-coast, had provided Britain with an excellent back-door into Europe through which had passed loads of British manufactured goods to the willing continental buyers. The door was now to be shut. In November 1807, Napoleon moved a French army under Junot through Spain, with the consent of his puppet, Godoy, the Spanish Chief Minister, and with astonishing speed occupied Portugal. British warships escorted the Portuguese royal family to Brazil. One more State had been added to the Grand Empire: but events had been set in train which were to bring that Empire to its ruin.

Napoleon had contrived the Spanish support for his invasion by Machiavellian diplomacy, and now the King of Spain, Charles IV, was induced to arrest his dissolute, but popular son, Ferdinand, on a charge of treason. The outcry which this arrest provoked pushed the king and queen

A*

into a premature abdication. French troops had been garrisoned in Spain to keep open the line of communication
between Junot in Portugal and France and now Murat led
a substantial army into Spain, ostensibly to protect the
Spanish king from his rebellious subjects. Napoleon, inviting all the Spanish royal family to Bayonne, persuaded
Ferdinand to abdicate in return for a pension, while a few
compliant Spanish grandees offered the vacant throne of
Spain to Joseph Bonaparte, which he was graciously pleased
to accept. French troops now poured into Spain as an
undisguised army of occupation and Napoleon planned to
take Gibraltar and North Africa, and shut the British out
of the Mediterranean.

But the Emperor had not allowed for the courage and
the pride of the Spanish people. Fully alive to the weak-
nesses of their royal family they yet preferred their own
to the usurper. In Madrid and in the provinces the people
turned furiously on the French invaders and the Spanish
officials who had accepted them. They organized committees
and formed Juntas, to enrol soldiers, gather armaments, to
declare loyal support to Prince Ferdinand and death to the
French. In 1808 Dupont's army of 30,000 was defeated at
Baylen by a ragged but jubilant Spanish force under
General Castaños, who reoccupied Madrid. The revolt
spread and the French fell back beyond the river Ebro
towards the Pyrénées. The hastily formed Juntas appealed
to Britain for military help and thus, in August, Sir Arthur
Wellesley landed at Mondego Bay with 13,000 British
troops. In three weeks he had won a skilful campaign at
Vimiero and the French made terms. Meanwhile in September 1808, Sir John Moore was ordered to Portugal with

35,000 men. A further 15,000 were to land at Corunna
under Sir David Baird, and leaving a strong garrison in
Portugal, Moore was to advance into Spain, join up with
Baird and give all possible assistance to the Spanish armies
in the expulsion of the French from that kingdom. This
was to be the largest British army assembled since Marlborough, and Moore, who had trained it, was not the man
to deploy it rashly. But the Spanish armies, though
courageous and determined, were proudly provincial and
had little communication with one another. Continued
local Spanish success encouraged Moore to move into
Spain, but Napoleon had not been idle. He had gathered
a grand army of 200,000 of his finest troops and crossed
the Pyrénées like a whirlwind. Spanish armies bravely stood
across the road of the new invader. General Blake was
defeated at Zornoza and two weeks later at Espinosa, and
this is the retreating army with which Forester's story
begins. The Estremadurans were beaten at Burgos and
General Castaños at Tudela. Moore had hoped to occupy
Madrid but Napoleon was already there. Fighting a
brilliant rearguard action, Moore retreated to Corunna
where he made his last stand.

In April 1809, Wellington landed in Portugal to take
over the British force, to train Portuguese forces and to
link up with the Spanish. Facing him was Victor with
30,000 men on the Portuguese frontier, Soult in northern
Portugal, while Ney held Galicia and the route to France.
Wellington defeated Soult at Oporto, clearing the French
out of Portugal; and, as Wellington advanced, the French
fell back upon Madrid, but with Soult threatening to come
between Wellington and his Lisbon base he prudently

retired to Badajoz and Masséna now came fresh from France with 80,000 men to finish off the campaign. But Wellington had prepared immensely strong defences at Torres Vedras across the peninsula above Lisbon, from the Tagus to the sea, and he fell back upon these, fighting tenaciously. Now, while Masséna cautiously probed the defences, Wellington enjoyed the advantage of sea power, with supplies and reinforcements coming from home, letters and instructions arriving in a matter of days and the wounded evacuated in the comparative comfort of transports. The French on the other hand were at the extreme end of a long and extremely vulnerable line. Masséna lost 25,000 men in the winter 1810-11 in skirmishes, sickness and desertion while waiting profitlessly outside the lines of Torres Vedras. Constant guerilla activity, often with arms supplied by British squadrons operating along the northern coast, tied up the French garrisons and weakened them slowly with ambush, sniping, poison and disease, and this is where the events of *The Gun* fit into the larger pattern of the Peninsula campaign.

Masséna in 1811 began to lose the initiative and, feeling Wellington's patrols probing ever more strongly, he fell back into Spain. In a series of hard-fought battles Wellington pushed back Masséna, then besieged and took Badajoz and Cuidad Rodrigo in 1812.

In every province the Spanish generals continued to fight against the French invaders. They lost the pitched battles but it was clear that the French occupied only the ground they stood on. Every citadel was beleaguered, every road cut. Napoleon had taken many of his veterans from Spain for his Russian campaign and the French Marshals

were often at loggerheads. Others were so cut off that they
knew little of the turning tide of war as Wellington pushed
steadily on. After Salamanca in 1812 Wellington entered
Madrid and continued in 1813 along the great road through
Burgos to Vittoria, and finally into France itself.

Perhaps as Wellington crossed the river Salas on his way
to Burgos he turned his head to see beside the empty
fortifications a bronze column which was its only memorial.
Perhaps like so many others he paused a moment to run
his fingers round the inscribed muzzle and read the words—

AND OUR MOUTHS SHALL SHEW FORTH THY PRAISE.

2—The Gun

> For want of a nail, the shoe was lost,
> For want of a shoe, the horse was lost,
> For want of a horse, the rider was lost,
> For want of a rider, the battle was lost,
> For want of a battle, the kingdom was lost,
> And all for the want of a horseshoe nail.

Napoleon lost his empire because Wellington was able to
defeat the French Marshals in Spain, because they could
not join forces, because the roads were in the hands of the
guerilleros, because with scattered remnants of the Spanish
army they fought on with whatever weapons they could
find, and because—perhaps—there was a Father Prieto who
did save a big gun from the French.

Even before Homer described the long siege of Troy, war

was the theme of many an ancient saga. Sometimes they told of human courage and endurance but often they revealed man's cruelty and destructiveness. Some stories of war are written from the lofty viewpoint of the historian, in which battles and campaigns are mere details in the elaborate tapestry of the period; others show in close-up the sufferings of men and women, children and animals, the easy return to barbarism and the futile destruction of familiar things. In either case the writer has a duty to describe events as they really were, without exaggeration and without shirking the full burden of truth. This is what C. S. Forester does when he takes his readers into the smoke of the battle with his great eighteen-pounder, but in between engagements he also reminds them of the wider issues of Wellington's Peninsular campaign and of Napoleon's conquest of Europe. Grandeur and comedy, the grotesque and the tragic appear in the same chapter, for these are all a part of the muddle of war which may bring out the best and the worst in men even in the same hour.

Many novels are successfully based on the life of the hero but this is much too limited for a war story such as *The Gun.* For a soldier sees war in vivid but disconnected scenes; he may be killed or taken prisoner and he is seldom aware of what is happening on some other part of the battlefield. By making the gun itself the central figure of his story, C. S. Forester builds up a motivating force which is much stronger than any human power, and from the little, chance-met lives of the Spanish guerilleros he constructs on a vast scale the classical tragic rise and fall of fortune. But within this design we are concerned with the lives of human beings, with their brief moments of glory when they were the masters of the gun.

The first of the gun's new masters was Father Prieto. The Galicians, remote from the capital, had never been vastly concerned by the often scandalous affairs of the royal family and the central government in Madrid. But when Napoleon took away their king and threatened their religion they discovered a patriotism which sprang from their sense of independence and a piety which had always directed their feudal lives. It was thus natural that the parish priests should serve as local government links between the Galician Junta and the peasant villages, for they were educated, were natural leaders and were ready to die for their faith. Father Prieto had spent his life among these people and he knew how to curb their exuberance. When he saw the gun he at once recognized its value to the Spanish irregular army. The peasants trusted Father Prieto and respected him as the fount of wisdom. They willingly worked as he bid them to set the gun upon its wheels again. He explained how to load and fire the monster, translated the motto on its mouth and, by a great effort of memory, recalled how such heavy gun trails were moved on a limber similar to the heavy cart that Isodore Botto so unwillingly provided. Under Father Prieto's direction the gun was painfully hauled up into the mountains and, thanks to his prudence, it was hidden under a pile of loose stone in a quarry when his band, which, because of the great gun, had swollen to over a thousand—joined the Galician army to attack Marshal Soult. The French had pursued the army of Moore to Corunna and, though now isolated in the mountains, swept aside the Spanish irregu-

lars who dared to try to cut them off. Father Prieto they
hanged in Vigo market square for his part in the 'rebellion'
and to make a special example of the priests.

But his contribution to the Spanish resistance was not
in vain. For two years the gun safely waited for its next
master.

El Bilbanito—the young man from Bilbao, for it was
too dangerous to use a real name—was a guerillero, not a
brigand, though in practice there was little difference. His
harsh, hunted life in the mountains had not impoverished
his love of picturesque clothes nor had it weakened his
fierce independence and burning hatred of the French, who
had deposed his king and tried to impose their ways upon
the proud traditions of Spain. Two years of bitter war
had eliminated all the weak and careless from the
guerilleros, for the French hanged all they caught. He had
been quick to react to the latest French attack and had
saved most of his men, though it had been prudent to shoot
accidentally his too ambitious second-in-command. He was
furious that he had lost irreplaceable pack-mules and stores
and was powerless to hit back. He understood all too well
the French strategy in building forts to guard the bridges
which were the only easy crossing places of the deep
ravines that seamed the plains. To be caught on the plains
by the French cavalry meant certain disaster and the forts
could not be captured without a heavy gun. His band were
surly after their losses, but he faced them courageously and
hanged the traitor Botto to impress his ruthless will upon
his men. Botto's blurted secret had given El Bilbanito the
weapon he needed and he acted with instant resolution.
He force-marched his men over secret paths to the quarry,

organized the complete rebuilding of the gun-carriage and proudly proved the gun with his first shot. It was his iron will alone which drove on his toiling men and animals over impossible paths in the mountains down towards the plains and the French. He took draught animals from starving peasants, conscripted labour, and overcame every obstacle. It was not surprising that his men proudly wore a cock's feather in their hats and that he wrote peremptory letters to the Junta and other guerillero leaders demanding supplies and disdainfully inviting them to come and serve under him. Even Hugh and Carlos O'Neill bowed respect-fully when they met such a man with such a gun. But El Bilbanito had neither the experience nor the mag-nanimity to win the service of men whose pride was as great as his own, and the inevitable quarrel flared up between him and Carlos. Although allowed to fight with his chosen weapon, the knife, his over-confidence cost him his life and all his brave plans for loot, destruction and revenge.

Hugh and Carlos O'Neill were professional soldiers, trained in the Military Academy and experienced in battle against the French. They fought not for loot but because it was their duty and they were loyal to the king whose commission they carried. Love of their country did not cause them to under-estimate the military power of the French nor overlook the Spanish weakness. But the gun added a new factor to their military calculations, justifying operations which would otherwise have been wild gambles.

Tall and slender, their blue eyes contrasting with their dark hair, they were the descendants of an earlier O'Neill, an Ulster Chieftain who had fled to Spain seeking refuge from religious persecution after his army had suffered a disastrous defeat at the hands of the English. Coming from a long line of soldiers and with the blood of Irish kings in their veins, they had an inborn arrogance that singled them out even in a nation of proud men.

Captain Hugh O'Neill of the Ultonia Regiment was the elder brother, more experienced in military decisions and with the gift of knowing how to handle men. It was he who won over the Princesa Regiment, speaking to them in their own dialect, persuading even the officers to join his enterprise. He trained his now considerable army while his brother searched for ammunition. He devised the plan of attack on La Merced, and in him the guerillos lost the one man who might have led them to sustained victory.

Captain Carlos O'Neill was trained for the artillery and although technically gifted in military skills he lacked the sympathy and sense of leadership which officers and men loved in Hugh. Between them the brothers had all the qualities to direct a great enterprise but Carlos alone was a fighter, not a leader. Carlos proved his courage in the duel with El Bilbanito and the accurate shooting at La Merced demonstrated his artillery skill, but in many other qualities he was sadly lacking. He hated the indignity of sea-sickness and the necessity of having to ask Captain Brett humbly for supplies of ammunition. He lost his temper with the Colonel of the Princesa Regiment, and the merciless slaughter at La Merced was due partly to his grief for his brother's loss and partly to his cruelty. His Irish ancestry made him subject to fits of brooding melancholy and the responsibility of high command, his hatred

of the French and impatience with his own men added to
the moods. He lashed with his tongue and cut with his
whip all those who roused his anger. He sneered at the
Spanish irregulars who would run away at the first serious
French attack; but then he did not think of them as men
but as expendable material of war. At twenty-four he was
too young to exercise the power of life and death, yet when
the army camped before Leon, citizens of wealth and position who had collaborated with the French came secretly
to him begging for mercy. The executions in Leon began
as instruments of justice but soon became the symbols of
O'Neill's power and cruel pleasure. His attack on the
citadel at Leon was correctly planned and he did not shrink
from the possibility of heavy losses, but Brother Bernard's
white arsenic did his work for him. The Duke of Menjibar
was treated with scant respect when he came to claim the
Junta's appointment as Captain General of Leon, O'Neill
graciously accepting this office for himself. But he allowed
himself no rest: he felt that the kingdom was at stake and
he knew what an effect the fall of Leon would have on
the whole French military strategy in Spain: it all rested
with him. The rain and the bad roads irritated him and
the stupidity of his soldiers, whose barbarous language he
could not understand, drove him to a frenzy. He destroyed
all the French strong-points in the area. He was constantly
worried for food, clothing and supplies. He could delegate
his work to nobody, for there was nobody he could trust.
In such a mood he treated even the guerillero leaders like
dogs. Jorge's slow decision not to arrest El Platero was like
a warm glow of hope that lit up the black gloom
which had hypnotized them all. O'Neill could not at first

believe that they would dare to disobey. Too late he tried to recover his command but he was surrounded by men who had insults and blows to avenge, and he died fighting like an animal.

There was no obvious successor to O'Neill; but Jorge, who had taken charge of the gun after the death of El Bilbanito and who had led the revolt against O'Neill, was the only leader prepared to accept the responsibility for future decisions. Although a man of few words, this big boy from Rioja, with his quiet smile, had been El Bilbanito's deputy. He had learned to work the gun and led one half of the guerillero attack on the walls of Leon. As the chief of O'Neill's bodyguard he had arrested many men, including the Duke of Menjibar. Although not given to sudden anger, it was the weal on his neck from O'Neill's whip that had stung him to mutiny. Now that it was left to Jorge to make the decisions he relied more and more with simple peasant faith on the big gun which had never failed them. They would go to attack one French post after another, he thought, everywhere gaining strength until the war was won. And so they found themselves on the great road besieging the strong fortress of Salas. Other guerillero leaders characteristically began to worry over lines of retreat, but with all the confidence of a simple man Jorge worked out his plan of attack. A trained soldier would have realized that one eighteen-pounder was not enough to reduce a fortress such as Salas. But Jorge was an un-educated peasant, not accustomed to thinking in abstract terms. He had learned his skills through practice and his plan of attack on Salas proceeded step by step as he worked it out there on the ground. His parallels, approaches and battery were to Jorge commonsense solutions to a series of simple problems, but were in fact perfect examples of text-book siegecraft. An even better example of Jorge's genius for working out his problems on the ground was seen in his destruction of the regiment of the Imperial Guard. A number of guerillero bands had scurried away from Salas with no real plan to prevent the French regiment from reinforcing it, but at the ravine Jorge could visualize the battle; the mass of infantry, the gun firing grape from the side and the cavalry waiting the signal to charge through the shattered columns of the French. Jorge had by instinct a true general's sense of ground and sense of timing to use all the forces under his command in the best place at the best time.

After this complete success Jorge was undisputed head of all the forces before Salas and with peasant patience and persistence he resumed the difficult siege of Salas. Shrewd commonsense told him to fire at the base of the wall so that the collapsing masonry would fill the ditch and leave a slope to the breach. He also realized that the enemy would do all they could to destroy his gun and he was quick to counter-attack the sally from the fortress. A more experienced soldier would have guessed that the French might build up a gun-position to fire directly into his battery, but Jorge learned too late. With his gun destroyed, Jorge led a desperate attack on the unbroken walls of Salas but they were repulsed with heavy losses. Without the gun, the guerilleros had no common plan to continue the siege or resist the powerful French relieving forces. The vast army melted away and Jorge, not un-happily, returned to his mountains.

The shot that wounded Hugh O'Neill and robbed the gun of its best commander was fired by a Dutchman, Major Jonquier. He was typical of many of the foreign officers who served in the French Imperial Army. He was a soldier by trade and was content to do his duty. His own country was now a part of the French Empire and in contrast to the burning patriotism of the Spanish, he felt no resentment. He missed the little luxuries of his homeland but did his best to make life tolerable at La Merced with his own cows and chickens and tender care for his stomach. He had fortified the convent to cover the bridge and the road with fire from his six-pounders. He was not unduly alarmed when the sentries reported guerilleros on the march, as he had met them before and had every faith in his own defences even though his garrison was made up of young recruits. He was a careful commander and having checked the defences and taken precautions against a night attack he went to bed. Early next morning he made sure that all the garrison had hot food and he made his rounds giving instructions and making jokes to relieve their nerves. The first shot from the eighteen-pounder told him that La Merced was doomed, for they were out-gunned, outnumbered and could expect no relief from any other French force. But Jonquier refused to consider terms of surrender. His military training and some stubborn streak in his character determined him to resist. He himself shot back with his little six-pounder until it was destroyed and he steadied his men during the long bombardment which breached his walls. When the Spanish infantry attacked he rushed into the breach but no French soldier followed him. And so he died alone; a brave, unheroic, almost comic figure: a stranger fighting in a foreign country for an alien cause.

Captain Luke Brett of His Britannic Majesty's forty-gun frigate *Parnassus* was true to the pattern of senior naval officers. Lonely because of his rank and the long periods spent at sea, he had developed the habit of using few words and of religious meditation. But loneliness had not diminished his alertness. He could take in at a glance the whole situation when he came on deck, and although he ran his ship with the least possible orders his eye missed nothing. He received Carlos O'Neill's ceremonious greetings with quiet dignity and was concerned for his visitor's seasickness. When he heard the request for powder and shot he gave it without demur, for he knew well the value of such a gun in the hands of the guerilleros and how it could help Wellington in his battles in the south. He was prudent to consider the possibility of an ambush of his boat on shore and wisely kept O'Neill as a hostage until the stores were landed. Five days later he was rather shocked to find that the Junta wanted O'Neill on many charges, but he kept his feelings hidden behind his outward mask of dignified duty.

War produces as many cowards as it does heroes, traitors as well as patriots and more quiet suffering than victories or spectacular outrage. The sufferings of Isidoro Botto were typical of many. He was a peasant, not rich, but better off than his poor neighbours. He was compelled, unwillingly, to lend Father Prieto his fine strong cart to pull the gun over the rough mountain tracks. But this was only the first of his losses. French troops foraging took the crops from his field, others commandeered his cattle. His barns were burned, he lost not only his stock but also the tools of his farming trade. Starving, penniless and in rags, robbed by French and Spanish alike, it was easy for him to forget his loyalty to a country which had treated him so badly and to think only of himself. He could get his own back on the guerilleros who had robbed him, and earn money to set himself up again by showing the French the secret path that led to El Bilbanito's hiding place. But the guerilleros survived and Botto was traced through the newly minted coins which he had been paid as the price of his treachery. Jorge brought him in for trial. With the rope around his neck, Botto bargained desperately for his life. Too late he realized his mistake in giving away the hiding place of the gun, and the guerilleros took from the unhappy Botto all he had left—his life.

War can also fan into flames the strange fires that smoulder in us all. Courage, comradeship, cruelty and deceit are magnified, but sometimes great evil is given the appearance of good. Who could guess at the real motives that drove on Brother Bernard? The gaunt figure of the huge Franciscan friar with his massive black beard and ragged grey-brown robe mounted incongruously on a white mule was legendary in the northern plains. The peasants believed that he had strange powers that made him invisible and immune to all enemies and dangers. They feared him as they feared the devil. He had fought at Saragossa and Marshal Bessières had put a price of a thousand dollars on his head, but although he went about quite openly the reward was not yet claimed. Only a ruthless fanatic could have rejoiced at the slaughter in La Merced, could have deliberately poisoned the French garri-

son by mixing white arsenic with their flour and called
his deed the hand of God. No man did more for his
country in rousing the people and attacking the French
military government; no man killed more Frenchmen in
all Spain than Brother Bernard. He and his followers
harassed the regiment of the Imperial Guard as it tried to
join up with the forces in Salas and his warning to Jorge
brought about their annihilation. After the battle, Brother
Bernard visited the wounded where they lay and rever-
ently heard their confession before he slit their throats.
He already knew that strong French forces were on their
way to relieve Salas and recapture Leon. But without the
gun, the guerilleros were not equipped to fight a conven-
tional pitched battle against the French and they felt it
discreet to slip quietly away. Then Brother Bernard's madness burst through his enthusiasm and he called down the
curse of God upon the departing bands.

3—On Guns and Projectiles

The Chinese used gunpowder thousands of years ago to
make firecrackers to scare off evil spirits. In medieval
Europe, chemists were constantly experimenting with all
sorts of mixtures just to see what would happen, and we
may well suppose that some of these mixtures were
explosive.

The English friar, Roger Bacon, is credited with the
invention of the first orthodox gunpowder about 1250. Sixty
years later Vasi or Pot de Fer were manufactured in
Flanders and were used to shoot a thick arrow from the

vase-shaped iron pot. In 1346, at the battle of Crécy, large Bombards, mounted on heavy wooden carriages were used. The noise and smoke were more frightening than the short range of the shot, but perhaps, like the gun of this story, they had a certain moral effect. The primary military need was for some weapon to make a breach in the walls of fortified towns, and so the guns were made bigger and bigger to take a larger charge of powder and a heavier stone or iron ball. But the guns were made of wrought iron and they were of limited strength and endurance. Consequently accidents were frequent. The ordnance makers now tried to build a gun as a 'barrel' with long iron bars welded together and strengthened with hoops of iron shrunk on to them. These guns were much stronger but they were expensive and their manufacture took too long for them to be made in large numbers. The next big step forward was the manufacture of cast-iron guns. The first is supposed to have been made by Ralph Hog of Buxted, Sussex, in 1542. Great skill was needed to prepare the moulds and to pour the molten metal, but it was these guns that outshot the brass cannon of the Spaniards in the Battle of the Armada. Then in 1739 an invention from Geneva made it possible to cast the gun in one solid piece and to bore the firing chamber afterwards. This made casting easier, for there was less chance of small air-pockets flawing the metal, and the chamber could be bored to give a smooth and uniform calibre through the whole length of the barrel and an almost gas-tight fitting for the ball, making the shooting more accurate and more powerful. The gun of our story was made about this time. It was made of gun-metal, which resisted corrosive gases of burning powder and the weathering of rain better than iron.

Apart from the siege operations, the army commanders were not too sure how best to use artillery in the field. A well placed cannon ball might upset close packed cavalry or foot soldiers but the gunners could not reload quickly and were very vulnerable in the counter attack. At sea, however, the advantage of hitting your opponent before coming alongside and fighting hand to hand, by boarding, was apparent. Consequently a variety of projectiles was developed, such as bar shot and chain shot, whose purpose was to damage enemy masts, spars and rigging. To clear the decks a mixture of old iron, nails, bolts, and gravel flints was loaded loose into the barrel of the gun. This curious assortment was known as 'Langridge'. For ease of loading, the mixture was later made up in canvas bags which roughly fitted the bore of the gun and a parchment cartridge was attached. Later, small iron shot were packed into an iron case or canister and by the middle of the eighteenth century canister was made from standard musket balls and packed in thin metal cases in fourteen sizes for the British service from $1\frac{1}{2}$-pounder to 42-pounder. At this time a musket ball was about .54 calibre, weighing just under half an ounce, and canister for an 18-pounder contained 400 musket balls. The effect of the canister, which burst open as it left the barrel, was to limit the spread of the flying metal while yet allowing it to hit quite a large area at the short ranges over which it was possible to fire it. Whereas an 18-pounder round-shot would carry a mile to a mile and a half, canister would only cover 300 yards, but its deadly effect on massed troops was exploited by Jorge when his concealed gun smashed

the regiment of the Imperial Guard. There was still a need
for a projectile which would hit over a wider area than
roundshot but which would have a longer range and
greater hitting power than canister. Early gunners tried
loading their guns with a number of smaller calibre shot,
perhaps a dozen half-pound shot in a 6-pounder gun. This
was used to demolish the upper works of ships, to cut
large rents in sails so that they would no longer hold the
wind, to smash spars and cut rigging; or on land to break
down fieldworks such as palisades, as the O'Neills did at
La Merced, and against large bodies of troops. Soon the
shot were tied up in canvas bags ready for use so that they
could be easily pushed into the gun muzzle and each canvas was quilted by tying it with a strong line. In this form
it looked like a bunch of grapes and was so called. Later
a metal base plate with a central spindle was included in
the canvas bag to give the 'grape' shot a diameter much
closer to the bore of the gun. Later still the individual shot
were carefully arranged in tiers on circular plates which
were then tightened by a centre rod. Only a slight distor-
tion was needed as the assembly left the barrel for the shot
to separate and spread. At the time of the Napoleonic wars,
grapeshot was made for the British service in ten sizes
from 6-pounder to 10-inch. The 18-pounder contained
thirty half-pound balls but there was a good deal of
variation in their composition; ten, eleven or even thirteen
1½-pound balls sometimes being used. Explosive shells
were used at this time but they could only be fired from
mortars and howitzers using a modest propellant charge.
The more powerful charge used to fire roundshot would
have set off the explosive in the shell and burst the gun.

These early shells were little more than hollow spheres filled with powder and fitted with a long fuse. When a shell fired at Salas fell into the gun emplacement, one of the guerilleros had time to chop off the end of the fuse with his spade. The shell was put into the mortar, fuse downwards so that it was ignited as the charge was fired. Alternatively the fuse was first lit by the gunner who dropped it quickly into the mortar and then put fire to the main charge. It is not surprising to learn that there was a high mortality rate among these gunners.

An 18-pounder with a well-trained gun crew might get off ten rounds an hour, but careful team work and disciplined attention to detail were necessary if the gun was to be correctly reloaded in the heat of battle and under enemy fire.

After firing, the gun would contain burning fragments of powder and wad. These had to be extinguished and the gun cleaned and cooled by a 'spunge or scowrer'. At the time of our story, the British Navy stored its powder in bulk and it was made up on board ship into cartridges, consisting of a flannel bag into which the correct quantity of powder by weight was carefully measured and the bag sewn up. The guerilleros in this story were supplied with powder in barrels and so had to measure each charge with a ladle as our early gunners did. Six pounds of powder was needed to discharge an 18-pound roundshot. The powder in its long ladle was carefully inserted into the barrel and when it touched the far end it was turned over to spill the powder. At the command 'put up your powder' the loose powder was rammed home, but the gunner was careful to put his thumb over the touch-hole—a drill called 'serving the vent'. This was to prevent the sudden out-rush of air igniting any smouldering grains round the vent and setting off prematurely the newly rammed charge. The powder was held in place by a tompion or wad made of rope yarn or cloth, which also reduced the loss of power through the expanding gases escaping between the ball and the inner walls of the barrel. The shot was now gently placed inside the barrel and a further wad, ideally of wood wrapped with yarn, was rammed tightly home on top of the shot to hold it firmly. Accurate shooting was made easier for the British as the roundshot they used were more exact in weight and shape than those used by the French and followed a steadier path through the air.

A gunner could correct his aim after his first shot only if his powder was consistent and the charge of powder used for the second shot burned as quickly and as power-fully as the first. Here, too, the British had a great advan-tage over the French, whose powder was not so well made. The powder was made up of 75 parts of saltpetre, 15 parts of charcoal and 10 parts of sulphur. It was very carefully mixed, sieved and made up into grains in different sizes; the larger grain giving a longer burning time and so a 'softer' explosion.

Aiming the gun or laying it on a target was not a matter of great science in those days, as El Bilbanito discovered with his first shot. The target was nearly always visible and the aim could be corrected by observing the fall of each shot. This was clearly the procedure at the siege of La Merced and at Salas. The muzzle of the gun could be moved to the left and to the right—this was the traverse of the gun giving direction—and then up or down—this was the elevation governing the range. The gun was traversed by raising the heavy trail by its lifting handles and by the leverage of the long traversing spike which fitted into two iron clamps on the trail. Meanwhile, the gunner stood behind the breech and lined up a notch on the muzzle-swell with his target. The elevation was controlled by a hardwood wedge or quoin which was forced between the breech and the gun-carriage. The point-blank range for a gun this size was about 400 yards, and in this position a notch on the breech was level with the zero mark on the graduated iron bar fixed upright to the side of the gun-carriage. To increase the range the wedge was withdrawn, the muzzle would rise and the shot followed a parabolic curve or trajectory.

The gun was fired by applying a hot iron or a burning match to the vent, which had been previously primed with a little loose powder. As the gun recoiled some yards on firing, it was advisable to stand well clear while applying the match. In action, a linstock carrying a lighted slow-match was stuck in the ground near the gun and from this was lit a portfire or quick-match made of some inflammable material carried in a conveniently long holder. A portfire cutter fixed to the carriage nipped off the burning end of the portfire after each round to reduce the risk of unintended explosions. If the touch-hole were blocked the gun could not be fired, and clearing the blockage was likely to damage the gun further. For this reason regular troops carried specially made spikes of iron which could be hammered into the vent and broken off short to 'spike the enemy's guns', and this was doubtless the object of the sortie from Salas.

As Father Prieto discovered, the gun could not be dragged far without some extra carriage to take the dead weight of the heavy trail, and stoutly-made limbers were designed to take up the gun-trail and later were used to carry shot and powder as well.

Marlborough and Napoleon both saw the great capabilities of artillery, and in battle it became the third arm of the army with infantry and cavalry. Earlier, artillery had been used principally against fortifications but by the period of our story it was used in battles of manoeuvre on the right of each infantry battalion. Firing roundshot at long range and grape and canister at nearer advancing infantry or cavalry, the fire-power of field guns could have a decisive influence on the course of the battle.

A short book list for further reading has been included on pages 221-2.

D. J. TAYLOR

The Editor thanks the following for the help he has received in the preparation of this edition.

Lt. Colonel C. B. Appleby, D.S.O., F.S.A., Director, The National Army Museum, Sandhurst.

Colonel W. J. Cockerill, Headquarters 54 East Anglian District.

Brigadier C. F. G. Hogg, Royal Artillery.

Mr A. W. Kennard, F.S.A., Assistant to Master of the Armouries, H.M. Tower of London.

Señor Ernesto La Orden, Minister in charge of Cultural Affairs, The Spanish Embassy, London.

Mr Brian Patton, Research Assistant, The National Maritime Museum, Greenwich.

Captain J. G. Wells, D.S.C., Royal Navy, commanding the Royal Naval Gunnery School, H. M. S. *Excellent*.

THE GUN

B

The Peninsula
showing the
Great - Road

CATALONIA

NAVARRE

ARAGON

VALENCIA

MURCIA

OLD CASTILE

NEW CASTILE

ANDALUSIA

ASTURIAS

GALICIA

ESTREMADURA

LEON

Bayonne

Bilbao

Tudela

Saragossa

R.Ebro

Vitoria

Burgos

Madrid

Baylen

Ferrol

Coruña

Cape la Penas

Lugo

Monforte

Vigo

La Merced

Astorga

Benavente

Obispo

Oporto

Salamanca

Ciudad
Rodrigo

Almeida

R.Tagus

Talavera

Badajoz

Albuera

Torres
Vedras

Lisbon

Valladolid

Palencia

Carrion

Frandos

Mansilla

Leon

R.Douro

Scale
0   50   100
Miles

CHAPTER I

A DEFEATED army was falling back through the mountains from Espinosa. Such was its condition that an ignorant observer would find it easier to guess that it had been defeated than that it had been an army. The twenty thousand men of whom it was composed were strung out along twenty miles of road; its sick and its dead littered the edges of the road for a hundred miles to the rear. At the head came such of the cavalry as were fortunate enough still to have horses to ride; they felt safer there than in their proper place covering the retreat. Next came the infantry, in groups, in herds, or in ones and twos. Their white Bourbon uniforms were now in strips and tatters, and the skin, blue with disease and cold, showed through the rents. Perhaps half of them still retained their muskets, and of these perhaps a quarter had bayonets as well. Here and there little groups still displayed the soldierly bearing, and marched steadily beneath the cased regimental colours, but these groups were few, for most of the colours had been lost at Espinosa.

The long column of misery tended continually to grow longer, as the more robust struggled forward to get as far as possible from the pursuing French, and as the weaker fell farther and farther behind. There were enough weaklings in all conscience; even in summer the men had been badly clothed, and even in victory insufficiently fed, and

now it was winter, and Espinosa had been fought and
lost, and the route of the retreat lay away from the fertile
plains and up into the inhospitable mountains. The rain
had fallen upon them in deluges for days, and now as they
climbed higher it was turning into sleet, and a bitter cold
wind blew. Ahead of them they could see the snow lying
thick on the mountain passes through which they would
have to climb, without food or fuel or rest, and with the
terror of the French to urge them on. Disease had come,
inevitably, to complete the work so well begun by hunger,
exposure, and the sword. The typhus—the Black Death—
was in among them, along with dysentery and rheumatism
and pneumonia. Men dropped dying in the very middle of
the road, to be trodden and spurned by comrades too sick
and wearying to step out of the way, and whose shoeless
feet left blood at every step.

If such were the state of affairs at the head of the
column, the condition of the rear can hardly be imagined.
Here were the men whose legs had given way beneath
them, and who still tried to struggle along on hands and
knees. Here were the women and children, left ever
farther and farther behind, gazing back apprehensively
down the road to see when the dreaded helmets of the
French dragoons would appear over the rise. Here were
the last few relics of the impedimenta of the army, all that
had survived the disaster of Espinosa and the hundred
miles of the retreat. The horses were all dead, and the few
guns and wagons were being dragged along by dying
mules, goaded by the drivers who limped along at their
sides. It was bad luck on the sick who fell in the highway
incapable of moving, for the gun teams were quite in-

capable of hauling the guns out of the deep central ruts;
they could only go straight on regardless.

If any part of the wretched Spanish Bourbon army could
boast esprit de corps and devotion to duty, it was the
artillery. The gunners of the few guns which had escaped
from Espinosa had no real motive in imperilling their lives
in dragging their guns on in this fashion. They knew
that if they were to cut the traces and leave their pieces
behind no one would ever have the energy to make in-
quiries into the matter. But either their own natural
obstinacy or that ingrained by discipline had caused them
to drag the things thus far.

The very last unit in the Spanish column—if we except
the dying—was a bigger, heavier, and more imposing gun
than the iron six-pounders which led the artillery column.
Thirteen feet long it was, and two feet in diameter at the
breech, and a foot in diameter at the muzzle. It was an
eighteen-pounder bronze gun, of that handsome dark alloy
which is still known as 'gunmetal'. Around the vent and
forward along the barrel it was ornamented with blazonry
and heraldic traceries, beautifully designed, and cast as
part of the gun itself; it was evidently a gun which had
had a mould made expressly for itself at the time of casting,
and had clearly been intended as an ornament for some
wealthy noble's castle. Round the muzzle, in boldly raised
lettering, was a Latin inscription, a fragment of the liturgy
of Nocturne—'And our mouths shall show forth Thy
praise.' The gun must have been one of a pair; its brother
must have borne the inscription 'Oh Lord, open our lips,'
and the two must have stood one each side of the entrance
ramp of a castle in the South. When the Spaniards rose

against the French invaders, and the nation flew to arms after a French army had been engulfed at Baylen, these two guns must have been taken from their ornamental duties to help eke out the woefully inadequate equipment of the Spanish artillery. The other gun had fallen into French hands at some one or other of the disasters which had befallen Spain when Napoleon in his wrath led the Grand Army across the Pyrénées—at Gamonal, perhaps, or Rio Seco, or Tudela, and was probably relegated again by now to ornamental duties at the Tuileries or at Compiègne, to grace Imperial splendour.

It seemed likely enough that the same fate would overtake its fellow, trailing along at the rear of Blake's defeated army. The dozen mules which were dragging its three tons of weight along the rocky road were in the last stages of exhaustion. To force them to take every single step the drivers had to stick their goads into their raw and bleeding sides; the big lumbering gun only surged forward a yard at a time, and every yard with pain and difficulty, crashing and bumping over the rocks which surfaced the road. They reached a point where all the gradients which they had already climbed up into the mountains were inconsiderable compared with the one which now faced them. It seemed to rise before them like the sides of a house; ahead they could see it at intervals winding on interminably, looping backwards and forwards up the mountain side, as far as the eye could see through the driving sleet. At every hairpin bend the pull of the long string of mules was necessarily at an angle to the length of the gun, with much consequent wastage of power. The drivers shouted, and stuck their goads into the mules' sides until the blood ran in streams; the gunners toiled at the spokes of the wheels with what feeble strength was left them. The wind shrieked round them, dazing them with its force and with the sleet which it hurled along with it. Then the inevitable occurred. One last spasmodic effort carried one wheel up to the top of the rock which had been impeding it; the mules lunged forward under the goads, and the whole thing tottered and fell over on its side in the midst of the road, dragging the limber over with it, and the wheelers in their traces, and they the pair in front, and so on until half the team was down, while the gun lay, huge and ungainly, on its side with one wheel still slowly rotating.

In this fashion the question was settled for the gunners. It would take hours to put that three tons of bronze on to its wheels again. And the mules were past further effort. Those which had fallen lay quietly on the rocky road, their only movement being the distressed heaving of their flanks. With most of them no amount of goading or kicking or cursing could get them on their feet again. When a dying mule finds himself lying down he nearly always decides to lie and die quietly, and no stimulus whatever will get him on his feet again to expend his last few breaths in the service of mankind. The wretched animals who were still on their feet huddled together and tried, as well as their traces would allow, to turn their tails to the sleet-laden wind. At any moment the dragoons might appear in pursuit; the gunners had seen them in among the rearguard once or twice already during the retreat, slashing about with their swords like a schoolboy among thistles. The wind and the cold and fatigue and hunger had left the gunners too dazed for intelligent effort with levers and ramps. They had just sense enough to open the limber and allow its small content of ammunition to cascade into the road, and then, detaching the limber from the gun, they were able to right the former and hitch the last few mules to it. With this light load they were able to struggle forward again up the interminable mountain road, into the fast falling winter night, while the gun still lay grotesquely with one wheel in the air and the dying mules around it, like some fantastic god surrounded by sacrificed animals—a simile which is not so far from the truth.

The Spanish army went on its way, leaving the gun behind it. Thirty thousand men had fought at Espinosa, and twenty thousand had escaped from that disaster. The march through the mountains, and a winter among their desolate slopes, left some eight thousand fever-ridden phantoms alive next spring to appear again in another corner of Spain and to be sacrificed in some further foolish battle. For the French left their retreat unharried from the morning of the day when the gun was abandoned. Not even a French army could penetrate further into that desolate tangle of mountains, with no more motive than the destruction of a beaten enemy; they wheeled aside and marched down into the plains to Madrid.

CHAPTER II

THE MEN of the mountain valleys, the charcoal burners and the miners, found the gun still lying in the road when next they descended to it. They eyed it with curiosity; for familiar though they were with small arms a cannon was a rare sight among those precipices. So far in this lost corner of the Peninsula the war had barely touched them. Indeed, they had suffered more up to now from the depredation of the starving Spaniards than from the French. The sight of the long desolate road, littered with dead men and dead animals and all the pitiful paraphernalia abandoned in the retreat, was their first introduction to the horrors which were to overwhelm Spain during the next four years. They were men of the mountains, not of the towns. The news that the French Emperor had kidnapped their King and had determined on setting his own brother in his place had been slow in reaching them, and these Galician peasantry did not feel the same intense national pride as did the Castilians and the townsfolk. It was the sight of the dead men along the road, and the tales told by the few living stragglers, and the shameful news of Espinosa, which roused them at last to take their part in the national uprising.

In every mountain village the parish priest mounted his mule and rode off to the nearest town for news, and came back with stories of the formation of provincial governments, of decrees of universal military service, of the

7   B*

organization of new armies to take the place of the old.
So that when Father Ciro Prieto came riding up the road
in reply to a hurried message, and saw the group of
peasants round the gun, he reined in and dismounted with
a thrill of pleasure. Artillery was rare among the mountains.

"Good morning, children," said Father Ciro Prieto, shaking his cassock out of the disorder consequent upon riding
astride.

"Good morning, Father," said they respectfully, and
waited for him to take charge of operations. He was a little
man with sharp grey eyes, and a great snuff-taker, and
much respected all round about as a fount of wisdom.
Those sharp eyes of his took in the whole story; the wheel-
marks in the road, the position of the gun, turned over at
a bend, and the dead mules, made it all obvious to him.

"The French are no further off than Camino Reale," he
said. "The sooner we get this gun into a place of safety
the better."

"Yes, Father, certainly," said Vigil the woodcutter. "But
how?"

The priest spread his hands.

"I leave that to you, my sons," he said. "Use any
means you think will serve."

Father Prieto's worldly wisdom stopped short at the problem of righting three-ton guns, but he was not going to
admit it. He sat at the edge of the road holding the reins
of the mule and taking snuff, while his parishioners bustled
about the task.

At first their efforts were feeble and ill advised. It was
hard for them to realize the enormous weight with which

they were dealing. Their early pullings and pryings availed them not at all. It was the copper miners among them who initiated the correct method; they were more used to such difficulties. Two wood-cutters were despatched to get a couple of big tree branches as levers. When these were brought back there was at last a real promise of progress. A little hole was dug beneath the barrel of the gun, just in front of the swell of the breech, and the end of a lever thrust into it. Then when ten men flung all their weight upon the other end, behold, the gun moved! It stirred a little in the rut in which it had buried itself. Everyone else promptly flung himself upon the lever. It sank under the combined weight, the gun lifted itself a full foot, and then, the lever slipping from under it, it fell again with a shattering crash upon the road again.

"Gently, children, gently," said Father Prieto from the roadside. His life's experience among these wild mountain people had taught him that they needed far more to be restrained from headlong excess of zeal than to be urged on.

"Gently, you fools," said Comas the miner. "That is not the way. Listen—oh, Mother of God!"

Already the wild enthusiasts had pushed the lever under the gun again and were swinging on to it.

"Listen to Andres," said Father Prieto, sharply, and his flock ceased their heavings while Comas gave a hurried lecture on the use of alternating levers. This time when the gun was heaved up out of its bed Comas was ready. He pushed the second lever under the gun, and a rock beneath it as a fulcrum, and in response to his shouts half the party now flung themselves upon the second lever.

The gun rose farther still—Andres' wild exhortations, backed up by Father Prieto, just sufficed to stop them overdoing it again. While the gun hung precariously on the tip of the lever Comas built yet a higher fulcrum, rested the first lever upon it, thrust the lever under the gun, and called to the others to heave again. In this fashion the gun rose steadily, turning over with its carriage to an upright position. There was a tense moment when the rim of the lower wheel took the ground and the gun began to rise upon it. Comas imperilled his life by rushing beneath the swaying mass to pile rocks against the wheel rim when it threatened to slip. As the fulcrums grew higher and higher the effort of turning the gun grew greater and greater; to the very end success hovered in the balance. Just before the gun was ready to fall into the upright position it seemed as if they would never be able to lift it the last necessary six inches. Every one piled upon the lever, their feet seeking out some grip which might increase their weight; they tugged and they strained, their joints cracking and the sweat running in streams in the cold mountain air. At last Father Prieto left his mule by the roadside and ran to the lever. He found a foot of it unoccupied, grasped it, and lifted his feet from the ground, his legs kicking absurdly within his cassock. His little additional weight turned the scale. The gun swung over, falling with a crash upon its other wheel, tottered, and kept its position, on two wheels again, pointing with defiance down the road towards the French while the lever, slipping from beneath it, deposited the whole mass of mountaineers in an ungraceful heap on the ground.

Everybody rose, panting and full of pride. They swarmed

about the gun, examining it with curiosity. They plied
Father Prieto with questions about it, most of which the
poor man was quite unable to answer. The minute education of a Spanish parish priest did not extend to a knowledge of siege artillery. He could tell them nothing about
the employment of the elevating screw and wedge beneath
the breech, but he could at least read out the legend round
the muzzle—they heard the Latin words with a respectful
intake of breath—and translate it for them—" And our
mouths shall show forth Thy praise "—and he found the
touch-hole for them (the gun did not boast the elaborate
firing arrangements with lock and lanyard which modern
artillery possessed) and was able to explain how to load
and fire. His flock could understand that; it was just the
same simple method as they used in their own muskets,
and Father Prieto's economic use of the little knowledge he
possessed quite concealed from them his complete ignorance of anything like laying and elevating an eighteen-
pounder. They were quite enthralled by his little lecture.
Diego Cabrera picked up one of the half-dozen rusty
cannon-balls which the gunners had spilt from the limber,
and weighed it in his hands. Everyone looked longingly at
everyone else. The thought was in the minds of all, big
children that they were, that it would be fine to load the
gun and fire it off, just once. But they looked at the width
of the bore and at the cavernous depths of the barrel. A
single charge for the monster would consume as much
powder as the whole community possessed. Diego let the
cannon-ball fall reluctantly from his hands.

"Now, into a place of safety with it, children," said
Father Prieto.

That started a new discussion. Anyone could guess that
an enormous team would be necessary to drag the gun up
the mountain side. Although these peasantry were ready
enough to risk their lives, they were all of them peculiarly
unwilling to risk their cattle. Horses and mules and
draught oxen had been hurried away along with the flocks
and herds into safe recesses of the upper valleys even before
there was fear of the French coming—the unpaid Spanish
armies were just as careless about the rights of property.
But no one could disclaim the possession of draught animals
to neighbours who knew every detail of his affairs, whatever tales he was willing to tell to commissaries and tax
gatherers. Each in turn was gradually provoked into offering the use of a mule or a yoke of oxen, and at last there
was a general dispersion to assemble a team, while the few
unpropertied men remained behind with the gun, fingering
the relief work along its barrel, peeping into the muzzle
to see the tiny bit of light which crept in through the
touch-hole, passing wise comment on the solidity of the
carriage work, while all the time the gun, huge and im-
passive, stood glaring defiantly down the mountain side.
It was well that the French made no move.

Then when the team was got together, in the late afternoon, and harness had been devised, a new difficulty arose.
They began by attaching the traces to the iron loop at the
tip of the trail of the gun, and found that thus it was
impossible to pull the thing along. The trail was devised
for limiting recoil, and simply dug itself into the ground
when they applied any pull. Clearly the trail must be
lifted, and the muzzle depressed, and the gun drawn along
in that position. But no cattle on earth were strong enough

to maintain sufficient tension on the traces to hold the ponderous weight of the trail in the air. Even Clemente Cagorno's renowned yoke of draught oxen, weighing a ton and a half between them, were dragged backwards as though they had been no more than a pair of nannygoats, while the trail sank back to the ground.

A stray memory came into Father Prieto's mind at last, illuminating it like day. It was a memory ten years old, of an occasion when he had ridden into Burgos, an enormous journey, to consult with the Bishop's secretary. In Burgos he had seen an army on the march, on its way to the Pyrénées to fight the French, who were then red revolutionaries instead of Imperial king makers. There had been guns with that army, clattering through Burgos, and by an excruciating effort Father Prieto remembered how they had been pulled along. The trails of the guns had been swung from limbers—stout two-wheeled carts, to which the horses were harnessed.

With dignity Father Prieto intervened in his parishioners' despairing discussion and explained how the thing should be done, and every one instantly saw the soundness of the advice. And at the same time everyone—save one— instantly decided who should supply the cart which would take the place of the limber. Isidoro Botto had been the least helpful of any of the group. He had not done much in the matter of righting the gun, and his contribution to the team had been only one unhappy ass, which every one knew to be sixteen years old if a day. Yet he was the wealthiest of them all, and they knew he owned just the right cart for the business. Each solid pair of wheels was of one piece with the six-inch axles, and they were attached to the wooden cheek pieces with iron staples of best Galician smiths' work, and every bit of wood was of solid Spanish oak. A clamour arose for Botto to offer his cart. He demurred; it was unsuitable for the job in hand; it was out of repair; he had lent it last week to a man from the Asturias; he could not afford to be without it. But he swallowed his objections when Diego Cabrera drew his knife and was imitated by half a dozen others. He went sullenly off with them to his farm to fetch the cart.

It was nearly nightfall when they returned, and humorists declared they could still hear Granny Botto's imprecations, which she had hurled at them when she saw that beloved cart being commandeered, and was presumably still continuing to hurl, some four miles away.

And now the trail of the gun was swung up and fastened to the back axle of the cart, and the motley team was harnessed up. Those who had whips cracked them joyfully; those who had goads plied them with a will, and those with neither ran up and down shouting encouragement. Cart and gun lurched, heaved, and then unmistakably got under way. The difficult corner was rounded, and they set themselves to the climb. Lanterns made their appearance from here and from there, and by their light each successive hairpin bend was negotiated, and the rising of the moon found them over the shoulder of the mountain. Then every one decided they had done enough for that day.

The further progress of the gun into the heart of the mountains can hardly be followed in so much detail. Certainly it was the very next day that the would-be gunners discovered a truth which the artillery teamster learns speedily enough—that going downhill is more difficult even than going uphill. Three tons of solid metal on a steep slope constitutes a Juggernaut which exacts a cruel toll of lives and broken limbs. The first runaway was only terminated by a crash into the ditch at a bend, with half the team disabled, and incredible labour necessitated in the way of building ramps and working with levers to get the thing on the road again. If the wheels were locked for a descent they ploughed so deep into the road that it was necessary to dig them out again. And if the strain on the ropes which locked the wheels rose above breaking point so that one wheel was suddenly released, that meant another capsizing and more heartbreaking toil to right the gun. Diego Cabrera and Clemente Cagorno and the others came to hate the huge thing which had taken possession of their lives. Isidoro Botto watched with dismay the gradual disintegration of his beloved cart under the shocks and strains to which it was subjected.

But there was some compensation in the fact that the passage of the gun through the mountain villages excited enormous attention. Men who were still hesitating to take up arms were carried away by the spectacle and attached themselves to the party, which increased in snowball fashion. To those unsophisticated mountaineers a force of a thousand peasants with an eighteen-pounder appeared an irresistible army. Father Prieto, rather to his dismay, found himself at the head of one of the most considerable forces of the province, and in consequence a man of weight in the councils of the Junta when the point of concentration was at last reached.

It was one of Fate's bitter ironies that not one of these men who had toiled so Homerically to bear the gun on its

way was to see it in action. For more news reached the
Junta. The tide of war had oscillated violently back and
forth across the Peninsula. Madrid had fallen to the French
despite all the boastings of the government. Moore and the
English had struck their blow, and had marched the length
and breadth of Spain pursued by treble numbers, even
along a part of the very road where the gun had been
abandoned. Now Moore's army had taken ship at Corunna,
leaving their beloved leader buried in the ramparts, and
the rumour sped round the countryside that their baulked
pursuers were to plunge on through Galicia to complete
the conquest of the country. Every available man must be
marched by the quickest route to head them off. Father
Prieto's Galician band must come, of course. With any
luck Soult might be completely surrounded and compelled
to surrender, which would bring more glory to Galicia
than Baylen did to Andalusia. The gun could not accom-
pany them, however. The route would be by mountain
paths, and their experience even on roads had shown how
slow was the movement of an eighteen-pounder. Every
moment was precious when resounding victory was so near
their grasp. The gun must be left, and the men must
march at once.

To Father Prieto's credit he improved on the hot-headed
Junta's instructions. Perhaps he may have foreseen disaster.
The gun was not left standing, as the Junta's orders would
have had it, in the street of the little village where they
found themselves at the moment. It made one more
journey, to where a quarry, unworked now in these tur-
bulent times, had been hacked out of the side of a hill at
the edge of the road. The gun was hauled into the basin

of the quarry, and lumps of stone were heaped on and around it until a cairn was formed over it. No one would ever suspect that a siege gun was concealed within that mass of stones; the passer-by would naturally assume that the latter was a pile formed during the working of the quarry.

And having completed this good piece of work for Spain Father Prieto and his men marched on to the promised surrounding and destruction of Soult. Of course that promise was not fulfilled. Soult and his veterans of the Grand Army tore their way through the flimsy lines of armed peasants. They rubbed in their easy victories by shooting or hanging or dropping over precipices the prisoners they caught—as indeed they were authorized to do by the laws of war, because their opponents wore no uniform. Father Prieto, poor little man, they hanged in the market square of Vigo because it was well to make a special example of priests, and most of his followers who did not die by violence died by disease. Only a few crept back to their farms and forests among the mountains to try and eke out a living from what was left to them after the exactions of Spanish irregulars and French armies had been met. The gun stayed where it was, hidden in its cairn of stones, month after month, until two years of the interminable war had gone by. French armies came and went; more than once they passed actually beside the gun without discovering it, on their occasional expeditions into the mountain country in pursuit of what they called brigands and the Spaniards called guerilleros.

CHAPTER III

A T T H E end of that period of two years a man stood on
the southernmost ridge of the Cantabrian mountains gazing down into the fertile plain of Leon. The contrast
between the scenery close about him and that on the
horizon was astonishing. The Cantabrian sierras are formed
of row on row of mountain chains, each roughly parallel
to the southern coast of the Bay of Biscay, each rocky,
steep, and scarped, clothed with forests for most of their
height, and their summits nothing more than jagged peaks
of naked rock. They are pierced by few paths and by fewer
roads, although here and there they enclose rich upland
valleys.

But at the very foot of the escarpment above which the
man stood gazing down began the plainland, the 'tierra
de campos', the 'land of fields', the richest portion of all
Spain. Here, as far as the eye could see, stretched rolling
cornfields, unbroken by hedges, with hardly a tree to
diversify the scene. There were numerous roads which
formed a network of yellow streaks over the surface, and
which connected the villages which dotted the plain—
clusters of one-storeyed cottages, for the most part constructed of sun-dried bricks, whitewashed. There were no
rivers to be seen, but the man gazing down from the sierra
knew that there were many, that the plain was one of the
few Spanish plateaux rich in water. For the rivers had cut
themselves beds far below the level of the plain, and flowed

18

at the bottom of deep-sunk ravines, so that only a very keen eye could discern from the mountain top the dark marking of the cañons as they wound about through the folds of the plain. The best way of ascertaining their course, in fact, was to note the little white bridges at the points where the rivers were crossed by the country roads.

The man who stood on the sierra looking over the plain was a guerillero chief, whom his followers knew as 'El Bilbanito', 'the young man from Bilbao'. The Spanish habit of conferring nicknames on anyone of note, from kings to bull-fighters, was specially in evidence in the case of the guerillero leaders. There were the 'Empecinado'—the 'swarthy one'—the 'Cura'—the 'priest'—and the 'Marquesito'—the 'little marquis'—and a hundred others. Between them they were teaching a new lesson in war to the Napoleonic armies who had themselves taught so many to the rest of the world. Unstable and fickle and wayward as they were, the Spanish irregulars were never discouraged, never wholly put down, and were always ready for some new raid on a vulnerable point in the widespread French army of occupation.

El Bilbanito, looking out over the plains as he had looked scores of times before, had an additional motive today for longing to strike a new blow. His forces had just received a most irritating and annoying defeat of a kind to which they were unaccustomed. Two companies of French infantry, marching by night from the plain, had attacked them at dawn after scaling a path which el Bilbanito had been quite certain was unknown to anyone in the French army. There had been a few casualties, although most of the men made their escape easily enough over the face of a precipice and through forest paths where the French had not dared to follow, but what was more exasperating was the loss of everything the band possessed save what was on their persons. Half a dozen pack mules had fallen into the hands of the French, all they had save one, and after two years of war a pack mule was worth its weight in gold. With them had been taken five hundredweight of powder, quantities of cartridges, some salt meat and biscuits, and much of the treasure which had been accumulated by much harrying of Frenchmen who had already harried Spaniards. The band was sorely annoyed and el Bilbanito's position was badly undermined; indeed had not Pablo, the ambitious second in command, been killed in the fray by a stray bullet (which might possibly have been fired from el Bilbanito's musket) he might have been already deposed. The need to achieve some striking feat of arms was therefore all the more pressing.

Yet by itself the sight of those rich plains was enough to rouse el Bilbanito's zeal. For two years now French garrisons had held those plains, plundering them only moderately, growing fat on their ample products, and with their dominion hardly challenged. No Spanish force could face the French on those plains, for the French possessed discipline, artillery, and cavalry, in all of which the Spaniards were conspicuously lacking. Not even a raid could be attempted on account of those cursed rivers. At every strategic point—which in the plains meant at every river crossing—the French had set down a small sedentary garrison, established sometimes in some strong isolated building or in fieldworks built for the purpose—some of them were visible to el Bilbanito's keen eye. That did not in itself stop raids, for a small party could cross the rivers anywhere, by night if necessary. But sooner or later that small party would encounter a superior force and would have to retreat. And what then? There could be no crossing of those difficult ravines when closely pursued, probably by the dreaded dragoons. They would be hemmed in, taken, and hanged for certain. Before they could run that risk they must make sure of a line of retreat, and to do that they must hold the bridges, and to do that they must capture the covering works. And to do that they must have artillery, which no guerillero band possessed, or could possess, considering the hunted life they led among the mountains.

El Bilbanito followed up this train of thought for the hundredth time, and for the hundredth time came to the same exasperated conclusion. The thing could not be done, although its desirability was so apparent. He stamped with vexation as he turned away from his viewpoint, and walked back along the ridge, over the perfect green turf which the abundant Cantabrian rains caused to grow here, halfway up the mountain side. He was a picturesque enough figure in his loose black trousers, and his red sash with the pistols and the knives in it, and his blouse with the big gilt buttons, and his flowing black cloak buttoned at the neck and billowing out behind him with the speed of his step.

A quarter of a mile along the ridge there was a narrow neck which joined this outpost of the mountains to the main mass of the sierras. At each side here a steep path ran down into the plains, and, uniting, continued along the neck and steeply upwards to the forest-clad slopes.

Here, as was to be expected, a sentry was posted, keeping watch along the protruding ridge and down both paths. He stood aside for el Bilbanito, but with small enough respect, so that el Bilbanito watched him out of the corner of his eye as he went by, and felt a creeping of the skin over his spine as he went on up the path lest a shot in the back should end his career then and there. Something would have to be done to keep these mutinous dogs busy.

The path plunged into the pine forest, rising sharply all the time, and only when he had turned a corner among the trees out of sight did el Bilbanito breathe more freely again. His sense of his own dignity had withheld him from looking back. Deep in the forest at a dividing of the ways was another sentry, who displayed a little more deference.

"Jorge has returned, captain," he said as el Bilbanito went by.

El Bilbanito's only reply was a growl which might have meant anything, but he quickened his step until he reached the clearing which was his temporary headquarters. Of the hundred men of his band the one or two energetic ones were busied making themselves little huts of pine branches. Half a dozen more were occupied at the fires; apparently Jorge had brought back food from his raid into the mountain village. Perhaps fifty, wrapped in their cloaks, were stretched out here and there in the clearing indulging in their siesta; the rest were sitting idly about awaiting his arrival.

As he made his appearance one of these men arose and came to meet him; it was Jorge, the big smiling boy from the Rioja, who was tacitly assumed to have taken the lately deceased Pablo's place as second in command and was naturally suspected of having designs on that of el Bilbanito himself.

"We have laid our hands on the criminal, captain," said Jorge with his usual grin.

"Which one?" snapped el Bilbanito.

"The one who caused us to be attacked last week. He is here, captain."

El Bilbanito brushed Jorge aside and walked over to the seated group.

"He has confessed already, captain," said Jorge, hurrying after him.

"Why did you not hang him at once, then?" demanded el Bilbanito.

"Because——" but Jorge's explanation was cut short when el Bilbanito reached the group round the prisoner.

It was Isidoro Botto. The loss of his fine cart had been the first step towards a poverty he could not bear; two years of war had stripped him of the possessions of which he had once been so proud. One of Bonnet's infantry columns, marching through the mountains, had stripped his fields of their crops; Frenchmen and Spaniards between them had commandeered his cattle, his barn had been burned, and Botto was now on the point of starvation, just as were most of his compatriots in the debatable land which could be reached but not occupied by French armies. And his brief experience of soldiering when Soult invaded Galicia had quite cured him of any tastes in that direction.

His brown cloth clothes were in rags, but that might have been the result of the mishandling he had just

received from the guerilleros; his hands and his feet were
tied, and one eye was closed and blackened by a blow. On
el Bilbanito's arrival he scrambled awkwardly to his feet
and tried to stumble towards him, but his feet were tied
too closely, and he only succeeded in falling on his face
amid a roar of laughter from the others. His elbows flapped
and his legs kicked absurdly. Some one grabbed his collar
and hauled him to his feet.

"You won't hang me, Your Excellency?" he said; there
were tears on his checks. "You won't have me hanged?"

"I will," said el Bilbanito.

"But you can't, you can't," expostulated Botto. The
enormity of such a proceeding seemed to make it an im-
possibility to his mind, but all the same there were horrid
doubts within him.

"I can," said el Bilbanito.

"Oh, Your Excellency——"

"What is the proof against this man?" asked el Bilbanito of Jorge.

"He was out late a week ago. He must have gone down
to the French outposts. He knows the path by which the
French came—he used to use it for his sheep. And two
days back his mother tried to buy food with this."

Jorge handed over a silver coin to his captain, who
scanned it closely. It was a Saragossa dollar—money struck
by the French for use in the occupied districts.

"And anyway," concluded Jorge, "he has confessed. He
admitted his guilt when we were going to hang him over
there."

Jorge jerked his head to indicate the area where this
story begins.

"Yes, it is quite true," said the tearful Botto. He was hysterical with terror. "But don't hang me. You will lose if you hang me. I can do it again. I can tell them another path by which they can come by night. And then you can be waiting for them. Your Excellency—señores——"

Botto's hands were tied, and this handicap to his gesticulatory powers combined with his fright to reduce him to silence.

For a moment El Bilbanito was tempted. With his inward eye he could picture the ambush at dawn, the slaughter of the wretched French conscripts, the triumph of the day. But no man could survive two years of guerilla warfare without being able to see the disadvantages of the proposed plan. The employment of double traitors, tempting though it might be at first sight, was fraught with too much danger; no one could be certain on which side the balance of treachery would eventually rest. Moreover, in this special case there were practical difficulties. Half the district knew that the man had been arrested and brought into the guerilla camp; if the French were to hear of it it would either be impossible or dangerous to use him. Moreover, if Botto were given the opportunity of another visit to the French outposts the chances were that he would stay there, and the opportunity would be lost of either using him or hanging him. The man's proposal was absurd.

"No," said el Bilbanito, turning away.

Botto shrieked with despair.

"Hang him," said el Bilbanito to Jorge.

Willing hands laid hold of the wretched man. They dragged him screaming to a tree. A boy climbed it eagerly and slung a rope over a bough. They fastened the rope about his neck. Botto, gazing at the sky through the noose, saw, like a drowning man, his past life rising before him, from the peccadilloes of childhood to the horrors of the recent past, to his only experience of fighting at Vigo, to the dragging of the gun through the mountains. That memory gave him a fresh wild hope.

"The cannon!" he shrieked. "I know where the cannon is."

El Bilbanito heard the words and turned sharply on his heel. They chimed in so exactly with his thoughts of half an hour ago, when he had been asking himself where he could find artillery. He hurried back just as they swung Botto off his feet, just as the last shriek of "The cannon!" was cut in half by the tightening noose. At his signal they lowered Botto to the ground again; fortunately the jerk had not broken his neck.

"What was that you said?" demanded el Bilbanito.

Botto tore at the noose with his bound hands; his eyes bulged; even when they loosened the rope he had to gasp and swallow for some minutes before he could speak.

"We buried a cannon," he said at length. "A big, big cannon, when I was with Father Prieto. Before you came here, Your Excellency. I am sure no one has found it since. I am the last of those who were there."

"Where was it you buried it?"

"Over the mountains, a hundred miles from here. I can take you there, Your Excellency."

"Where was it?"

"On the side road to Lugo, two villages beyond Monforte. A great big cannon, Your Excellency."

"In what place did you bury it? "

"In a quarry just outside the village, Your Excellency."

"H'm," said el Bilbanito. "Are there many quarries there? "

"I don't think so, Your Excellency. There will be no difficulty——"

Botto choked anew as he saw the trap into which he had fallen, and he began to beg again for his life.

"Oh, you won't hang me now, Your Excellency? " he screamed. "You must take me with you to find the cannon. You can hang me if my story is not true. It is true, by all——"

"What else have you to tell me? "

A little spontaneous inventive power might at this moment have saved Botto's life. If he could only, with some verisimilitude, have laid claim to further knowledge, and offered to barter it against a promise of pardon, he might have prolonged his wretched existence, for a space at least. But he was not endowed with creative ability. He had to stop and think, to try to devise something, and el Bilbanito, watching him closely through his narrowed eyes, saw the truth, saw that no further useful revelations were to be expected.

"Bah ! " he said, and he called to the men who still held the rope: "Up with him."

It was only five minutes more of life that Botto had gained for himself, and the five minutes were now ended.

El Bilbanito was grimly satisfied with himself as he walked away. He had a reputation for ferocity to maintain; he hoped the incident had made a suitable impression on his band. It had been rather amusing to have the poor fool blab out all he knew and then hang him after all; it would not be difficult to find the gun, in a quarry two villages beyond Montforte on the road to Lugo, without him. And it was just as well the man was dead. That saved a good deal of the possibility that the news that the guerilleros would soon be armed with artillery might leak out to the French—trust a guerilla chief to know the value of surprise. There might be traitors among his own followers, all the same—el Bilbanito's pensive expression hardened, and he put his hand to his pistols at the thought —well, the recent hanging would make them cautious, at any rate.

El Bilbanito's mind went on making plans, devising how he could make best use of this possible gun. It would have to be a hard, sudden stroke. El Bilbanito's motives in making his plans with such care were only very slightly selfish. True, he certainly wished to regain his prestige among his followers. And there was a good deal of the spirit of the true craftsman in wishing to make the best job possible of the work he found to his hand. But also there was Spanish patriotism within him, a hatred of the French invader, a desire to bring back the king whom the French had kidnapped, a passionate resentment against the nation which had meddled so gratuitously with Spanish affairs, a longing for revenge upon the enemy who had brought such calamities upon the country. Spanish pride and Spanish patriotism were in this case working hand in hand with the instinct of self-preservation.

El Bilbanito's decision was reached quickly enough. He signalled to Jorge.

"Call the men together," he said, curtly. "We march in ten minutes."

That was all the order necessary in a guerilla band. They marched with all they had, and they were unused to having explanations offered them by their high-handed leaders.

CHAPTER IV

THE ROUTE which el Bilbanito's Cantabrian band had
to follow was complicated by the fact that most of the
main passes in the Asturias and in part of Galicia were
commanded by French garrisons, but el Bilbanito was perfectly capable of devising a route which would steer clear
of them, and that without a map and without a moment's
reflection. Two years of guerilla warfare had taught him
every mountain path in the province; at any moment he
could say instantly which passes were likely to be blocked
with snow, and which fords impassable with floods, accord-
inging to the season. That kind of knowledge was part of
his stock in trade; it was in consequence of it that he was
able (on most occasions, at least) to elude the pursuit of the
French columns which were sent after him on the rare
occasions when the garrisons of the plains were able to
scrape together a surplus of men for the purpose.

There were moments during the march when his heart
misgave him slightly. If the expedition were to prove a
wild goose chase his men were likely to get out of hand.
The possibility had to be faced, but he had encountered
mutiny before and the likelihood did not worry him unduly; he only saw to it that his pistols were invariably
primed and loaded. If he wanted the gun there was no
other course open to him than the one he was following.
Had he merely sent a small party to find if the gun were
there he knew perfectly well that before he could bring it

up to join him it would be commandeered by some other band or by the hunted group of refugees who called themselves the Galician Junta, and if he went for it himself he would not only meet the same difficulty, but his band would elect another leader in his absence. Besides, a hundred miles of rapid marching would do his men good; they were growing fat and lazy and it was important to conserve the incredible marching capacity which they were capable of displaying.

The villagers of Molinos Reales resigned themselves to the inevitable when a new band of guerilleros descended upon them from the mountains. They were used to it by now, and guerilleros were at any rate one degree better than French. El Bilbanito billeted himself on the house of the alcalde, and distributed his men among the stone-built cottages which clustered about the church. Every householder found himself with one or two men to feed and house, and if these men's boots and clothes were worn out, as they mostly were, he had to resign himself to handing over the small contents of his wardrobe to them and donning instead their cast-off rags. The worst of guerilleros was their habit of descending without warning from the hills; if regular troops or French came along there was nearly always sufficient time to hide what few valuables were left, drive the sheep and cattle into the mountains, and assume an aspect of poverty even more abject than was really the case.

El Bilbanito allowed his men the luxury of twenty-four hours under roofs, with as much food as they could coerce from their unwilling hosts. He himself, with Jorge and two chosen aides-de-camp, went off immediately to the

C

quarry which the alcalde indicated to them. The fact that there was such a quarry certainly boded well for the confirmation of the story of the man they had left dangling from a pine tree on the borders of Leon. And the basin of the quarry was level with the road, surrounded only on three sides by the steep-cut sides—a further indication of probability. And there, in the centre of the basin, there was a huge pile of broken stone, which must have been there some time because two or three blades of grass were growing on it.

With a little feeling of excitement el Bilbanito pulled a stone or two from the heap, and then, remembering his dignity, desisted.

" Pull that heap down," he said to his followers, and, turning his back, he strolled away with a magnificent assumption of indifference.

He heard the clatter and rattle of the stones as Jorge and the others set to work, and when he heard their cry of delight he turned hastily back and rejoined them. The gun was there, surely enough. Already its huge long barrel was visible above the dwindling pile, and they were digging away the stones from about its carriage.

El Bilbanito examined it carefully. Its metal had assumed a dull green colour with all the moisture to which it had been exposed, but that was a reassuring sign. It proved that the gun was of bronze, and bronze will endure centuries of exposure; an iron gun would be honeycombed with rust by now. Indeed, the ironwork of the mounting, the screw controlling the wedge below the breech, the staples of the carriage, the rims of the wheels, were red and rotten and crumbling. Even the stout oak and chestnut of the carriage had suffered. Lichens had grown up on them. But the gun itself, the irreplaceable, was intact. El Bilbanito ran his fingers with joy over the relief work along the barrel, and slapped its fat trunnions, and with the needle that his dandyism caused him always to carry he dug the dirt out of the touch hole. Then he hastened back to the village.

The alcade was confronted with a demand for carpenters and smiths. He spread his hands deprecatingly. He explained in his barbarous Gallego dialect that skilled workmen of that sort were scarce nowadays. But el Bilbanito would listen to no excuses. The village carpenter was sent for, and within an hour the alcalde, escorted by Jorge and half a dozen men, was on his way over the hills to the next village in search of a smith of repute who was known to live there. El Bilbanito with a working party and the armourer of the band—a gunsmith who had strayed into the band from Aragon—hurried back to the gun.

The armourer knew nothing about artillery, nor did el Bilbanito, but they were men of experience and common sense, of inventive capacity and ingenuity, as befitted survivors of two years of mountain warfare. Men who had bridged crevasses with an enemy in hot pursuit, who could swing loaded mules over precipices and set them unhurt on their feet at the bottom, were not likely to be deterred by the difficulties of handling a three-ton gun. El Bilbanito set his party—partly his own men, partly impressed villagers—to work on the construction of tall shears over the gun. The armourer sketched the elevating apparatus for future reference. The carpenter examined the carriage, noting measurements and dimensions; as he could neither read nor write he had to notch them cabalistically on pieces of wood, but he was used to doing his work like that.

Plans were complete by the time Jorge returned with both a smith and carpenter whom he had torn from their homes with the comforting assurance that it would not be more than a week or two before they would be allowed to return. The armourer was already improvising a forge, and a detachment detailed by el Bilbanito was conducting a house to house search for all the iron which could be discovered, brazeros and such-like. By the next morning the smiths and carpenters between them had constructed the necessary pulley blocks, the shears were reared over the gun, and el Bilbanito was anxiously supervising the swinging of the vast mass of metal cut out of its carriage.

Jorge selected, with the aid of the carpenter, the best pieces of weathered oak from the latter's stock. Jorge knew nothing about timber, but, as he explained with his eternal grin, he made sure of getting the best and most valuable pieces by simply insisting on taking those which the carpenter was most voluble in explaining would not do.

The gun swung in its slings over its carriage. Thanks to the quadruple pulleys in the blocks a dozen men had sufficed to lift it far enough for the trunnions to clear the deep notches in which they rested. The wreck of the carriage was run from beneath it, and then, ever so carefully —el Bilbanito would have shot the man who was clumsy —the huge thing was lowered to the ground, and el Bilbanito turned his attention to urging on the smiths and the carpenters to complete their work of fashioning a new carriage.

The man was in a fever of excitement. He knew, even

better than unfortunate Father Prieto had suspected two years before, what prestige the possession of artillery would bring him among the guerilleros of the province. But more than that, he carried in his mind's eye that mental picture of the fat plains, and the helpless garrisons dotted over them—helpless, that is to say, in face of an eighteen-pounder—and the ruin he could wreak upon the long vulnerable lines of communication stretching far to the rear of the French armies in the field.

All day long and for days afterwards the little village rang with the beat of the hammers on the extemporized anvils. There were iron rims to be made, fitting so exactly the broad wooden wheels which the carpenters were making that only when they were strongly heated would they slip over the felloes, so that when they were cool they would hold the wheels together despite the strain to which they were to be subjected. The screw handle which forced in and out the elevating wedge beneath the breech had to be painfully forged by hand out of bar iron, and, more difficult still, the threaded sockets in which it had to revolve. Axle pins and so forth were easy enough—the Galician smith had passed his days on that sort of work.

Even el Bilbanito had to grant an occasional rest to the weary ironworkers. He chafed at their taking six hours for sleep, but he allowed them to do so each night. He confiscated for them the best of wine and provender, and he sent his detachments far and wide to secure for them a sufficiency of charcoal. In four days the work was completed—a perfect new carriage was made for the gun. Perhaps it was not quite so prepossessing in appearance as the old one had been at its best, but it was a wonderful piece of work. The cheeks, on which the trunnions were to rest, were of four-inch oak, and the notches themselves were faced with beech. The axle was of oak too, six inches in diameter. The spokes of the wheels were of the finest ash that could be found; those wheels were the wonder of a district which had never seen other than plain solid discs cut from trees. El Bilbanito grudgingly gave his approval when he came to inspect it finally, but he reserved his final decision until a trial should be made.

The carriage was run out to the quarry, the gun slung up again by the shears, and the carriage pushed beneath it. Then the gun was slowly lowered into position, with the armourer rushing back and forth to see that it was properly done. Slowly the trunnions entered into the sockets, and bedded themselves down. The vast breech settled itself upon its block, and the sling ropes slacked off as the carriage took the strain. The woodwork creaked at the first imposition of its three-ton burden, but everything held firm. The armourer clamped down the iron holdfasts over the notches, and passed on to examine the rest. Everything was perfect. Zero on the newly forged scale exactly corresponded with the groove on the gun's breech—or within a quarter of an inch, which was good enough for siege artillery work. The trunnions fitted the sockets exactly; there was no trace of rocking or rolling. When the elevating screw was wound out the wedge below the breech slid sweetly backwards, and the muzzle of the gun rose steadily, and the notch on the breech moved regularly down the ranging scale. The gun, so the armourer declared, was ready to work, and el Bilbanito issued his order to prepare it for firing.

The armourer was delighted; it would be a further opportunity of demonstrating his attention to detail and anticipation of instructions. One of the two reserve powder kegs was brought up and opened. A liberal measure of powder was scooped up and poured into the muzzle of the gun, a rammer which the armourer had prepared of a bundle of rags on the end of a pole was pushed up the barrel so that all the powder was packed into the breech, and then a piece of blanket was stuffed up after it to hold it firm. Next the armourer produced his masterpiece—a big round boulder selected from the bed of a stream and bound round with leather so as to fit the bore of the gun. This was pushed in on top of the wadding, and the gun was loaded.

At the armourer's order half a dozen men laid hold of the trail, two others worked with levers at the wheels, and the gun was swung round until it pointed out of the quarry, across the road. The armourer mounted on the trail and fussed with the laying screw—which gave the necessary amount of fine adjustments in the lateral aiming of the gun which mere pulling round of the gun and carriage could not give with certainty. Looking through the notch on the bar of the backsight he had made yesterday, the armourer aligned the groove on the muzzle swell with a patch of white rock showing up through the undergrowth of the mountain side across the valley. Then he turned the elevating screw until the mark on the breech corresponded with the figure ' 250 ' on the elevation scale. The armourer had never in his life fired at such a range as two hundred and fifty varas, not even with the long Tyrolese rifle his lordship the Marquis of Lazan had brought him to repair before the war, but he estimated the distance as well as he could by the light of Nature. Next he scooped a little more powder from the keg, and with it filled the touch-hole. Last of all he produced flint and steel and tinder, caught, after many attempts, a spark upon this last, and transferred it to a length of slow match which he blew into a glow. All excitement, he was about to lay the match on the touch-hole when the harsh voice of el Bilbanito called him back. He was not to be the man to fire first shot from the gun.

El Bilbanito took the match, hardly hearing the armourer's pattered instructions. He had sense enough without them to stand clear of the wheel in the recoil, and he knew well enough that the way to fire a gun was to apply a match to the touch-hole. Leaning far over he pressed the spark against the loose grains of powder visible round the edge. There was a sharp fizzling noise, instantly drowned in an immense, a gigantic bellowing explosion. The enormous volume of the noise quite dazed el Bilbanito; it was much bigger than he had expected. The gun rushed from beside him in its recoil, crushing the fragments of rock beneath its wheels, and a huge cloud of smoke enveloped him. Through the smoke he could hear a wild cheer from his men.

Then the smoke cleared away. He was still standing holding the smouldering match, and the gun was four yards away. His men were gesticulating and pointing, and, looking in the direction they indicated, he saw that a little cloud of dust still hung over the patch of rock at which the gun had been aimed. The armourer had indeed achieved a miracle.

And the gun stood there with a faint wisp of smoke

still trickling from its muzzle, immense, imposing, huge. It almost looked as if it were filled with contempt for the little marionettes of men who capered round it, little things whose lives could be measured, at the best, in scores of years, and who were quite incapable unaided of hurling death across five hundred yards of valley.

C*

CHAPTER V

IT WAS not until the gun had been tried and proved that el Bilbanito allowed himself to send out the letters he had looked forward so eagerly to dispatching. Haughty letters they were, as befitted the only chieftain in Galicia who possessed an eighteen-pounder. All save one were addressed to the other guerillero leaders in this debatable land. They announced the brief fact that el Bilbanito now disposed of siege artillery and was intending an attack upon Leon; anyone who cared to come and serve under him would be welcomed. That the offer would be eagerly accepted el Bilbanito had not the least doubt; no one could lead the life of a guerillero and not yearn to push down into the plains; so great would be the desire that the chiefs would swallow their pride and consent to act as his subordinates —or, if they did not, their men would desert and flock to join the leader who could offer them with so much certainty plunder and victory beyond anything achieved up to now.

The other letter was just as peremptory and was addressed to the Junta—the hunted local government—of Galicia. It, too, announced that el Bilbanito now owned a gun, and it demanded instant supplies of powder and eighteen-pound shot, with plenty of pack animals to carry them, and ample forage, and muleteers. As an afterthought el Bilbanito included in his comprehensive demands a request for money, food, and clothing—not that he particularly hoped to get them, but because there was a faint chance that the Junta might have some stores for once in a way, and he felt he was just as entitled to a share as anyone else.

While he was awaiting answers to all his letters el Bil-banito took in hand the business of getting the gun back over to the edge of the plains. All the energy which Father Prieto and his party had expended in carrying the gun so far was not merely wasted, but was the source of a great deal of trouble, for el Bilbanito wished to bring the gun into action not many miles from the point where its regular gunners had abandoned it. And there was the question now of those French posts on the high road through the mountains; they would have to be circumvented. The gun would have to return by the route which el Bilbanito and his men had followed—over the crests, by the footpaths. The alternative was to use the gun to help storm the French posts, and from that el Bilbanito turned resolutely away. When he struck, he wished to strike at the heart; the reduction of the mountain garrisons would take time, and the plainlands would receive warning before he could be in among them.

Far and wide el Bilbanito sent his men in search of draught animals. They were hard to get nowadays. In one village where he came in person and demanded oxen the priest took him and, pointing down the valley, showed him a plough being dragged over a field by a strange team indeed—a little white ass, a man, and four women, the human beings bent double with the strain and only pre-serving their balance by supporting themselves on their hands, while an old white-haired man exerted his feeble

strength at the handles. El Bilbanito laughed and took the
ass, and the women were white to the lips as they saw
him and his men go off with it. Spring was near at hand,
the ploughing was not a quarter finished, and they would
starve before the year was out.

The asses and the one mule and the six oxen they
collected at last served their purpose in getting the gun
under way. Two wheels on an axle served as a limber to
which to attach the trail, and for some miles the gun moved
nobly along the high road. But soon they reached the point
where a footpath came down the mountain side and joined
the road. It was up this path that the gun had to go. El
Bilbanito had ordered it, and he was here with his pistols
to see that it was done. A mass of rocks was carried down
to bridge the ditch. The motley string of animals struggled
over it, the gun crashed after them, and the struggle began.

These lower crests of the Cantabrian mountains, on the
borders of Galicia and Asturias, are covered with that dense
growth of spiny bushes which is best known to English
people by its Corsican name of 'maquis', but which the
Galician peasant calls the 'monte bajo'—an impenetrable
tangle of small evergreen trees of different species, growing precariously on the rocky slopes. The mountain side,
too, is not a continuous uphill, but is broken up into a
precipitous switchback with a general upward tendency,
but alternated with down slopes as steep as the roof of a
house.

Ten men went on ahead with axes, cutting the undergrowth at each side of the path to allow the animals
following them to push along it two abreast. Beside the
team walked the drivers, one man to each animal, with

whips and goads, ready at a shout from el Bilbanito in the
rear to stimulate their charges into fresh frantic efforts.
Forty men walked beside the gun and limber, distributed
along the trail ropes; they had to be ready to pull forward
or back, or to turn the gun round corners, as the difficulties
of the path dictated. Then came a dozen men carrying two
thick trunks of trees, and ready to drop these behind or in
front of the wheels to act as 'scotches' where necessary.

It was el Bilbanito's personality which carried the gun
over those mountains. His men would soon have abandoned
the task as hopeless, despite the assistance which their
leader got for them by conscripting the aid of all the
peasants, men and women, whom he could catch. There
were times when an hour's labour meant only ten yards of
progress. That was up the steeper inclines, when they had
first to disperse and gather small rocks to make some sort
of road surface, and long ramps up and down at points
where the path charged over some steep minor ridge of
rock at gradients which would compel a man to go on
hands and knees. On these steep slopes men and animals
would rest to get their breath, while the gun was held up
by the scotches, until a warning shout from el Bilbanito
caused the men at the drag ropes to take the strain again,
and the drivers to hitch their goads ready in their hands.
Then el Bilbanito would shout 'Pull!' and the men would
tug, and the whips would crack, and the animals would
tug and flounder about on the uncertain foothold, and the
gun would move ever so little—a yard or two at most—up
the slope before the effort died away and the scotches were
dropped hastily behind the wheels again and the gasping
beasts of burden—on two legs or on four—could rest again.

The animals would fall and break their legs between rocks, but others could be got as the party moved on; a peasant threatened with instant death would generally reveal where an ass or an ox could be found. There was rarely any need to apply torture. Even cows had to be used—to this day the Galicians and Asturians use cows for draught purposes—but cows, with all the contrariness of their sex, persisted in dying under the strain without even the excuse of broken bones. The men did not die. They cursed el Bilbanito, they cursed the gun, and the cattle, but they lived. During this period el Bilbanito slept more securely than before; he knew that mutiny breeds in idleness, not in hardship or hard work. The men might curse, complain, grumble, but they were secretly proud of their efforts. There was a thrill in looking back down a seemingly endless mountain side and in knowing that they had dragged a gun all the way up it. Unremitting toil of the most exacting nature had always been the destiny of those peasants even in peace time, and now in war their labour was made more attractive for them because each man wore a plume of cock's feathers in his hat and belonged to the noted guerillero band of el Bilbanito, which was soon to sweep the plains of Leon by the aid of the gun.

In the mountains above Bembibre they found the first results of the letter writing el Bilbanito had done before setting out. As they came lumbering down into a village a band of ragged guerilleros came forth to welcome them from the houses in which they had been billeted. Foremost among them were two men not at all of the Galician type. They were tall and slender, with mobile humorous faces, and both of them had blue eyes and black hair—a most

unusual combination. El Bilbanito knew them by reputation. They were the brothers O'Neill, Hugh and Carlos,
who at the head of their Asturian band had distinguished
themselves the year before when the Spaniards had tried to
raise the siege of Astorga. Their surname explained their
colouring—they were the descendants of some Irishman,
possibly one who had 'left his country for his country's
good', or who had joined the Spanish army to avoid the
tyranny of Cromwell or of William III a hundred and
fifty years ago. Men with Irish names teemed in the
Spanish ranks; most of them were more Spanish than the
Spaniards by now, and few could speak English.

The two O'Neills bowed to el Bilbanito with much ceremony. They could appreciate what he had achieved in
bringing the gun thus far, and they could appreciate still
more the advantages the possession of the gun conferred.
El Bilbanito, on the other hand, was equally glad to see
them. He needed a large force for his projected raid into
Leon, and so was glad of the reinforcement; still more was
he glad of the promise it held out of further additions to
his force.

Carlos O'Neill was clearly all a-bubble with excitement
as he stepped up to the gun and examined it.

"My brother was in the artillery once," explained Hugh
to el Bilbanito.

"Indeed?" said the latter, with increasing interest. A
trained artillery officer was a most desirable acquisition.

They watched him as he looked over everything, examining the elevating and training gear, the detail of the
carriage work, the soundness of the metal of the gun itself.
Then he came back to them.

"Well?" asked el Bilbanito; for the life of him he could not keep a trance of anxiety out of his voice.

"May I congratulate you, señor?" said Carlos. "It is a magnificent weapon. Your Excellency must have good workmen to put together so good a mounting. They were artillerymen, I take it?"

"No," said el Bilbanito. "I have none with me."

"Indeed?" said Carlos in his turn, and the two brothers looked at each other.

"So you expected *us* to supply artillerymen when you wrote and invited us to join you, señor?" said Hugh, haughtily.

El Bilbanito shrugged his shoulders.

"You or the others. It was of no importance to me. I should contrive something, anyway. Call your men out and set them at the drag ropes. Mine are in need of a rest."

The inevitable quarrel between the chiefs might have flared out there and then. The Spaniard does not assume authority gracefully; he suffers from the defects of his qualities, and becomes overbearing when he finds himself in the position of leader. But at the moment the situation was eased by the rapid fraternization of the two bands. The O'Neills' men had in fact forestalled el Bilbanito's order, and, swarming out of the cottages, had relieved the new arrivals of their duties at the gun. At the moment they were going slightly downhill, and they were on a path which might almost be called a road from its width and regularity, so that the change was effected without difficulty. The two O'Neills had to break off the conversation in order to get their belongings from the house, hurriedly, for fear of being left behind. It was undignified, they felt.

They felt better when they came clattering up on their horses to catch up the column, for el Bilbanito was on foot like the rest of his men, like a true mountaineer. Carlos O'Neill, especially, could look down on el Bilbanito trudging along behind the gun, because his horse was an immense animal, a seventeen-hand grey, a most surprising sight in this land of fine mules and diminutive horses.

"Horses!" said el Bilbanito. "They will be useful when we leave the road again. Our team is weak, as you see."

"No, señor," replied Carlos O'Neill indignantly. "You will not have Gil to pull in traces. I value him far too much."

"I shall have him if I think it necessary," retorted el Bilbanito.

"No, no, no, never," said Carlos. "Take your hand away from your pistol, sir!"

El Bilbanito was determined to display his authority, and to nip any incipient rebellion in the bud. But as he drew and cocked his pistol, Hugh O'Neill's riding whip came down on his wrist, and the weapon exploded harmlessly. El Bilbanito flung the empty pistol into Carlos' face.

At the sound of the shot the two bands of men on ahead with the gun stopped and came running back, and the animals, grateful for the rest, began to munch the grass at the roadside. Carlos O'Neill had dismounted, and the big grey horse stood behind him looking over his shoulder like some wise counsellor whispering in his ear.

"You shall die for that blow," said Carlos, wiping the blood from his cheek. Hugh O'Neill came round beside him; the guerilleros began to draw up on each side of the road, the two bands facing each other. Muskets were being cocked; there seemed every likelihood of a bloody little battle on the spot.

"As you will," said el Bilbanito. "Here and now."

Jorge was at his elbow, Carlos drew his sword.

"Holy Mary, Mother of God!" said Carlos. "The fellow has no sword!"

"Not I," said el Bilbanito. "We settle our quarrels with the knife, we men of the mountains."

"Do you expect *me*, with the blood of kings in my veins, to fight like a brigand with knives?" demanded Carlos.

"Of course, if you are afraid, señor——" said el Bilbanito.

Carlos looked round him. His ragged Asturians for once had no sympathy with him. They knew nothing of the etiquette of the duel, and they took it for granted that knives should be used; as far as their knowledge went the knife was the national weapon of Spain. El Bilbanito was very sure of his ground.

"It is nothing to me," said Carlos, his fighting blood aflame. "Lend me your knife, you."

Even his brother could not remonstrate. An O'Neill could not be expected to refuse a challenge to fight with any weapon, at any time, against any opponent. All Hugh O'Neill could do was to watch to see that no unfair advantage was taken, and to hold himself ready to challenge el Bilbanito himself if—inconceivably—his brother should be defeated.

The sky was wintry and grey, and a cold wind blew down from the snow-covered peaks which closed in the horizon. At the edge of the road stood the gun, huge and immovable, with the weary animals harnessed to it in a long double line. The guerilleros were ranged in an irregular oblong, enclosing the piece of road where the quarrel was to be fought out, and in an angle of the oblong stood Hugh O'Neill, with the reins of the two horses over his arm; ever and anon he patted Gil's neck to reassure him in this matter of his master. In the middle of the oblong the two men seemed to dance a strange, formal dance. Each held his cloak over his left arm with the end fluttering loose; in his right hand each held a knife, the long slightly curved weapon of Spain, blade upwards, thumb towards the blade as a knife ought to be held. Each was bent a little at the knees and hips, and taut like a spring. They sidled round each other right-handed, their eyes narrowed with the strain of watching every movement of the enemy. Feint and counter-move followed each other like the steps of the dance which a casual observer might think they were dancing. Here and there in the ranks of the spectators men coughed nervously. In a fight with knives one man must die as soon as the opponents come within arm's length.

El Bilbanito had no fear of the result; he had fought too many of these duels, and, as he would simply say, he had not been killed yet. This man O'Neill handled his knife and cloak like a tyro, and caution was only forced on el Bilbanito on account of O'Neill's long reach and vigilant eyes. Yet they would not save O'Neill, not with el Bilbanito in front of him. If a feint did not throw him off his guard he could goad this beginner into making an attack which would lay him open to a deadly counter-stroke. El Bilbanito leaned to his left and dashed within O'Neill's guard. By a miracle O'Neill caught the knife on his cloak; it went through the cloak and through his arm, with satisfaction el Bilbanito felt the blade jar on the bone. He caught his enemy's right wrist in his left hand, and bent his knees and braced his thick body for the throw which would follow. The fight was won.

Perhaps his grip slipped; perhaps O'Neill's arms were stronger than he expected. O'Neill's wrist slipped from his hand. El Bilbanito was conscious of a violent blow on his side, which deprived him of his breath. There was a sharp pain in his chest, but it soon passed. El Bilbanito never knew that he had lost the fight; he never knew he was dying. With a strange dull curiosity he noticed his knees grow weak under him, and he felt himself, without knowing why, sink slowly on to the stones of the road. The light hurt his eyes, and he turned gently on to his face and lay limp. And over him stood Carlos O'Neill, with the knife in his right hand red to the hilt. El Bilbanito's knife still transfixed his left arm, from which the blood came in spouts, and ran down his wrist and fingers.

CHAPTER VI

THERE WAS Spanish regular infantry in the village
which looked out over the plain. They were the Princesa
Regiment, but they were not the least like the old regular
army, the men who had worn the white Bourbon uniforms,
with their cocked hats and the tight breeches and the black
gaiters. These men wore the rough brown home-spun of
the country; the coats were cut away in tails at the back,
and the trousers fastened with straps under the foot. And
they wore shakoes, too, so that altogether they looked like
gross caricatures of English soldiers.

   The appearance of caricature went farther than the clothing, for the men were at drill, and drilling grotesquely. The
lines were ragged, and there was no attempt at keeping step,
and when finally the colonel gave the word to form square
there was hesitation, muddle, until in the end the regiment fell together in one vast pudding-like mass, bayonets
pointing in all directions, while the colonel and the
adjutant raved from their saddles. In despair of ever sort-
ing out the confusion by drill-book methods the colonel
called out company markers, and gave the word for the
regiment to fall in on them, and while the men slouched
to their places the colonel made ready in his mind the
speech he determined to deliver, in which he would paint
in vivid terms the fate of the Princesa Regiment if ever it
tried to form square in that fashion with Kellermann's
dragoons charging down upon it.

It was unfortunate that at the moment when the colonel began his lecture there should come distraction from the mountain tops. Over the crest high up on the left a little procession came into view. The men and animals and vehicles composing it were dwarfed to specks by the distance, but in the clear mountain air they could be seen clearly enough, while even the sound of their progress, the shouts of the men leading the team, could be heard as a faint shrill piping. The spectacle was far more interesting than the colonel's hysterical lecture on tactics; every eye was turned up the mountain side, and soon every face was, and then in the end, while the colonel almost wept, the whole regiment broke up and lounged over to watch the fun.

The process of bringing the big gun down the mountain side was really exciting. There were four long drag ropes stretched out behind it, with thirty men to each, and every man lying back taking the strain and only allowing the gun to descend foot by foot to the accompaniment of the directing shouts of the leaders. In front a quaintly assorted team of draught animals was being led down, while round about the gun a dozen wildly energetic men were running back and forth, rolling the bigger rocks out of the way, working like fiends with levers when irregularities of surface tended to tip the gun on its side, and dropping scotches in front of the wheels when the drag-rope teams became disorganized and there was a chance that the gun might tear loose and come charging down the mountain on its own. Then when the angle of slope altered and the gun was faced by a short uphill the excitement redoubled. The team had to be harnessed up to the limber, a good momen-

tum imparted, to the accompaniment of deafening yells, to
the gun on the last bit of downhill, and then the drag-rope
crews had to rush round so as to pull forward instead of
back to carry the gun as far as possible up the slope until
the momentum died away and spasmodic efforts were
substituted for it, each painfully dragging the gun another
yard or two up until the next crest was reached. Altogether
it was a most entertaining spectacle.

When at last the gun reached the road the regiment eyed
it and its escort with curiosity. The gun was huge, enormous, in their eyes, accustomed only to the little field
six-pounders which were all the Spanish army could boast
nowadays. It came crashing and clattering down the road
on its vast five-foot wheels with a most intoxicating noise.
The odd team which drew it—three mules, six asses and
a couple of cows—did not appear so strange; they were
used to seeing the military train drawn by assorted teams.
And the men who came with it were not so unusual a
spectacle either; they had often seen guerillero bands
before, and more than half of them had been guerilleros
themselves before they had been caught and clapped into
the ranks of the army.

At the head of the band rode a tall young man in a
captain's uniform on a small brown horse; beside the gun
rode another man in the blue coat of the artillery, much
patched and very ragged, and the fact that his left arm
was in a sling accounted for his having mounted his horse
on the wrong side on reaching the road. His horse seemed
to have been proportioned to the gun, so colossal an animal
it was, a huge, bony grey like some horse out of a
picaresque romance.

The Princesa Regiment witnessed the meeting between the colonel and these two officers, and saw them escorted with much politeness to regimental headquarters beside the village church while the colonel's grooms attended to their horses. And then the regiment found itself, as frequently happens, with nothing to do. The men fraternized with the guerilleros, and examined the big gun with curiosity, and idled about as only Spaniards can, until their idling was interrupted by the sudden appearance of the guerillero captain in the little square outside the church. He clambered on to the breech of the gun, and all through the village they heard him shout, 'Princesa! Princesa!' and they came running to hear what he had to say.

CHAPTER VII

"I AM Colonel de Casariego y Castagnolt, of the Princesa Regiment of infantry," said the colonel, introducing himself, "and my adjutant, Captain Elizalde."

"I am Captain Hugh O'Neill, late of the Ultonia Regiment," said O'Neill. "May I present my brother, Don Carlos O'Neill, of the Artillery?"

The introductions were most ceremonious; it was not until they were comfortably seated in headquarters that any topic of business was mentioned.

"I understood from my orders," said the colonel, "that a certain el Bilbanito was bringing the gun here."

"We have el Bilbanito's men with us," replied Hugh O'Neill, "but el Bilbanito himself, most unfortunately, did not survive the difficulties of the journey."

"But how sad," said the colonel. "How did he die?"

"It was a sudden indigestion," interjected Carlos O'Neill.

"Very sudden," elaborated Hugh.

"I have heard of the disease before," said the colonel. "Was it steel or lead he was unable to digest? Or perhaps —perhaps he suddenly found himself unable to breathe?"

"It was something like that," said Hugh, airily.

"Quite so, of course," said the colonel, with his glance drifting over Carlos O'Neill's bandaged arm. "And now to business."

The colonel did not seem in too great a hurry to start,

all the same. He took a long pull at his cigar, and he made a searching examination of its ash, before he could bring himself to say what he had to say.

"In consequence of el Bilbanito's lamented dicease,' he began slowly, "I must address my orders to you, señores. Those orders are——"

"Yes?" prompted Hugh O'Neill, when the pause grew too long for his patience.

"My orders are that I take the gun out of your charge. The Junta has decided that it is too valuable to risk in the plains. They have decided to employ it in the fortifications of Ferrol, whither I am to escort it at once."

There was a shocked silence for a moment before O'Neill's anger blazed out.

"What?" he said. "Take it all the way back again? Take it away from us? Never!"

"Those are my orders from the Junta, señores," said the colonel, firmly. "It is my duty to obey them. And may I remind you that it is the duty even of guerilleros to obey the established government?"

"It is simple plain foolery," said Hugh.

"I could think of a worse name for it," said Carlos.

"Perhaps I could too," said the colonel, "but I would not say it to my superior officer."

"So they have sent no ammunition, nothing?" demanded Hugh.

"Naturally not. Why send ammunition from Ferrol when it is at Ferrol that the gun is to be used?"

"But el Bilbanito made all sorts of plans to use the gun on the plains," said Hugh.

"I am aware of that," said the colonel. "El Platero with

two hundred men is waiting to meet him between here and La Merced, Cesar Urquiola has brought up his cavalry. Even Mina has sent a battalion of his Navarrese to the rendezvous."

"With a thousand men and the gun we could raid as far as the great road," said Carlos O'Neill.

"I think it extremely likely," said the colonel. "You could set all Leon in an uproar. La Merced has only two hundred men in garrison, with two six-pounders."

"Indeed?" said Hugh, professional interest quickening. "I thought it was stronger than that. We can take it easily, then."

"You might, if you had a gun to do it with. But un- fortunately, señores, as I am the first to admit—you have no gun."

"But you cannot take our gun from us, colonel. It would be criminal folly to waste this chance."

The colonel had to brace himself before he could reiterate his determination. It was sad to disappoint these two young men; it was sadder still to throw away an oppor- tunity which even the colonel's limited military instinct told him was ideal. But he had his orders, and he must abide by them.

"I must repeat, gentlemen," he said, slowly, "that I start for Ferrol tomorrow with the gun."

Carlos O'Neill's chair fell over with a clatter as he got to his feet.

"We won't permit it," he said. "You shall *not* have our gun."

"This sounds like insubordination," said the colonel.

"So it is! The gun's ours and we shall keep it!"

"Don Carlos, that is not the way to speak to your superior officer. I might punish you severely if I did not make allowance for your youthful enthusiasm."

"You will *not* have the gun. Not if I die for it."

"Don't say words of ill omen like that, Don Carlos. Remember—gentlemen, you force me to say this—that outside I have three battalions of my regiment. Fifteen hundred men altogether. And you have—two hundred? Three hundred? If you force me to take strong measures you see that I can carry them out. And if your insubordination is maintained outside the privacy of this office I shall have to take official notice of it. I shall have to call a court-martial to try you for mutiny. There is only one penalty for mutiny, gentlemen, and you know what it is."

For the moment the colonel thought he had won his point. Neither of the young men spoke. Carlos O'Neill even replaced his arm in the sling whence he had withdrawn it in his excitement. Then Hugh O'Neill rose from his chair, where he had been seated all through the interview. He said nothing, but walked slowly to the door; the colonel and his adjutant followed him with the eyes. So lackadaisical were his movements that no one could have suspected him of any plan. He opened the door, walked through, and shut it behind him. The colonel was genuinely sorry for him; he thought that, overwhelmed by sorrow at being deprived of his beloved gun, he had gone out to work off his despair in drink, or, possibly—for mixed Spanish and Irish blood plays queer tricks—even in exercise. The colonel was only disillusioned when he heard O'Neill's voice ringing out like a trumpet, "Princesa!

Princesa! Oh, Princesa, come and hear about this new treachery in high places!"

The men came running to hear him. They massed themselves around the gun on to which he had climbed. Irish eloquence winged his Spanish words. He told of the mountain sides over which they had dragged the gun, and of the mustering of guerilleros at the rendezvous, of the coming of el Platero and of Mina. He told them of the helpless garrisons in the plain, the prisoners who would fall into their hands, the plunder which was there for the taking, the welcome they would receive when they freed the towns from the hated French dominion. He got a roar of laughter from the plainsmen among them when he said that he was tired of the belly-aching mountain cider and wanted to drink honest wine again—it was a deft argument which appealed both to those who looked on wine as a necessity of life and those who considered it a rare luxury.

Colonel Casariego made his appearance in the mob just as O'Neill was working up to his climax, telling the men that folly or worse at headquarters had decided to waste all these glorious opportunities. The Princesa Regiment was ordered back to rot again in garrison at Ferrol, and they were to drag the gun back with them over the mountains. Carlos O'Neill sidled up to Colonel Casariego as he made his way towards an excited group of his officers. Before the colonel realized what was happening something was dug uncomfortably into his ribs and, looking down, he saw that it was the muzzle of a pistol. At O'Neill's back there were half a dozen of his gang.

"I think we will go back to headquarters, colonel," said O'Neill, politely.

The only satisfaction Colonel Casariego found as he sat miserably in his headquarters with a sentry at his door, listening to the hullabaloo outside, was in the periodical arrival of his senior officers, who came to the house under O'Neill's escort, in ones and twos, and were incontinently locked up with him. The three majors commanding battalions, the older ones among the captains, the adjutant and the quartermaster, all came to share his captivity. What was significant was the absence of the junior officers. It was no surprise at all to the colonel when Hugh O'Neill made his appearance again and announced to the waiting officers, "Gentlemen, the Princesa Regiment has decided to follow me to the plains. Any of you officers who care to join me and serve under me, retaining your present rank, will be welcome. I only ask your word as gentlemen to give faithful service to me and the cause of Spain."

There was only a moment's silence before Captain Albano rose.

"I am with you, sir," he said.

And one after the other the majors, and the captains, and the quartermaster, came over to O'Neill. Only Colonel Casariego was left, sitting solitary at the table. There was nothing left for him to do but to make his way back to the Junta and confess his failure, to tell of the desertion of his whole regiment. He bowed under his misery. His face went down into his hands, and he wept. O'Neill shut the door quietly, and left the old man weeping.

CHAPTER VIII

CAPTAIN LUKE BRETT, of His Britannic Majesty's forty-gun frigate *Parnassus*, was in his cabin reading the Bible, for he was a religious man, when a midshipman knocked on the door.

"Come in," said Captain Brett.

"Please, sir," said the midshipman, "Mr. Hampton says there is a fishing boat coming off from the land, apparently signalling to us."

Captain Brett looked instinctively up at the tell-tale compass over his head.

"Tell Mr. Hampton I'll be on deck directly," he said.

He put the marker carefully between the pages of his Bible, and followed the midshipman to the quarter-deck. Last night's gale had died down by now. The *Parnassus*, close hauled under easy sail, heaved and swooped over a quartering sea, with every now and again a spatter of spray tumbling in over the starboard bow. Captain Brett's all-embracing eye swept over the ship; in that one encircling glance, as his officers well knew, he could inspect every detail of the routine of the deck. He looked at the trim of the sails, at the gleaming white decks, the shot in the racks and the hammocks in the nettings, the course of the ship, the working party overhauling cable on the forecastle. Away on the port side could be seen the brown cliffs of Spain, with Cape de las Peñas in the distance.

The first lieutenant was looking forward through his

62

telescope, and Captain Brett, following his gaze, saw a
little speck appear on the crest of a wave, disappear in a
trough, and appear again, bobbing violently. It was an
open fishing boat running down wind under a brown
lugsail to intercept them. As the captain looked through
the telescope which the lieutenant handed him he saw a
speck of white run up to the top of the little mast and
down again, up and down.

"Yes, they're signalling to us. Bear down two points,
Mr. Hampton. Heave to and let them come alongside when
we reach them."

"Shall I have a bo'sun's chair ready, sir? You know
what these dagoes are."

"As you wish, Mr. Hampton."

Lieutenant Hampton's suggestion was proved to be a
very sensible one, for the man who was swung eventually
on to the *Parnassus'* deck from the yard-arm clearly could
not have climbed a rope. He had one arm in a sling, but
that was not the most important of his disabilities. He
was green with sea-sickness as a result of the violent
motion of the fishing boat; moreover, to Mr. Hampton's
huge disgust, his feet were no sooner on the deck than he
vomited again, helplessly, holding on with his one hand
to the rope of the bo'sun's chair over his head.

"God damn all dagoes," said Mr. Hampton.

When the paroxysm passed the man looked about him.
He was a tall, slender man, dressed in something resembling
uniform—a much patched blue coat with some gold lace
still adherent, and white breeches and boots and spurs;
perhaps it was the first time that spurs had ever jingled on
the deck of the *Parnassus*.

"El capitan?" he asked, inquiringly.

"I am Captain Brett, of this ship."

Clearly the man spoke no English; the words meant nothing to him, but at sight of Captain Brett's uniform, shabby though it was, and air of authority, he decided that Captain Brett was the man he sought. He produced from his pocket a small leather wallet, and with infinite care he drew a letter from it and offered it to the captain. It was an innocent-looking enough letter, although it would have been his death warrant if he had fallen into the hands of the French with it on his person. The captain glanced through it, examined the signature with care, and passed it on to his lieutenant, who read:

OFFICE OF H.M.'S MISSION TO THE ASTURIAS
GIJON
10th June 1810

This is to make known to officers of His Britannic Majesty's forces by land or sea that the bearer of this recommendation, Captain Carlos O'Neill of the Spanish Artillery, is an officer in the Partisan forces of Spain, and to charge all such officers to render all assistance to Captain O'Neill as their duty permits and as they may judge will further the common cause.

HENRY BERKELY, Major
H.M.'s representative in the Asturias
Second Foot Guards

"That's Berkely's signature all right," said Captain Brett. "I've seen one of these things before. And what's this he's trying to show us now?"

D

Captain O'Neill was trying to draw another paper from his wallet, which fitted it so tightly that in his one-handed condition he found difficulty in drawing it out.

"Allow me, captain," said Captain Brett; the fellow's bowings and scrapings had actually infected him, too.

Captain Brett drew out the paper; it had been long folded and was in danger of tearing along the creases.

"Oh, it's his commission," said Captain Brett.

It was indeed a noble document, embossed at the head with the arms of Spain and bearing three seals at the foot; it was printed in type resembling a flowing italic hand, but quite incomprehensible to Captain Brett because it was in the Spanish language. But he could see that written in by hand here and there through the document in gaps purposely left were the words 'Don Carlos O'Neill'. It was obviously a genuine document, and established the identity of the bearer.

"If his name's O'Neill, why the devil doesn't he speak English?" asked Lieutenant Hampton.

"He's a Spanish-Irishman. I've seen his sort before," said Captain Brett. "He had better have a drink while we find out what he wants."

The gesture of offering a drink is an easy one, actually within the capacity of a stiff-necked naval captain; while he made it Captain Brett heard a chuckle from the midshipman of the watch at his side, but Lieutenant Hampton. that resolute disciplinarian, saved his captain's dignity.

"Fore to'ga'n masthead, Mr. Norman," he said. "And stay there until sunset."

And the midshipman went, crestfallen, while Captain Brett escorted Captain O'Neill with ceremony to the companion ladder. But once down below, where everything heaved and creaked and swayed, O'Neill's misgivings overpowered him. Unceremoniously he turned and rushed up the ladder again and fell limply across the leeside bulwarks.

"Poor fellow!" said Captain Brett. "A glass of my old port ought to do him good."

The captain's steward brought chairs and bottles and glasses, and, once seated, with a glass of brandied port inside him (where, for a miracle, it stayed), O'Neill seemed to get better.

"Now, captain, tell me what I can do for you," said Captain Brett.

The words meant nothing to the Spaniard, but the tone in which they were spoken did. He got out of his chair, and looked round the ship. The twelve-pounders down on the main deck clearly, from his attitude, were not what he sought. But he went across to the big eighteen-pounder quarterdeck carronade, looked at it with delight, took out the tompion, examined the bore, and then slapped the gun with pleasure, pointed to himself, and then at the distant shore.

"He wants to take our eighteen-pounder away with him!" said Lieutenant Hampton.

"I don't often swear," said Captain Brett, "but I'll see him damned before he does."

Both officers shook their heads violently, and O'Neill's face fell until he realized that they misunderstood him.

"What's he looking for now?" asked the lieutenant.

"He's found it," said the captain.

O'Neill, after staring anxiously round, had seen hanging by the wheel the slate and pencil of the log of the watch. He rushed and seized these, and began hurriedly drawing with the slate on his knee. After three minutes he showed them the results of his work—a neat drawing of a big gun on a military carriage. He pointed to the picture, and then he moved his hand in a circle round the muzzle of the carronade, and then out to the mountains again, and then to his chest.

"He's got an eighteen-pounder on shore," said Captain Brett, and nodded and smiled, trying not to look quite as foolish as he felt.

Thus encouraged, O'Neill started drawing again.

"What in God's name is this?" asked Hampton, who was looking at the drawing upside down as it progressed. "Grapes?"

"No, shot, of course," said Captain Brett. It was a picture of a pyramid of cannon balls.

Brett opened the shot rack beside the carronade, and lifted out one of the eighteen-pounder shot and offered it inquiringly to O'Neill.

"Si, si, si," said the latter, nodding ecstatically.

"At last!" said Brett.

But O'Neill was drawing again, excitedly.

Now that they were on the track only a cursory glance was necessary to recognize the new drawing as a picture of a powder barrel.

"He wants powder and shot for an eighteen-pounder siege gun on shore," decided Captain Brett. "He can have them."

One paragraph of his orders laid stress on the need to help the Spanish forces, and to co-operate with them wherever possible. It was only English sea power, reaching out across hundreds of miles of ocean, which sustained the Spaniards in their interminable struggle with the French Empire. But for that, the Spanish insurrection would long before have been quenched in blood as had been the Tyrolese revolt, and the Lombard revolt in preceding years.

"I don't know how he thinks he'll get them, sir," said Hampton inquiringly. "The French have got every port garrisoned between here and Ferrol."

"He knows some quiet inlet or other, never fear," replied Brett. "Look, he's drawing again."

The new picture was unmistakably a mule—not a donkey or a horse, because O'Neill's pencil point laid great stress on the ears and tail. Then O'Neill spread the fingers of his one sound hand ten times, and pointed down the coast.

"He's got fifty mules waiting somewhere," said Hampton.

It was Captain Brett who solved the difficulty of finding out the exact place; O'Neill could think of no method of conveying his meaning, for all his pointing and gesticulating.

"The chart, Mr. Hampton," said Captain Brett.

With the chart of the coast spread out before him O'Neill had no difficulty in pointing out the exact little bay he had in mind. Everybody this time was nodding and smiling, pleased with the progress made despite all difficulties.

"He's drawing again," said Hampton.

O'Neill was making an addition to his picture of the mule; when he passed it over it had along its side five cannon balls held in a sack over its back.

"That means ten altogether to each mule," commented Brett. "They always overload the poor brutes."

Next the cannon balls were rubbed out by O'Neill's wetted finger and replaced by a powder barrel. O'Neill pointed at the mule so adorned and then spread his fingers.

"He means he wants five loads of powder, and forty-five of shot—four hundred and fifty rounds. Let me see." Captain Brett was not of a really agile mental quality, but he succeeded in solving the problem of mental arithmetic presented to him.

"Yes, he's about right. That is not quite enough powder, but I suppose it is easier for them to get powder than eighteen-pounder shot."

"That's four tons of shot, besides the powder, sir," said Hampton, who also had been doing mental arithmetic. "It'll mean sending the cutter—that boat of his isn't nearly big enough."

"That is so," said Brett.

The two officers looked at each other and then found themselves glancing uneasily at O'Neill as if he could read their thoughts although not understanding their speech.

"It might be a trap, sir."

"Very true, Mr. Hampton. You will have to use all precautions. Have the four-pounder mounted in the cutter, and loaded with grape. Get that boat of his in tow, and I will stand in after dark. You can cast off *here*"—Brett's stubby finger indicated the mouth of the inlet—"and I will wait for you."

"Yes, sir."

"And call the gunner and see to breaking out the shot and powder he wants. Offer him a few rounds of canister and grape as well as round shot. He may need 'em, some-time."

"Aye, aye, sir."

"If it *is* a trap, Mr. Hampton, that boat will be just ahead of the cutter as you go in. Fire the gun into it, and then come back, bringing this gentleman with you. We will see how he looks at the yard-arm."

There is no need to follow Captain Brett and Mr. Hampton through the complicated task of explaining to Carlos O'Neill in dumb show the fact that he was their prisoner until the cutter should leave the inlet after nightfall unharmed. The rising moon found the *Parnassus*, a shimmering white ghost of a ship, hove to off the mouth of the bay. Captain Brett, leaning on the quarter-deck rail, had felt so much confidence in O'Neill's obvious honesty that he was not in the least surprised or relieved when he heard the splash of oars returning down the bay and knew that the munitions had been safely landed. Mr. Hampton came on board to make his report.

"Yes, Mr. Hampton?"

"Everything was as he said, sir. The mules were waiting on the beach. I saw them loaded and start up a little path up the cliff."

"Very good, Mr. Hampton, hoist the cutter in."

But it was a different story five days afterwards when Captain Brett came on board again after going on shore for orders at Ferrol.

"Oh, Mr. Hampton," he said, "do you remember that man O'Neill who came on board when we were off Cape de las Peñas? If ever we see him again we are to put him in irons and bring him here for trial."

"For trial, sir?"

"Yes, they want him for treason, and mutiny, and—bless my soul, there's no end to his crimes. Berkely gobbled like a turkey at the mention of his name."

"Was that recommendation of his a forgery, then, sir?"

"No, but it was a year old. We noticed that. And since Berkely gave it to him—just before he came off to us, in fact—he has got half the Spanish army to mutiny and taken them off on the opposite course to what Berkely ordered. The Junta is sick with rage about it."

"But what did he want the ammunition for, sir?"

"For his eighteen-pounder. It's the only siege gun in all Galicia, it appears. The Junta wanted it for themselves, it appears, and O'Neill thought otherwise."

"He seemed to me to be a man of sound judgment, sir."

But Captain Brett did not try to countenance any criticism, however veiled, of the government of His Majesty's Peninsular allies.

CHAPTER IX

WHILE HUGH O'NEILL was waiting for his brother's return he came to know all the sensations of a man in a powder magazine with the building on fire. The idiocy of the Junta in not sending the ammunition which el Bilbanito had demanded was imposing delays on the invasion of Leon, and delays were dangerous. There was no fear of the French; with Wellington loose again in the South and every French resource at strain to hold him in check the French were content to sit quiet in their garrisons in the North and hope not to be attacked. Every movable body of troops in Leon was on the march for the Tagus, as O'Neill well knew, and he had little to fear that any news of the concentration in the mountains would leak out to them. Nor was there much to fear at the moment from the Junta. That was two hundred miles away, at Ferrol, and it would be long before the news of the defection of the Princesa Regiment reached it; it would be longer still before they could move up troops—if they had any to spare—to interfere with him.

The danger lay round about him, close upon him. Troops which had mutinied once might mutiny again. He had seduced them from their allegiance by a promise of an invasion of Leon; with every day that the invasion was postponed their turbulence increased. The fact that there was no ammunition for the gun would be attributed to his negligence, and no mob ever stops to listen to excuses.

O'Neill, a year or two ago while he was still with the army, had seen San Juan, a real general, hung up in a tree by his mutinous troops and then used as a target. Something like that would be his fate if he had to hold these undisciplined villains in check much longer.

It was a blessing that Carlos had been able to move off at once in search of ammunition. The Princesa Regiment's mule train had been at his disposition, and fortunately Carlos still had the recommendation to the English which Colonel Berkely had given him nearly a year before. The sea was only thirty miles away, across three ranges of mountains. Hugh O'Neill tried to be pessimistic in his estimate of the time Carlos would be gone. He decided that Carlos might be back in a week, and he set himself to keep things quiet for that time. He called out the Princesa Regiment for manoeuvres and worked them until they were ready to drop. He sent the guerilleros, both those of his own band and those of the deceased el Bilbanito, on expeditions hither and thither to harry the wretched villages for food—he had nearly two thousand men to feed, and the whole district had been plundered and re-plundered for years. He sent urgent messages to el Platero —the silversmith—and to Joaquin Alvarez, Mina's lieu-tenant, and to Don Cesar Urquiola, begging them to have patience and await his arrival at the rendezvous. But all the same it was a mighty relief to the young man when a boy rode up on a pony with a note from Carlos. He was on his way back with the ammunition, and would reach them shortly. O'Neill called down a blessing on the British Navy and issued the order to his motley forces to make ready to get on the move. The animals were harnessed up to the gun and they set out on the last stage of the journey through the mountains.

The gun, the big lumbering thing, was responsible for much already. Here, on the edge of the mountains, was assembled the biggest concentration of irregular troops the war had seen as yet. Besides the Princesa Regiment there was O'Neill's band and el Bilbanito's. There was Alvarez with his Navarrese, whom Mina had sent from their Pyrenean hunting grounds. There was el Platero with his Biscayans, and Urquiola with his Castilian horsemen—the only guerilla troops who had dared to carry on the war in the plains. They were of a different type from the mountaineers, lean, dignified men, who wore their clothes and their beards with an air. Pennons fluttered at their lance points when they trotted up to meet the descending column, and their spurs and accoutrements jingled bravely. Yet Urquiola and el Platero and Joaquin Alvarez all greeted O'Neill with deference when they came up to him as he rode beside the gun. It was not the two thousand men whom he commanded who made them so respectful; it was the gun. Its thirteen feet of length, its five-foot wheels, its immense breech, all indicated its colossal power. One and all, those men had chafed at the restraint imposed upon them by the little fortresses in the plains. This gun would knock those places to pieces.

On the evening when the forces were all met, O'Neill and his brother walked out to where the mountains definitely ceased, along a path which ran along the top of a huge green spur jutting from the mountains into the plain. Here, where the hill fell away in a steep escarpment, they could look out over the plain, and note the winding rivers and the scattered villages, and the rich fields and the numerous roads. It was from this very point that el Bilbanito had stood gazing out over the plain, a long time ago, wishing that he had artillery with which to descend into it, but neither of the young men was aware of that, and perhaps if they had been they would not have considered it a matter of ill omen. Their hearts were high, and they laughed as they laid their plans. Carlos O'Neill even considered it now worth that loss of his dignity which he had suffered on his visit to H.M.S. *Parnassus*, worth the sea-sickness and the childish drawing on the slate and the gesticulations which had (in his opinion) consorted ill with the gravity of a Spanish gentleman with the blood of kings in his veins.

CHAPTER X

MAJOR JONQUIER was a Dutchman. He was a fat, pale, fair man with pale blue eyes, slightly protruding. He was not much given to thought; he never meditated upon the strangeness of the fate which made Holland a part of France, and which had carried him off from his land of dykes and windmills, and had set him down in command of a mass of French conscripts in the sun-soaked plains of Spain, and had bestowed upon him the high-sounding title of Governor of La Merced, and had set him to hold Spaniards in subjection to a Corsican who was known as Emperor of the French.

He was a man of phlegmatic temperament, but he was a little annoyed when a message came to him, just when he was comfortably dining, to the effect that there were enemies in sight. With a sigh he got up from the table, and rebuttoned his tunic, and refastened his stock, and buckled his sword-belt round his bulging waist, and drained his glass of wine, and took his telescope from its hooks on the wall, and then, sighing again, he addressed himself to the climb up the steep stone stairs to the first floor, and he positively grunted with the exertion of climbing the vertical ladder which led to the roof. If the sentry had allowed his imagination to run away with him, he would get a week's *salle de police* for disturbing him at this, the most sacred hour of the day.

Determined to get the business over and done with

75

without delay, he did not linger on the roof, but walked straightaway over to the bell tower, bowed his head to enter by the low door, and climbed ponderously up the little ladder to the little square platform at the summit, where the French flag flapped languidly in the slight wind. The sentry was there, and the sergeant of the guard, and the addition of Major Jonquier's portly form made the platform uncomfortably crowded when he squeezed through the trapdoor.

He extended his telescope and looked about him, and the sergeant of the guard pointed excitedly towards where the mountains towered up from the plain.

"Hum!" said the major to himself, and again "Hum!"

There was something which looked like a snake a mile long advancing up the road from the mountains, where the sun was about to set in scarlet glory. From the length it must be a small army, but it was so wreathed in dust that nothing could be definitely ascertained, except that through the dust occasionally could be seen the flash of weapons. But ahead of the column the governor could plainly see more of the enemy. There was a small column of horsemen on the road, and out to right and to left of it were smaller groups of cavalry winding their way along the field-paths parallel to the road. Clearly there was a strong force of the enemy advancing to the attack of the fort, screened, as the best military opinion dictated, by an advance guard of cavalry. As the major's glass swept the plain again his eye caught sight of something fluttering where the cavalry rode. They were lance pennons—it must be Urquiola and his mounted brigands come up from Castile. Once before they had penetrated this far. There must be a concentration of guerilleros—an event often expected but never witnessed before.

Major Jonquier began issuing his orders even before he left the platform. The messenger was to ride at once to Leon with the news of the attack. Major Jonquier was quite certain that the messenger would not do any good; he knew that in all the province there was no relieving force which could be sent to him at present. The monthly convoy of supplies with its heavy escort was only due to arrive in three weeks' time. But the garrison—an unreliable lot—would be more cheerful if they knew the messenger had ridden off.

Meanwhile for three weeks the major was equally certain that he could hold off the attack of any mob of irregulars, who of course would be without artillery. He came down into the fort and began a rapid inspection of the defences.

La Merced had been a convent, a large square building of grey stone built round a central courtyard. Its position for the defence of the bridge was ideal. It stood on a rounded hillock just away from the river and a complete hundred yards from the roadway where it joined the bridge. At one time the land on which it stood had been enclosed by a high stone wall, but this had been torn down because of the protection it might offer an attacking force, and had been replaced by a high strong palisade of wood, of which the posts stood just far enough apart to prevent a man squeezing through. This palisade would delay any storming party, and as it stood within comfortable musket range of the convent it formed an important part of the defences. The building itself, like many Spanish convents, offered windows only towards the courtyard; the four exterior walls were quite blank, save for the loopholes which the garrison had knocked in them all round. The stone which had once formed the park wall had all been carted up to the convent and built into two little bastions at opposite corners, in each of which was mounted a six-pounder, one commanding the bridge and the other the road. Each gun could fire along two faces of the building, so that if the attackers were even able to climb the palisade they would find themselves merely at the foot of the blank walls, pelted with musketry from the loopholes and scourged with an enfilading fire of grape from the guns. No wonder Major Jonquier felt easy in his mind as he went along the corridors seeing that everything was in order.

One of his two companies of infantry was on duty, the men standing at the loopholes looking out; the other company, instead of making the most of its period off duty, like sensible men, were gathered about in groups in the barrack rooms, or peeping out of the loopholes, discussing the new development. But then, they were only recruits, not veteran troops.

Major Jonquier went out on to each bastion in turn. At each gun were five artillerymen. The linstocks were burning and the guns were loaded ready with grape. With a grunt of satisfaction he waddled back again into the convent. He peeped into the courtyard. His six cows were there, in improvised wooden stalls—Major Jonquier was a man who insisted on milk in his coffee and butter on his bread. He saw that the sentries keeping guard over the doors of the cellars in which were the stores were at their posts. He gave orders for carcasses—bundles of rags soaked in oil—to be made ready on the parapets. If these were to be lighted and tossed over they would give all the light necessary to shoot down the attackers in the event of a night attack. Night was already falling rapidly, and it would be dark before the raiding army reached the convent.

He went back into his own room and shouted to his servant for his dinner. That servant was a perfect fool. He had the incredible imbecility to bring in to the major the omelet which had been ready to serve before the alarm— it was a nightmare of an omelet now; as the major said, with oaths, it was the colour, shape, consistency, and toughness of the sole of a shoe. He drove the man out to the kitchen to prepare another.

It was no excuse for the man that he was a Spaniard and would be hanged for certain if the place were taken. The place was not going to be taken, and an omelet was a more important matter than a Spaniard's neck, anyway. The second omelet was only a slight improvement. Major Jonquier groaned as he ate it; the man's nerve must have been completely ruined by his fright. But the braised beef with red pepper would be better—Major Jonquier had prepared that dish with his own painstaking hands before this bother about guerilleros had begun. He ate it hungrily, heard with annoyance that there was no soft cheese to complete the meal, and contented himself with hard. He finished his wine, and shouted for his coffee and brandy. He stretched his legs beneath the oak table and tried to feel like a man who has dined satisfactorily. It was a useless effort. A dinner interrupted half-way through can never be a good dinner. The bleak grey stone room was too Spartan by far for his tastes, and it was so infernally cold, despite its miserable brazero of charcoal, that he had to wrap his cloak round his legs. The tallow dips gave only a suspicion of light. The coffee was not coffee at all, but only a horrible chicory substitute which the continental blockade forced him to drink. His cigar was perfectly foul. Major Jonquier thought of his native Holland, of white-tiled stoves and oil lamps and good coffee and a black cigar with a straw up the middle. The only thing which was satisfactory was the brandy, and even of that he did not think it advisable to drink more than three glasses after his couple of litres of wine. The horrors of war were decidedly unpleasant.

He could not even drink his brandy in peace because that young fool Captain Dupont insisted on coming in to tell him that the guerilleros were in earshot. The major growled like a bear, climbed up to the roof again, and peered through the night over the parapet. Decidedly there was activity out there in the darkness. The major and the captain could hear voices, shouting, and laughter. The neighing of a horse came distinctly up to them. Then a new sound reached their ears—the chink of spades and pickaxes. Some working party out there was digging vigorously. Major Jonquier decided it must be on the summit of the mound lower down the road, a quarter of a mile away. What they could be digging was more than he could guess—barricades, probably, across the road as a defence against cavalry. He knew by experience that those guerilleros from the mountains, who had half of them been miners in the days of honest work, would dig like badgers on the slightest provocation, huge, useless fortifications, always in the wrong place.

He was tempted to go down to the bastion and order a shot or two in that direction, but he decided against it; ranging and aiming were too difficult in the dark. He impressed upon Dupont the need to keep the sentries well awake, so that they would hear if anyone tried to chop down a section of the palisade under cover of the darkness. He himself repeated his tour of inspection, and testily ordered the young men of the company off duty to get to bed and go to sleep. The whole garrison would have to be on duty an hour before dawn. Major Jonquier confidently expected that the guerilleros would try their usual tactics—a wild rush in the grey of the early morning.

They could do so if they liked. He could predict the result, having fought guerilleros often enough before. Many men would die at the palisades. A few ardent spirits would perhaps hew a little gap. A few others would haul heavy scaling ladders up the slope, but they would not even reach the foot of the wall. They would be shot as they climbed under their burdens, and then finally the whole mob would break up and run and probably not stop until they reached the mountains again. It would be a salutary lesson for them, and for another few weeks he would be able to dine undisturbed and sleep in peace. As it was he went and lay down on his bed with all his clothes on, even his sword as well, leaving strict orders that he should be called before daylight.

In the dark morning when his servant came to wake him he started out of bed as soon as he was called. Pulling his cloak close round him in the biting cold he walked out

into the dark corridors. The passages rang with the sound
of the heavy boots of the men coming up to take their
posts at the loopholes. All of them were shuddering with
cold. Jonquier turned to the sergeant at his side.

"Have the soup heated and brought to the men at their
posts," he ordered.

He went up on to the flat roof where Dupont was nervously pacing about. The young fool had evidently not
been to bed, and the major was about to reprimand him
severely when his words were cut short by a new series of
sounds down by the road. There was a cracking of whips
and a clanking of chains. Lights showed, flickering, over
by the mound.

"What in hell——?" said Jonquier, peering vainly
through the darkness. The lights moved vaguely about.
Someone shouted hoarsely. There was a terrific bustle over
there.

"Oh, well, we shall know soon enough," said Jonquier,
philosophically.

The eastern horizon was just beginning to grow a little
paler, and it became evident that it was going to be a misty
morning.

"Keep your men awake up here, Dupont," said Major
Jonquier. "And remember never to leave any side of the
fort unguarded, however hard they may be attacking the
other ones."

He lowered himself down the ladder and reached the
first floor. The men were all at their posts here, and as he
descended a private came clattering along with a pail of
soup, and another followed behind with a basket of bread.

"If they attack," he said to the nearest group, "don't

get muddled. Don't drink your muskets and fire your soup
out of the loopholes."

The men laughed. Everyone liked old pot-bellied Jonquier
and his funny guttural French.

"And aim low," said Jonquier more seriously. "Aim for
their legs and put an end to their fandangoes."

He waddled down the staircase to the ground floor.
Everyone down here had finished their breakfast.

"Feeling better for your breakfasts, men?" he asked.
"That's good. Now you won't——" He made the same
joke as he had made on the first floor, and got the same
laugh.

"And aim low," he went on just as before. "Aim——"
Jonquier was doing his duty. He was cheering up his
soldiers, and embedding the pill of good advice in the jam
of banter.

He went to a loophole and peered out. By now it was
nearly full light, and the mist was beginning to shred
away. If the guerilleros were going to attack, they were
losing their best opportunity. The big bulk of the fort must
be fully visible to them by now. It was strange that they
should delay. He walked through into the big grey stone
room which had been the refectory and which ran along
the whole of one side of the building, facing towards the
mound down by the road.

"Feeling better for your breakfasts, men?" he asked.
"That's——"

A terrific crash interrupted him. The building shook, and
the whole hall was filled with stone dust and flying chips
of stone. Someone screamed. Something fell on the stone
floor with a clang and rolled towards Jonquier. It was a

big cannon ball—a most certain indication that La Merced was doomed. Jonquier looked at it as though death itself was rolling towards him over the floor—as indeed it was. A big section of the two-foot thick wall had been knocked in, leaving a nearly circular hole two feet in diameter between two loopholes. The unhewn stones of which the wall was composed had been sent flying to all parts of the room. A man with a shattered wrist was still screaming, as much with fright as with pain.

"Stop that noise!" said Jonquier, pulling himself together. "Go down into the store-room and get one of the servants to bandage that arm for you. Get to your posts, men."

With all the appearance of nonchalance that he could assume he walked to the hole the cannon ball had made and looked through it. There was still a slight mist outside, but it would hardly last five minutes longer with the thirsty sun drinking it up. Down there by the mound the mist seemed thicker. No, it was a cloud of powder smoke which was gradually dissipating. Jonquier could make out the raw brown of the newly turned earth; five seconds later the smoke had drifted sufficiently away for him to see, vaguely, a rude breastwork which had been dug. And pointing out through the embrasure of the earthwork he could see the muzzle of a big gun. Even as he looked the gun disappeared in a burst of white smoke, and in the same instant the building shook again to a splintering crash as the shot hit the wall twenty feet from where he was standing. The concussion threw him to the floor.

There was panic in the long hall, but Jonquier dragged himself to his feet in time to check it.

"Back to your posts, you cowards!" he roared. "You, sergeant, shoot the next man to flinch."

The men hesitated, but Jonquier stood firm.

"Each man must lie down by his loophole," he said. "And stand up and aim straight when the rush comes. I am going to turn the guns on their battery. We'll not be hit without hitting back."

On the first floor he saw young Lieutenant Lecamus fidgeting with his sword hilt and biting his lips with nervousness. Even as they met the building shook again as another shot hit the wall below.

"Go down to the refectory and keep the men there up to the mark," Jonquier ordered. "And pull yourself together first, man."

He brushed the grey dust from his salient abdomen, and, wheezing a little, hurried on to the bastion. Here the gunners were standing to their gun.

"Why the devil haven't you opened fire?" he demanded.

"No orders, sir," said the sergeant in charge.

"Orders? Who waits for orders in a siege? You're not fit for your job. Slew the gun round and open fire with round shot on that breastwork. No, don't stop to draw that charge. Fire the grape out."

The gun roared out its defiance, but it was a much more insignificant sound than the deep-mouthed bellow of the big siege gun which the guerilleros had somehow acquired. In the smoke the artillerymen sponged out the gun, rammed in cartridge and ball, and the sergeant crouched over the breech to aim. He stepped aside and jerked the lanyard. Jonquier saw the earth fly from the wing of the breastwork.

"High and to the right," he said. "Reload."

Then the big gun on the mound fired back, and this time the shot hit the solid mass of the bastion six feet below their feet.

"Ha ! " said Jonquier. "We've taught them to leave the wall alone."

The sergeant fired the gun again, but this time it was a clean miss. No one saw where the shot fell.

"Reload," said Jonquier. "I will lay the gun next time."

As he spoke the big gun on the mound thundered forth its reply, and the ball screamed through the air close over their heads.

"Devilish good gunners down there," said Jonquier to himself. "And a devilish good gun."

He crouched over the breech, looking through the notch on the elevator bar and the groove on the muzzle swell. In the bit of the interior of the breastwork which he could see through the embrasure he saw bare-armed figures labouring over the siege gun. He aimed carefully, and signed to the sergeant to fire while he moved aside to note the effect. This time earth flew from the face of the earthwork close to the embrasure.

"We'll hit him next round," said Jonquier. The gun was wiped out, the cartridge rammed, and a gunner was about to thrust the ball into the muzzle when the reply came. Eighteen pounds of solid iron, flying at three hundred yards a second, hit the little six-pounder square on the mouth. The air was full of flying bits, and the gun was flung back off its carriage. It was split clean open for half its length, one trunnion broken off, the carriage knocked to pieces. The gunner with the cannon ball fell dead with a fragment of iron through his neck.

Jonquier looked down at the wreck and ruin. He was of the type that failure merely makes angry, not despairing. The blood surged into his face. He clenched his hands and stamped his feet. But by an effort of will be prevented himself from shaking his impotent fists at the enemy and compelled himself to speak calmly and carelessly.

"Our gun receives an honourable discharge," he said. "Get your muskets and lie down, you men. Save your fire when the rush comes until they are at the foot of the wall."

He climbed back out of the bastion on to the roof again, and walked over to the other bastion. As he went he felt the fort tremble again as another shot hit the wall below. The Spaniards had recommenced, pitilessly, pounding at the main building to open a breach.

The reason why the other gun had not opened fire was obvious. The angle of the fort projected between it and the siege battery. There was nothing to fire at. Jonquier played with the idea of hoisting the gun up to the roof, running it across, and lowering it down to take the place of the injured gun, but he abandoned it. Even a six-pounder is a difficult and ponderous thing to hoist about, and the breach might be achieved and the assault made while the gun was still out of action. Besides, this gun had been mounted to sweep the bridge; the whole reason of La Merced's existence was to guard the bridge. Removing the gun from this bastion would leave to the Spaniards practically free passage over the river.

He looked down towards the bridge and the river and

caught his breath. The enemy were already over the river. He could see little knots and groups of men on the farther bank. Presumably they had crossed lower down during the night by small boats. Now a little group of men ran on to the bridge. Some of them waved their arms. Jonquier wished he had his telescope with him so that he could make out details, but he was only three hundred yards from the bridge and could see well enough. One member of the group seemed to be walking unwillingly, as if he were being dragged along. Another leaned over the parapet of the bridge as if he were fastening something to it. Then, with a bustle and a scurry the unwilling man was hoisted up and flung over the parapet. Jonquier heard the artillerymen standing beside him breathing suddenly hard. The unwilling man's fall from the parapet was abruptly checked. It ended with a jerk, which threw his arms and legs into the air in grotesque attitudes like a child's toy. Then he swung idly like a pendulum in a little arc, turning first his back to the fort and then his face, and his bald head shone in the newly risen sun. Then Jonquier recognized him; it was Julio Coppola, the renegade Spanish postboy, whom he had sent out the night before with the news of the attack. Jonquier shrugged his shoulders. Even if he had got through, it was much to be doubted if help could have come for another fortnight; but all the same, it was annoying that the Spaniards should have hanged him so publicly, because otherwise he might have told his men that help might come any moment, and so stimulated them to beat off the attack.

"Don't hang about gaping like this," he snarled to the artillerymen. "Sweep that rabble off the bridge."

The men seemed to wake from an evil dream, and sprang guiltily to the gun; the whole hanging had only taken a few seconds. While they were aiming the Spaniards were scuttling back across the river like naughty boys discovered in mischief. It was almost too late when at last the gun was fired. The grape shot plunged down to the roadway of the bridge, ploughing it up, and sending chips flying from the parapets. Only one shot found its target. One of the men, hit in the leg, was thrown to the ground, and, prostrate, continued to writhe comically towards safety. The others were all safely hidden in the undergrowth along the river bank.

"Reload," growled Jonquier, "and keep that bridge clear in future."

He went back over the roof and down to the refectory. The room here was thick with dust. but enough light came in through the gaping holes in the wall to show the damage which had been done. There were big ragged rents everywhere along it; the floor was littered with the stones which had been flung in. As Jonquier stood gazing round another cannon ball arrived, sent flying a big stone which was projecting into one of the holes, passed across the room, knocking a table into splinters, and crashed through the inner wall into the kitchen beyond. The men were crouching as close to the floor as they could, lying still like dead men, all save Lieutenant Lecamus, who was walking up and down trying to be brave.

"Can't I take the men out of here?" said Lecamus, as plaintively as he could whisper. "They would be safe enough in the cellars, and we could call them out when the attack comes."

"If we once let them down into the cellars," replied Jonquier, "there will be no getting them out again when the attack comes. You know that as well as I do. It will do them good to be shot over a little." He did not add "and you, too," although he thought it.

The pitiless pounding went on. Monotonously, every few minutes, a fresh hole appeared in the wall. The Spaniards were breaking it from end to end, and a good gun they must have had, and reliable powder, because there was very little variation in the height up the wall at which the balls hit—three feet or so. Then with a rumble and a crash a whole section of the wall, completely cut away at the bottom, came tumbling down, cascading partly into the room. Jonquier sprang forward. He was sure that the sight of that wall falling would draw the Spaniards to make their assault. One good attack, beaten back with heavy loss, would take the heart out of them and stiffen up his men. But the attack did not come. Looking out from the breach Jonquier saw no enemies. The gentle wind had blown a long smear of smoke across the country from the enemy's battery, and that was all. The dazzling sunshine revealed no column of attack. The enemy were all hidden away out of sight, behind the mound, and under the embankment of the road.

"How much ammunition have the bastards got?" asked Jonquier of himself. "Are they going to pound the whole place into ruins before they attack?"

The only answer to the question was another shot, which hit the wall towards one end and brought down yet another big section of the crumbling structure, and another shot after that, and another, remorselessly.

Then at last came a break. Jonquier heard the high notes of a cavalry trumpet twice repeated. Two men appeared over the earthwork on the mound, and began to walk steadily towards the fort, first down the slope, and then up the gentle incline to the palisades. One had a bit of white cloth on a stick; the other blew his call upon his trumpet.

"All the etiquette of war!" sneered Jonquier to himself. "A flag of truce and a trumpet like one gentleman to another."

He was about to step through the breach to meet them, but checked himself. There was no need to make too much disclosure of the practicability of the gap. He turned back through the kitchen and the hall, and went out through the main door, and round the building to where the trumpeter and the flag of truce were standing at the palisades.

The trumpeter was a Basque to judge by his round blue cap—some Pyrenean smuggler, doubtless. The other wore some fragments of the blue uniform of one of the mercenary regiments of the Bourbon kings of Spain. Jonquier stopped five yards from them and stood waiting for them to speak. The officer turned to the trumpeter and said something to him, and in turn the trumpeter addressed Jonquier, speaking the vilest French.

"You must surrender," said he.

"I shall not surrender," said Jonquier.

The trumpeter and the officer conferred, and then the trumpeter turned to Jonquier again.

"If you surrender," he said, "we shall grant you your

lives. If you do not, you will all be killed. That is what the laws of war say."

"I do not discuss the laws of war with brigands," said Jonquier. "I am an officer of the Emperor. And I trust that when General Kellermann's dragoons arrive this afternoon I shall have the pleasure of seeing you on the end of a rope."

That was the best he could think of in the way of stimulating the besiegers to make a premature assault. He turned his back and walked away, striving to be as dignified as possible in the eyes of his men, who he knew would be watching this interview from the parapets and loopholes. He trailed his sword and he stuck out his chest and cocked his shako.

"This is your last chance," called the trumpeter harshly through the palisades after him.

Jonquier made no sign of having heard, and left them to turn away with no appearance of dignity. Even trifles like that may affect the spirits of troops.

It is hard to say what motive made Jonquier so obstinate in the face of death. He cannot have had overwhelming confidence in his troops to beat off an attack. He had no hope of relief. He was fighting in a cause in which he did not feel any interest. Possibly it was sheer blind obstinacy, the obstinacy of a man who finds a piece of work to his hand and will not abandon it though it kills him. Perhaps it was fighting madness, or its latter-day equivalent, professional pride. But it was hard to associate either of these qualities with the fat little man—whose blue tunic rode up in horizontal creases over his belly—despite the military splendour of his red epaulets and glittering buttons.

Lieutenant Lecamus awaited him anxiously in the refectory, and the men stood about wishful to hear what he had to say.

"You had better lie down, men," was what he vouchsafed, "they will be opening fire again soon."

And then, when they had obeyed, disappointed, he continued:

"You'll soon get your revenge for being shot at. Each of you can kill six of them, while they come up the slope. But one or two each will be enough to set them running back again."

His words were emphasized by the bellowing roar once more of the siege gun on the mound. But no shot hit the fort.

Curious that they should have missed, thought Jonquier. There came another roar from the gun, and still no sound of the impact of the ball. He went up to the roof where Captain Dupont still stood with his company crouched behind the parapet. From the roof he could see the explanation. The enemy were firing grape at the palisades. They were making good practice, too. Jonquier saw a blast of grape hit the ground six feet before the palisades, tear it up, and then, continuing on, cut off short a full dozen of the stout posts. Five rounds of grape cut enough gaps in the palisade for fifty men to make their way through at once.

Still Jonquier did not care. From the parapet of the roof, from the bastion, and from the breach itself he could turn a hundred muskets upon the attackers when they came up over the glacis. If his men held their weapons straight the enemy could not break in. Struck with a new thought he sent Captain Dupont's drummer flying down to the servants huddled in the cellars—renegade Spaniards, all of them. They were to bring up to the roof all the spare muskets and ammunition. All the men there could have two muskets each, and the servants could help with the reloading.

Until this reinforcement arrived Jonquier was in a fever lest the assault should be launched before the new arrangement was settled, but there was no need for this anxiety. The gun in the breastwork had opened fire again with round shot, and was resuming its remorseless, monotonous pounding of the walls.

Jonquier left to Dupont the marshalling of the trembling civilians and went down again to the breach. The whole side wall was now blasted away, and was represented by a long heap of stones piled up from ground level. The sun was pouring into the long room, illuminating the chaos within—shattered furniture, huddled corpses, scattered stonework.

The firing was now being directed at the corner of the building, where the walls were trebled in thickness in a solid pillar to support the weight of the floors above. At every impact of a ball the building trembled, and they heard the fall of a little avalanche of stone outside. Jonquier wondered grimly what would happen when the pillar gave way. He looked out through the breach at where the gun was firing away, remorselessly, one shot every four minutes. There was only death or captivity in store for him if it continued. Yet there was no means of silencing it. Jonquier thought of a sally; he might gather the greater part of the garrison together and charge out and try to capture and damage the gun. But he put the project away as hopeless. There was no possible chance of it succeeding. Two hundred men could not charge across four hundred yards of open country against two thousand enemies. To attempt it would only precipitate the end. The only thing to do was to fight it out to the last where he stood—a determination which suited his temperament admirably. He set his teeth with sullen ferocity.

There was not much longer to wait. One last shot knocked away so much of the supporting pillar that it collapsed with a rending crash. The whole building was full of the sound of smashing rafters. Stones and plaster rained down from above as the whole angle of the building collapsed. The dust hung thick as fog round the fort. It seemed for a brief space that the whole structure would fall like a house of cards. The men at the loopholes on the first floor and on the roof were flung down as the floor heaved beneath them. Then with a horrid sound the bell tower which surmounted the angle buckled in the middle and came crashing down on to and through the roof, flinging the look-out sentry in a wide arc a hundred feet to the ground.

Jonquier wiped the blood from his forehead where it had been cut by a flying chip of stone, and peered through the dust.

"Stand to your arms, men!" he roared. "Here they come!"

Masses of the enemy had broken out from their cover behind the mound, at the roadside, in the ditches. They were racing up the hill. Their wild yells reached Jonquier's consciousness as only a shrill piping—rage and excitement

E

having forced up his blood pressure to such a pitch that his hearing played him tricks. His own stentorian shouts, the reports of the muskets, seemed to him no louder than the sound of children at play.

"Don't fire until you can see the buttons on their clothes!" he yelled. "Aim low!"

But half his men were too numb and dazed to fire. Others loosed off their muskets at hopelessly long ranges. A solid wave of stormers reached the palisades and burst through the gaps. Only one or two fell to the firing. The others poured forward up to the breach and began to pick their way through the littered stones.

"Back with them!" yelled Jonquier.

With his blood aflame he leaped on to the breach. Somehow he had lost his shako, so that his sparse fair hair gleamed in the sunshine. He plunged down the ruins sword in hand, but none followed him. He struck someone down, and found himself in the midst of enemies. For yards on either side of him Spaniards were pouring up the breach. Some gathered round him, and he slashed at them impotently with his sword—an odd, ungainly figure he made with his pot belly, plunging about on the heaped stones, cutting at his wary enemies. He felt the blade rasp down a musket barrel. Then he became conscious that someone was shouting at him, the same word, over and over again. They were calling on him to surrender.

"Never!" he said, and slashed once more.

Ten yards away a Spaniard dropped on one knee and took aim. The musket cracked, and Jonquier fell on his face among the piled-up stones. His little short legs moved pathetically for a moment.

And the breach was won and La Merced was taken. The Spaniards raged through the corridors and the halls and the chapel. They were as merciless as only men can be who have taken a place by storm, as merciless as may be expected of men with uncounted defeats to avenge, with uncounted oppressions to make payments for. Some of the groups they met here and there tried to fight, and some tried to surrender, and each attempt was equally unavailing. The wretched French boys died on the bayonets, or were shot at close range so that the flash of the muskets scorched their clothes. They were hunted down in the cellars like rats. They were killed as they huddled round the chapel altar. They were flung over the parapets of the roof, and were finished off as they writhed with broken bones at the foot of the wall.

CHAPTER XI

So La Merced was taken, and the passage was won across the Orbigo. Great was the plunder. The cellars were heaped with food—there was enough there to supply the starving Spaniards for a week at least. There were chests of silver coin, the accumulated tribute wrung from unhappy Leon. There were clothes for the naked, and weapons for the unarmed. There was a six-pounder field gun to add to the artillery train of the besiegers, and there were welcome supplies of powder. And lying among the ruins, easily to be found, were the cannon balls that the siege gun had fired at the place. Some were in fragments and useless, but quite half were still round enough to be used again. Ninety rounds had sufficed to batter in the walls of La Merced, and there were still four hundred to load on to the ammunition mules.

And the wine, the vast barrels of last year's vintage, was a delight to these men, who for months had lived lives of severe hardship. It was not long before every nook and cranny of La Merced was filled with shouting quarrelling groups, who drank and fought and fell asleep and woke to drink again. The natural abstemiousness of the Spaniard and the peasant was forgotten in the flush of victory. By midnight three-quarters of the victorious army was dead drunk. The tiniest fraction of the French army would have won a resounding victory over them if such had been near, but there was none. There were some among the

Spaniards who kept their wits—especially those who had first reached the treasure chests. They must have borne in mind the cry of the irregulars at the beginning of the war —'*Viva Fernando y vamos robando*'—'Long live King Ferdinand and let's go robbing'—for during the night several little parties of men made unobtrusive departure from the fort, with heavy haversacks, which might have emitted the musical jingle of coined silver if they had not been so carefully packed. The disintegrating effect of victory upon undisciplined forces was thus early marked.

But the morning and the rising sun found at least the most important unit of the attacking force still at its post. The gun still stood in its redoubt, glaring motionless over the earthen parapet. The heavy timbers which had been laid beneath its wheels were splintered and cracked under the shock of the recoil of its ninety discharges. Heaped up beside it were cannon balls in depleted pyramids, opened barrels of powder, all the litter which the gun's crew had hastily left behind when they ran forward to join in the plunder of the fort. The commanding officers of the army, even, were not there. They were in a peasant's cottage a mile away.

It had been a deadly shot that Jonquier had fired, the one that had flicked those masses of earth from the parapet. Hugh O'Neill had received the full blast of pebbles and sand right in his face, driven with enormous force, as he had stood in the redoubt directing the fire. They had borne him away stunned; the quick blood had masked his face so that Carlos O'Neill did not know the extent of his brother's injuries, while he stayed to continue the

battering, and to conduct the parley with the French commander, and to let his yelling hordes loose in the assault
when the corner of the fortress collapsed. He did not know
how badly Hugh was hurt until the afternoon, when he
mounted his big horse and rode back to the cottage, intent
on cheering his wounded brother with the news of the
success.

Hugh was in no mood to be cheered by any news whatever. Consciousness had returned to him, and all he could
think of was the agony in his face and eyes—his eyes were
sightless pits of pain from the sand which had been flung
into them. There were no medicines, no dressings. The
men who were with him could only lave his ragged face
with cold water and hold his arms when his hands sought
in his madness to increase the damage done, while he
screamed and choked with the pain, uttering horrid shapeless sounds from the tongue and through the cheeks that
the stones had riddled, revealing the shattered stumps of
the teeth the stones had broken.

He would have asked them to kill him and end his
agonies, Carlos guessed, if he had been able to articulate,
and more than once he thought of using the pistol in his
belt on this brotherly duty, but he could not bring himself
to do it. He could only sit there beside him, listening to
the horrid sounds, until at last pain brought its own relief
and Hugh fell unconscious again. Mortification and blood-
poisoning might in the end save Hugh from his fate, of
dragging on his existence blind and with a face no one
could see without shuddering, a blinded officer, dependent
until the end of his days upon charity.

The gun called insistently for all the attention Carlos

could give. The blow must be struck hard and quick and now that the way had been opened for it. There must be no dallying now. The French dominion over the plains must be shattered before they could draw together sufficient forces to parry the blow. Carlos had never been anything other than a soldier. His childhood had been passed in barracks, and his adolescence in the ranks. His father and his grandfather and his great-grandfather before him had been soldiers. Family tradition and the professional pride of the soldier by birth forbade him to think of abandoning his task. The possibility never occurred to him. His brother might die of disease or starvation, but he himself must go on. The government he served was notorious for its in-efficiency and its ingratitude, but the soldier does not bear that in mind. He knew nothing, or next to nothing, of the peasants he wished to set free—the monasticism of barracks gave few opportunities to a soldier of meeting the people who found the money to clothe and feed him—but that was beside the point; it was as inconsiderable as the fact that he knew nothing of the men he was to kill. His sole task was to go on fighting. He was undoubtedly glad that the fortune of war had brought him his present important command instead of the obscurity of an artillery captaincy, just as in the old days he had been glad that Fate had given him the dignified occupation of man-killer instead of relegating him to the lowly ranks of farmers or doctors or shopkeepers, but this again had no influence on his decision to continue with his duty. Heredity and environment left him incapable of considering any other course. He must go on fighting as a river must run down-hill.

So that in the morning the soldiers and the brigands who were sleeping off their debauch in and around La Merced were roused by their commander with bitter words. The lash of his tongue drove them back into the ranks, and set the teamsters hurriedly harnessing up the draught animals to the gun, and the muleteers loading their mules again with cannon balls and barrels of powder. The column was formed quickly enough, the Castilian lancers riding ahead, the infantry trailing along the road with no more trace of formation than a flock of sheep. They were over the river at last, pouring forward on to the rich plains, chattering and laughing and singing, while in their midst rode O'Neill on his huge grey horse. He was silent and dry-eyed, although he looked back to the cottage where his brother lay awaiting death in charge of the half-dozen lightly wounded. Behind came the gun, rumbling and clattering along the stony road, with its long team extending fifty yards ahead of it, and the attendant gunners walking at its side, while after it rambled the fifty pack mules of the ammunition train, with their balanced nets of cannon balls or barrels of powder rubbing their raw backs rawer still.

It was a typical day of the Spanish spring, with winter left behind. The sky was a hard blue, with scarcely a cloud, and the sun that glared down upon the plains bore more than a promise of its midsummer tyranny. As far as the eye could reach the plain rolled away on all sides in gentle undulations, green and pleasant now with the young corn, and only broken here and there by the scattered villages of greyish-brown brick.

Over the plain and into the villages the invasion swept

like a flood. Urquiola and his lancers came clattering in. Haughtily they made their demands. Who was there who had shown signs of acquiescing too readily in the French dominion? The villagers pointed to one and another whose fate was sealed. What carts, what draught animals were there? Each village must find food in proportion to its size, twenty loaves to every house, one sheep to every three, delivered immediately in the carts. Money? Communion plate? Powder and shot? All was swept in. Young men of military age? They must join the ranks. The liberation of the plains proceeded satisfactorily.

At the next river there was a force of the enemy, only half a company, a hundred men. They had no fort here to guard the bridge, there was only an entrenched redoubt covering the approaches, in which the garrison could retire on the approach of an enemy; normally the men lived in billets in the village. The garrison had taken refuge here the day before, as soon as they heard the noise of the bombardment of La Merced, like a minute gun proclaiming the end of the French dominion over the province of Leon.

They had no artillery and little food, and they knew that the message they had sent to the town of Leon asking for help would bring small response, and they had had a chilly night huddled in the trenches, and when they saw three thousand enemies pouring down the road towards them their hearts misgave them. Jonquier had died rather than yield; the elderly lieutenant in command here preferred to yield rather than die. He guessed what must have happened at La Merced, and when he saw the big gun run up and preparation made to batter a gap in his flimsy

E*

earthworks he had one of his white shirts hoisted on a
pole in sign of surrender. He had a strong card to play.
The bridge behind him was of wood. He would burn it
unless their lives were spared.

O'Neill rode up to the redoubt on his grey horse, with
his interpreter running by his stirrup, and granted the
terms demanded without argument; time was valuable
now. The garrison marched out feeling a little sheepish,
and laid their arms on the ground while the Spaniards
clustered round them. The French had been promised their
lives, but they had been promised nothing else. They were
stripped of most of their clothes, of their invaluable shoes,
of their haversacks and pouches. Finally, half naked and
barefooted, they were handed over to a sergeant to escort
to the rear.

What their fate was to be was rather worse than the
elderly lieutenant had ever contemplated. Ferrol was the
nearest place where the Spaniards could lodge prisoners in
security, and Ferrol was two hundred miles away, beyond
the Cantabrian mountains. French prisoners, barefooted
and half naked, guarded by men without the least interest
in keeping them alive, would fare badly in a mountain
march of two hundred miles through a hostile population.
But they were fools, of course, to have expected anything
better.

Then the column pressed on, over the wooden bridge.
The Asturians and the Galicians, and the Navarrese whom
Mina had sent, were prodigious marchers. The regulars—
for what the name is worth—of the Princesa Regiment
kept up as best they could. The sun began to sink
towards the west, behind them. Still they toiled on, down

one long incline and up the next. Every little crest they reached displayed the same interminable landscape before them, in which the villages came as welcome but only transient breaks. Still they tramped along the narrow road, sandy here and rocky there, while the sun beat upon their backs and the dust caked upon their mouths, and O'Neill sat silent on his horse in the midst of them.

In the late afternoon there came a sudden flurry of excitement. One of Urquiola's lancers came riding up to the column, and the news he bore caused O'Neill to drive in his spurs and gallop forward hastily to the head of the line. There was cavalry out ahead of them; it might be Kellermann's dreaded dragoons come up from Estremadura. The rumours that Leon was bare of troops save garrisons might be false. A thousand dragoons, led by the man whose charge had won the battle of Marengo, would sweep the flimsy infantry away, capture the gun, and bring this expedition to a ridiculous end.

However, O'Neill found his alarm unjustified. There was only a single squadron of French cavalry out on the plain; presumably they were the recruits with remounts whom report had described as detained in Leon on their way south. Urquiola's two hundred lancers hung round them, neither side daring to subject their shaky troops to the trial of a charge. O'Neill could see the French commander riding in front of his men, shading his eyes with his hand as he peered forward into the setting sun to ascertain what was this unexpected army pouring into Leon.

At sight of the French a yell of defiance went up from

the marching infantry. The Spaniards shook their fists and waved their weapons, and called to their enemies to come on. At the sound O'Neill's lips wrinkled in a sneer, although he did not let his men see it. Three times already he had marched with Spanish armies which had yelled defiance at the sight of the enemy and which had called just as eagerly for battle. And every one of those three Spanish armies had been shivered into fragments at the first charge of the French cavalry—brave words forgotten, heroic determinations thrown away, weapons cast aside, running terrified in all directions. O'Neill had no illusions about the quality of this fourth army. Mina's disciplined Navarrese might stand firm. The others would run. He could only hope to achieve anything with this mob by the inglorious method of avoiding all collisions in the open country, attacking garrisons while he might and hurrying to the shelter of the mountains at the first approach of a field army.

The commander of the French cavalry, having noted the length of the column on the road, and the gun and the wagons at the rear, and the bearing of the troops, and all else concerning which he would have to make report to his master, wheeled his men about and trotted off, Urquiola and his lancers trailing after him at a safe distance. And at the same moment the milk-white spires of Leon cathedral, tinged to pale rose in the reflected light of the sunset, showed at last upon the horizon. Not for two long years of war had any Spanish army—save those marching back to captivity in France—set eyes upon them. It was with some consciousness of achievement that O'Neill gave orders for the march to end, for pickets to be sent on up the roads while the men found shelter in billets or bivouacs where they could, and for the gun to be halted under his own supervision in the roadside inn which he decided should be his headquarters for the night.

CHAPTER XII

O'NEILL DINED that night in the company of his senior officers; el Platero sat at the foot of the table, uncouth in his stubby black beard—he never seemed to have more or less than four days' growth—and with him were the majors commanding the three battalions of the Princesa Regiment, and Don Cesar Urquiola, and Alvarez, who commanded the Navarrese, all of them light-hearted and gay. They ate the tough chickens with relish, and they drank the best wine the worried innkeeper could provide.

This latter individual fluttered round them anxiously. It was nervous work satisfying the wants of the new conquerors; the fact that there was not the least chance of his being paid for this dinner, or for the accommodation of the two hundred men who were billeted in the outbuildings, was the least of his anxieties. His inn had been a favourite rendezvous for young French officers riding out from Leon, who had even been known to pay for their meals, and he feared lest this should be held to indicate that he was a 'Josefino'—one who had become reconciled to Joseph Bonaparte's rule over Spain—and if that were the case his existence would end abruptly in a noose of a rope.

No wonder he did his poor best to see that his visitors were comfortable, and he eyed with increasing trepidation the stony melancholy of O'Neill, who sat heedless of the gaiety of his companions, drinking glass after glass of wine with no visible effect. The dim candlelight shining on his face showed his expression to be desperately unhappy. He looked out over the heads of his officers, and seemingly through the blotched white-washed walls into the darkness beyond. It was only that morning that he had left his brother blinded and with his face in tatters. And the Irish blood in his veins, small in proportion though it might be, made him specially liable to these fits of brooding melancholy.

Yet there were moments of satisfaction even during this nightmare depression. They came when his glance wandered out through the window, out to the courtyard lit by the lanterns of the headquarters guard. For there, solid and immovable in the centre of the court, stood the ponderous mass of the gun. O'Neill found something supremely comforting in its presence. He had come to love that colossal eighteen-pounder.

Outside, at the door of the inn, an argument arose. The sound of it drifted into the main room where the officers sat. They could hear men expostulating, and a deep booming voice, unknown to them, overriding the expostulations. Finally the door opened and a Franciscan friar entered. He was a huge, burly man; his hood fell back over his shoulders revealing a close-cropped head of black hair and a wild tangle of black beard. His greyish-brown robe was in rags so that his bare legs could be seen. His sandalled feet were filthy with road travel. Behind him were visible the frightened innkeeper and an equally frightened Jorge, who were responsible for admitting him.

The huge Franciscan—his head seemed to brush the low

ceiling—gazed down at the men around the table, and
addressed himself without hesitation to O'Neill.

"You are the general of the army?" he demanded.

"Yes," said O'Neill.

"I have a message for you."

O'Neill signed to Jorge to withdraw and close the door,
but the friar checked him.

"It does not matter who hears my message," he said.
"It is one of good cheer. Go up boldly against Leon. The
walls will fall before you, and the atheists will die—will
die—will die. The hand of God is at work in Leon, and
those whom God may spare for *you* to kill must be killed
without mercy. They were all killed at La Merced?"

"Yes," said O'Neill.

"All? Everyone? That is well. But you spared those
others today at the bridge of Santa Maria. That is evil.
The atheists must be slain, and you have spared a hundred
of them to fatten in idleness."

El Platero laughed; he knew—none better—how in-
appropriate a description this was of the prospective fate
of the wretched prisoners sent back to Galicia. But his
laugh ended on a wrong note as the Franciscan turned his
terrible eyes upon him.

"The hand of God may reach those who laugh in the
hour of the Church's agony," said the Franciscan solemnly.

Then he looked deliberately at each person at the table,
and each one dropped his eyes before his glance.

"Kill, and spare no one," he said. "Remember that the
hand of God is at work in Leon. I am going on to be the
instrument of God elsewhere."

With that, he turned about. They heard him stride

down the little passage, and they heard him bless the
sentry at the main door as he passed him.

"Who the devil is that?" asked el Platero.

"God knows," replied Urquiola. "Here, innkeeper, innkeeper!"

The worried host came in, wiping his hands nervously
on his grey apron.

"Who was that friar?" snapped Urquiola.

"Really, sirs, I do not know for certain. They say——"

"Well?"

"They say that he was one of those that fought at
Saragossa. Brother Bernard, the world calls him. They say
he is more than human. A year ago Marshal Bessières at
Valladolid offered a thousand dollars for his head, and as
you see, gentlemen, he has not paid it yet. He was in the
city of Leon for three weeks past. He walked in the streets,
but the French did not arrest him. They say he can make
himself invisible to French eyes, but I do not know
whether that is true."

"Neither do I," said el Platero with grotesque solemnity.

"That will do, innkeeper," put in O'Neill, unexpectedly,
and the innkeeper withdrew relieved.

O'Neill sat brooding at the head of the table. Suddenly
he looked up.

"Gentlemen, I hope you have enjoyed your dinner," he
said.

That was one way of dismissing them. El Platero remembered he had to go round the outposts to see that his men
were awake. Urquiola had problems of forage and farriery
to solve. The officers bade O'Neill good night; he hardly
condescended a monosyllable in reply, still sitting there,

with his hands resting on the table, looking into vacancy.
They were all a little piqued at this aloofness, and
grumbled at it as they emerged into the keen night air.
The thought was in the minds of all of them that this boy
of four-and-twenty had no business usurping the command over grown men of experience. They had not minded
obeying Hugh O'Neill, but this young Carlos. . . . It was
a pity he was the only artillery officer of them all. Still,
that did not make him entirely indispensable. The men
would follow him while he gave them victory and plunder,
but at the first check . . .

O'Neill, who had not slept for two nights, allowed his
forehead to droop down to the table. Among the three
thousand men whom chance had brought under his command there was not one to whom it occurred to see that
O'Neill had a bed to sleep in. The groom who had brought
in his saddlebags was now comfortably drunk in the cow-
stall where Gil was tethered. It did not occur to his Spanish
mind to seek out any additional duty. It was left to the
innkeeper to suggest bed to O'Neill, and to bring in a sack
of straw and lay it on the floor for him—the innkeeper
slept in the pleasant warmth of the kitchen, with his wife
and serving maid and ostler and five small children. Now
that Hugh O'Neill was disabled, there would be no one to
dress the wound which el Bilbanito's knife had made in
Carlos O'Neill's arm three weeks before. Fortunately a
clean stab heals best when bound up in the blood, so that
Carlos had no need now for the sling, and the wound itself
was nearly healed and hardly troubled him.

Yet O'Neill's night was disturbed. There were numerous
people who urgently wanted to see him, people who had

somehow, despite guards and curfew orders, contrived to
escape from Leon and had walked or ridden out to where,
as rumour had soon spread the news, the headquarters of
the raiding army were to be found. Most of them were
pitifully anxious to interview O'Neill. They pressed actual
gold—and gold was a very rare commodity in Northern
Spain at that time—into Jorge's hand to bribe him into
ushering them into O'Neill's room, and once there they
were ready to talk at incredible length. They all had something to explain, they all sought to compensate for past
misdeeds. The Spanish interpreter to General Paris,
Governor of Leon, wanted to explain why he had accepted
this employment, and why he had translated Paris's brutal
proclamations into Spanish. It was done with the most
patriotic motives, he assured O'Neill, and in proof of it he
was ready to tell O'Neill all he knew about the organization of the French garrisons in the province. The Mayor
of Leon came out; he wanted to explain that he accepted
office under the French occupation solely to be able
to soften down the French demands upon his long-
suffering people. Now he was delighted to be able to tell
O'Neill all about the arrangements made for guarding the
town in the event of a siege. There were other men most
unjustly suspected of having favoured the French cause
who were anxious to clear themselves of this charge by
denouncing others—some of whom had already made their
appearance at headquarters with reciprocal denunciations.

All night long there was a constant trickle of people out
from the town, and O'Neill had to deal with them all.
Delegation of authority is a difficult matter with an improvised army, and especially so when internal jealousies

are present. O'Neill could leave the cavalry scouting to Urquiola, and the outpost work to el Platero—they could be relied on to do such work well. But it was a very different matter when it came to the business of a staff. The men who might be expected to do staff work well were not to be trusted at all in an army where anyone might hope to succeed to the command if he guided chance the right way. O'Neill was acutely conscious that he did not possess the gift, almost essential to a leader of irregulars, of making men love him. Unlike Hugh, who could crack jokes in Gallego and Asturian, and who won the hearts of everyone he met, Carlos could only speak his own Castilian and left everyone in his army indifferent as to whether he lived or died. He had to watch every move of his subordinates, and he had to lock within his bosom any information which came his way—and he had to reserve for himself, in consequence, the labour of gathering such information.

He was a good soldier, nevertheless. He knew what information he needed, and he did his best to acquire it. In two years of desperate warfare he had amplified the theoretical knowledge acquired from his father, and in barracks, and in the military college at Zamora. He knew just how much he could ask of his men and how far they could be relied on. Most important of all, he knew what he wanted to do and was utterly determined to do it. There would be neither divided counsels nor dilatory execution in the handling of O'Neill's army.

This was confirmed again the next morning, when an hour before dawn saw the invaders roused from their billets and assembled on the road; by two hours after sunrise Urquiola's lancers were prowling round the walls of Leon and the infantry were forming up in a mass outside the Benavente gate. General Paris within the walls was a wily old soldier. He had a thousand men under his command, and he knew well enough that it was an insufficient force to defend a long medieval wall against a serious attack and at the same time hold down a rebellious population of fifteen thousand or more. He intended to make his real defence within the citadel he had built up inside the town, but at the same time he had not the least intention of abandoning walls and city before he was sure that the attackers were capable of capturing them. He was not to be bluffed into yielding an inch prematurely.

It did not take long to convince him that the attacking force was in earnest and had the means to enforce their will. A column of troops, in the brown clothing which now indicated the Spanish regular army, marched off round to the east side of the town. Paris's telescope saw that they had scaling ladders with them. Meanwhile, up the road to the Benavente gate, he saw a big gun come lumber-up. His cavalry reconnaissance had made no mistake when it credited the invaders with siege artillery. The gun was brought up to within a quarter of a mile of the gate, and was swung round into position with the utmost deliberation. A train of mules followed behind with ammunition. Through his glass Paris could see an officer on a grey horse directing operations. Presumably that must be the O'Neill he had heard about.

Paris could do nothing to discommode the Spaniards while this was going on. He had no artillery at this point which could have the slightest effect. The flimsy medieval

wall was not wide enough to bear big guns, even if he
had any to spare, and even if the Emperor who had sent
him into the country had condescended to supply him with
them. He had two or three two-pounders—'wallpieces'—
but they were not accurate enough to have any effect at
a quarter of a mile. The besiegers had chosen the weakest
spot in the whole circumference.

O'Neill dismounted from his horse and straddled the
trail of the gun. His target practice against La Merced two
days before had given him an exact knowledge of the
capabilities of the gun. It was a beautiful weapon, shooting with an accuracy which had surprised him, accustomed
as he was to the rough and ready equipment of the Spanish
regular artillery. As he looked along the sights he knew
exactly where the shot would hit, and his expectation was
fulfilled. The cannon ball crashed into the huge wooden
gate exactly over the lock. The timber shattered in all
directions. Methodically, O'Neill changed his target. Half
a dozen rounds left the whole gate hanging in splinters.
The gate had been built up with sandbags behind the
timber, but sandbags could not be expected to stand long
against eighteen-pound cannon balls hurled against them.
At every shot the shape of the heap changed, as the contents of torn bags at the bottom poured out and the full
ones from the top came rolling down. Before long the
steep-sided mass of sandbags had degenerated into a mere
mound, easy to climb and difficult to defend. O'Neill sent
one of Urquiola's lancers flying to the Princesa Regiment
with the order to attack. Alvarez drew his sword and ran
to set himself at the head of his Navarrese. With a yell
they all poured forward. To the right of the gate went

el Platero; to the left Jorge led the other guerilleros. Their duty was to open musketry fire on the defenders of the wall while Alvarez burst through the gate with his solid column. Yet as they charged forward they saw spots of colour appearing on the top of the wall. Men up there were waving their arms, waving flags, waving scarves, dancing with delight. General Paris had withdrawn his garrison into the citadel in the nick of time. He was not going to try to defend that wall against an assault and an escalade with a furious civilian population at his back and only a thousand men all told.

CHAPTER XIII

THE SUCCESSFUL army poured through the steep and narrow streets. The population was mad with joy. Bright shawls waved from the windows. The streets were full of cheering mobs. The men clapped their deliverers on the back, and the women tore their arms and equipment from them and carried them themselves. Patriotic persons and those with guilty consciences rolled barrels of wine out to the street corners and stood with cups in their hands beseeching passers-by to drink. A bevy of women surrounded O'Neill, stroking the big grey horse, spreading scarves under his feet, kissing O'Neill's hands and even his boots and breeches if his hands were not attainable.

O'Neill was too preoccupied with urgent business to enter into the spirit of the thing. He had to shout his orders over the heads of the people to where Urquiola rode beside him. The half-dozen troopers who accompanied him went clattering off, each despatched on a separate errand. He was too much of a soldier to allow civilians to delay him when he had a course of action mapped out. The municipal deputation which came to meet him was heard with scant attention, and they pulled long faces when a few brief words in reply told them the number of shoes, and of suits of clothes, and the amount of solid hard cash the city was expected to contribute to the cause, and that within three days. Every householder must be ready to lodge and maintain two soldiers from now on, indefinitely.

But O'Neill's final order excited a different kind of interest. There must be a scaffold and the municipal garotte erected within two hours in the Plaza Mayor, and the town executioner must be in attendance.

The news of the request sent a buzz of excitement round the town, for no Spanish fiesta could be really complete without a public execution; when the chapter of the Cathedral heard of it the arrangements for the celebration of the thanksgiving Mass were abruptly cancelled; the clergy would not risk their dignity in hopeless competition with the spectacle.

O'Neill rode off to where, against the north wall, the garrison had concentrated to stand a siege. Leon could not boast a military citadel, like Burgos, but General Paris had done his best to compensate for the omission. The thick-walled prison and the town hospital stood side by side beyond the Plaza Menor in complete isolation; he had torn down, long before, one or two houses which offered points of vantage to any who might attack. He had built solid works connecting the two buildings and strengthening weak points. Here with a clear space all round him, with six weeks' provisions in his cellars, and four field guns to keep the mob at a distance, he felt confident that he could beat off any attack until the concentration of outlying garrisons or the despatch of some other army of relief should set him free again.

Paris would have felt happier in his mind if the guerilleros had not possessed a powerful siege gun—as was the case everywhere else, his arrangements had only en-visaged a spasmodic attack by an enemy without artillery —but even as things were he felt few qualms. He had

more troops and more guns than Jonquier had at La Merced, and an infinitely stronger fortress whose peculiar construction afforded several concentric rings of defence.

O'Neill, reconnoitring cautiously from an upper window
of a house on the corner of the Plaza Menor, recognized
the difficulties before him. He could breach those walls
with the gun, doubtless, but one breach would not suffice.
When that breach was won the gun would have to be
brought up to it to breach the wall behind, and when the
prison was finally taken there would still be the hospital.
If the French fought with spirit there would be bloody
fighting and tedious battering—weeks of it, presumably—
before the whole place was taken. One gun would do its
work so slowly, and in the progress of the siege there was
always the chance—particularly at close quarters—of a
lucky shot from the besieged, or a well-timed sally, disabling the gun completely. It would be a hard task to keep
his wayward followers up to the effort and the self-sacrifice
involved. If once they tired, or if he could not continually
gratify them with success, his army would fall to pieces.
There was some excuse for the gloom which still clouded
O'Neill's brow when he rode back; he bore too heavy a
responsibility for a young man of twenty-four.

At the corner of the Plaza Mayor and the Rambla there
were more women awaiting him. But these had not come
to kiss his hands, or to spread shawls under his horse's
feet. There were two or three small children, and a young
and lovely woman, and one or two older women with
white hair. They fell on their knees as he approached, and
held out clasped hands to him. Unconsciously he began to
rein Gil in as he neared them, but his ear caught a few

words of their petition, and at once he loosened his reins
and drove in his spurs so that Gil plunged forward again.
They were asking for the life of a man; apparently they
had discovered for whom the garotte was being prepared.
O'Neill's black eyebrows came together, scowling. A young
man with the fate of a kingdom in his hands, called upon
to dispense the power of life and death, does not welcome
arguments about his decisions. He had judged the men
guilty, and they must die.

The young woman scrambled to her feet and ran and
seized his arm, but he shook her off so that she fell on her
face in the road, and the orderlies clattering behind him
had to swerve to avoid her. He saw the white lips of the
old women moving in prayer, but his ears refused to hear
their words.

Alvarez and Captain Elizalde had done good work in
the scant time allowed them, here in the Plaza Mayor.
The scaffold and the garotte stood ready in the centre, with
the executioner and his assistant gracefully at ease—the
executioner was seated in the chair to which he would
shortly bind his victims. On one side of the scaffold were
the half-dozen drums of the Princesa Regiment; on the
other, in a vivid mass were the clergy in their vestments
with the Bishop at their head, ready to give their blessings
and countenance to this display of justice. Round the
sides of the square, and thronging the windows of the
houses, were the poulation of the town—a thin line of
soldiers prevented them from encroaching too near the
scaffold.

Alvarez came up and saluted.

" Everything is ready," he said. " Shall I give the word? "

"Yes," said O'Neill.

"There are one or two others," said Alvarez, "beside the ones you had arrested last night. The mob brought them to me, and the town council said they were traitors. I put them in with the rest."

"Quite right," said O'Neill, hoarsely.

Alvarez turned and waved his arm to a group of his men who stood, apparently awaiting this signal, round the portal of the Cathedral. They disappeared inside. In the beautiful Cathedral tower a bell began to toll, its deep note vibrating oppressively through the silence of the square. A procession emerged from the Cathedral door. Pablo Vigil, Alvarez's lieutenant, came first, strutting along much elated by the dignity and solemnity of the occasion. Then, three by three, came the victims and their guards, each man who was to die between two guerilleros. Some were old men and some were young; mostly they were of the type of portly citizen.

O'Neill recognized in most of them the men who had come to plead with him for their lives the night before. He remembered the arguments they had used, one after the other, and the bribes they had offered. Most of them had knelt to plead with him; some of them had wept when, after hearing all they had to say, he had called to the guard and had them locked up.

They had no dignity now, for Alvarez had stripped them to their shirts for greater shame. The wind flapped the garments round their thighs; one or two of them, unable to walk for weakness, were being dragged along by their guards. One of them was shrieking in a high treble. Round the square they went, right round to the Cathedral door again, and then out to the middle where stood the scaffold. The guards flung the first of them on to the wooden flooring, and the executioners fell upon him and hoisted him, nerveless but resisting feebly, into the chair. They made fast the straps, and clasped the iron collar round his neck. The executioner applied himself to the lever, while Alvarez, his showman's instinct working double tides, signed to the drummers. To the roll of the drums the wretched man's limbs contorted themselves horribly within their bonds. It seemed as if all the thousands watching caught their breath simultaneously. The executioner put all his weight upon the lever and the screw broke the man's neck.

At that moment something crashed into the square, ploughing up the cobbles, and, ricochetting, crashed into the face of a house. The French were firing field guns from the citadel. There was panic in the square. The crowds of spectators began to push and struggle to get away; the soldiers broke their formation; the executioners hesitated in the midst of the business of taking the corpse out of the garotte. A flash of hope illuminated the features of the unhappy men waiting their turn to die. One of them actually, on his knees and with clasped hands, began to render thanks to God in a cracked voice.

A second cannon ball, pitching near where the first had fallen, intensified the panic. It seemed as if all Alvarez's carefully planned ceremonial was to be stultified. But O'Neill's voice, blaring like the bellowing of a bull, steadied the mob. He sat his horse rigidly in the centre of the square, keeping the big brute still while another shot fell only twenty yards from him. As he pointed out in his terrible voice, only a small part of the Plaza Mayor was exposed to the first of the guns of the citadel. They were firing straight up the Rambla, and their shot could only reach the small portion of the square which lay in a direct continuation of this road. If the weak-kneed fools in that corner would only move—*quietly*—over to the other side of the square they would come to no harm and business could proceed.

So it was done. While one side of the square was deserted the crowds thronged the other three sides, and the executions went on with decency, the drums rolling, the bell tolling, and O'Neill on his horse like an equestrian statue watching the work being done.

This was as severe a blow to French rule of Spain as even the taking of La Merced. When the news of the executions at Leon went round no Josefino would feel himself safe. Every Spaniard would think twice before he made himself a tool of the usurper. French rule in Northern Spain could never be so secure in future. The knowledge was a source of satisfaction to O'Neill, but unhappily it is to be doubted if he had been entirely influenced by the need to achieve this result when he ordered the executions. Two years of savage warfare, the overwhelming responsibility of his position, the horrible wounding of his brother, and the present strain upon his nerves had brought out a vein of cruelty which had laid unsuspected within him. The mixture of blood which so often makes for cruelty may have been partly responsible as well, and at La Merced he had ample temptation to acquire the taste for slaughter. O'Neill on his horse was conscious of an inward delicious satisfaction at the sight of the contortions of the men in the garotte, even though he kept his face unmoved. It boded ill for the enemy he had to fight and for the people he had to govern.

With the conclusion of the killings and the approach of evening the city of Leon gave itself up to riot and revelry. During eighteen months of French occupation the people had been subjected to a severe curfew ordinance. The evening life of the streets in which the Spaniard takes so much delight had been denied to them, but now, with the French shut up in the citadel they could swarm here and there as they wished. They did not care that all the Rambla, from the Plaza Menor to the Plaza Mayor, was dangerous ground—the French sent a blast of grape up it whenever there were sufficient saunterers to justify the expenditure of a round of ammunition. They did not care that the peace of the evening was occasionally broken by musket shots, for the Navarrese were distributed in a semicircle in the houses round the citadel and were taking long shots at any sentries who might be visible within. They did not care that the gun, wreathed incongruously in greenery by patriotic ladies, was being dragged by devious alleys to a corner where a working party under O'Neill's own super-vision was toiling to build up solid the lower rooms of two houses to act as a battery for the bombardment of the morrow.

All the troops were not on duty. There still remained a thousand or two to join in the music and the dancing and light-hearted merriment. Anyone might have thought who saw the gay throngs that the war was over, that Spain was set free, instead of that a handful of irregular troops had gained a precarious hold over one little patch of the vast expanse of Spain. No one minded. No one could mind who for the first time for eighteen months was not compelled to go to bed at sunset. The night was all too short for them to wring all the pleasure they wanted out of its passing hours.

Even morning found them still gay. They demonstrated the ability of the Spaniard to make merry all night and still be able to face the day without depression. There was talk of a bull-fight. The aged, patriotic and wealthy Conde de la Meria was rumoured to have sent out of the town in search of bulls which Don Cesar Urquiola's Castilian gentlemen could ride down with their lances in accordance with the high tradition of Spanish chivalry—the day of the professional bull-fighter on foot was not yet come, by half a century.

A few of the more military minded and inquisitive among the inhabitants wandered down to the alleys round the Plaza Menor to see what was being done in the matter of the siege of the citadel. They found the soldiers busy barricading the alleys, knocking loopholes in walls, making ready to beat back the sorties which O'Neill judged would be launched upon them as soon as the big gun should open fire. To capture or disable that gun the French would pour out their blood like water.

He himself had hardly slept again that night. He had lain down and dozed in snatches now and then in the midst of the working parties. The lower rooms of the two houses he had selected were now filled with earth; the gun had been dragged into the narrow passage between them and earth had been heaped round it so that only its muzzle protruded, concealed as far as might be. At a hundred yards—the range which circumstances dictated—even the

light guns of the garrison might disable this, the only
siege gun at his disposal.

His heart almost misgave him when he looked out at
the massive defences he had to penetrate, the palisades and
earthworks and walls, the ditches and escarpments. He
remembered with bitter amusement the words of Brother
Bernard—"Go up boldly against Leon—the hand of God
is at work in Leon." Brother Bernard could not be very
well versed in siege warfare. There was no chance even of
starving out the French, for O'Neill knew that General
Paris had filled the cellars of the citadel with food long
before. Many people had pressed upon him information
regarding the stores there. They had counted the barrels
of flour, and the tubs of salted meat, and the sacks of
grain, and the barrels of wine which had been accumulated
there during the occupation. It was the Spaniards who had
had to make up that store; there were people in the town
who had had to labour in the milling of the flour. And
while the hundred and fifty thousand rations were being
accumulated in the citadel the French had lived on further
rations drawn from the luckless countryside. There was
not the least chance that the stores might turn out to have
been depleted by rash indents upon them to save trouble.
Why, before O'Neill's very eyes arose the smoke of the
French fires, cooking their morning soup. The two tricolour
flags flaunted themselves from the flagstaffs at each end
of the long fortress. O'Neill set his teeth and turned away
to supervise the completion of the arrangements for the
siege. He saw no sign of the hand of God being at work.

By noon he had everything ready. The gun was ready
to open fire; its ammunition was hidden away behind

F

masses of earth where no stray shot could find it out. Close at hand a hundred men stood with trusses of straw. These were to be thrown into the prison ditch when an assault was made, after the palisades had been shot down and a breach battered in the west wall of the prison. How many casualties would be incurred even if the attack succeeded O'Neill did not like to consider—and the greatest success which could be anticipated could only result in the capture of one-twentieth of the citadel. All the open space of the Plaza Menor would have to be crossed under a fire of point-blank musketry and of grape and canister from the artillery. But still, these losses would have to be faced. Perfectly conscious of what would be the result to him of a severe check, O'Neill went down to the gun to open fire.

The noise of the gun in that confined space was appalling. O'Neill and the gun team felt as if their heads were being beaten open with sledge hammers every time the gun went off. But the practice was good. A few rounds of grape tore a huge gap in the palisades, and then O'Neill began with round shot on the angle on the hospital. He would not direct his fire upon the main gateway, as the approach there was exposed too much to cross fire, and he shrewdly expected that within the courtyard, unseen, lay a field gun crammed with canister trained upon the entrance. He preferred to attack a spot not so easily defended. Round after round crashed against the wall. The bricks flew at every blow, but owing to the angle of impact it took some time before any hole was apparent in the wall.

It was strange that so little return fire was directed upon the gun by the defenders. There was a light gun in an embrasure some way down the wall from the point of attack, but it only fired twice, and each time the aim was dreadfully bad. The shots only brought down a shower of bricks from the face of a house twenty yards from the gun. O'Neill could not understand the reason for this silence. A further shot from the big gun brought down a little cascade of bricks from the angle of the wall. O'Neill left the gun for a moment, and went up to the first floor of the house beside it in order to inspect the progress of the bombardment without having his view impeded by smoke.

There seemed to be no sign of life in the citadel. Then he noticed that one of the two tricolour flags was invisible now. Someone must have hauled it down. As he looked, wondering, he saw the ponderous hospital gate swing open. He rushed back down the stairs shouting to his men—the anticipated sortie must be about to be delivered. Yet so quickly did he move, that by the time he was on ground level again it was only half open.

But no stream of soldiers yelling, '*Vive l'Empereur*' appeared. There was a distinct pause while O'Neill stood and wondered. Then someone came staggering out round the gate. He walked unsteadily a few yards towards the gap in the palisades and fell down. After him came a few more men, reeling and tottering. One of them, walking like a blind man, fell with a crash over the recumbent figure, and made no attempt to rise. Another suddenly doubled up with pain, sat down, and then fell over on his side. Not one of the group succeeded in reaching the palisades. The wondering O'Neill, completely puzzled, suspected a trap and yet, unable to see wherein it lay, stepped out into the open. He strode forward across the open space, and his men began to follow him. Not a shot was fired from the citadel. O'Neill pressed forward through the broken palisades, and reached the men writhing on the ground. He could gain no enlightenment from them. He went on, sword in one hand and pistol in the other, through the gate, and under the *porte cochère*, into the courtyard.

Here the sight presented to his gaze was horrible. The courtyard was heaped with men in the last stages of agony. They lay here and there raving in delirium, torn with pain, vomiting and retching. Some were dead, and they seemed the most fortunate. A field gun, just as he had expected, stood defiantly in the centre of the court facing him, but its crew lay dead around it. The guerilleros would take no further step forward; they clustered about the gate peering into the yard; most of them were praying and crossing themselves.

O'Neill shook off his superstitious fears. Alone, he opened the door beside him, and entered the building. The long room in which he found himself seemed full of groans and cries, and as his eyes grew accustomed to the lessened light he saw more men in agony writhing under the loop-holes, and throughout the citadel he found more tortured humanity—dying men on the staircases, dying men on the parapets, dying men everywhere.

As Brother Bernard had promised, the hand of God had been at work in Leon—or rather, the white arsenic which he had caused to be mixed with the flour of the garrison's stores had had its effect.

CHAPTER XIV

THE LEONESE knew pity. When they heard the news they came, men and women alike, to try and care for the unhappy men whose bowels were being seared and torn by the poison within them. But arsenic knows no pity. It slew and slew and went on slaying. Many of the men who did not die at once survived only a few days, lingering until the secondary effects of the poison extinguished the flickering life in their wasted bodies. Only a few score of the garrison survived, bent and crippled. It had been a most notable slaughter, redounding to the credit of Brother Bernard. If a few more patriotic Spaniards would arise who could kill a thousand Frenchmen apiece the invasion of Spain would end abruptly.

But the fall of Leon, the capture of the citadel, was an event which was of first-class importance in the course of the war. At the news of it the whole province shook off its sullen fear of the French and took up arms. Every village contributed its band of half-armed irregulars; it was a rising more violent even than the one which had opened the war—the one which Bessières had extinguished in blood two years before. The other small garrisons scattered through the province were forced to take shelter within their little fortresses, round which prowled the rebels in their thousands, unable to do any harm to the stone walls, but watching and waiting, with the patience of wild animals and the same thirst for blood.

Nevertheless, these peasants had a proper respect for the outward signs of authority, and when a glittering cortège, all hung with orders and dazzling with gold lace, rode down from the mountains of Galicia and across the plains of Leon, it was received everywhere with deference. The horsemen who composed it seemed to be in a hurry to reach the city of Leon, and they rode fifty miles along the sandy roads with hardly a halt, clattering up to the town and through the gates with all the pomp and dignity they could display. They drew up outside the palace of the Conde de la Meria, where soldiers lounged before the doors.

"Go and tell Captain O'Neill," said the leader to one of them, "that the Duke of Menjibar, Captain-General of Leon, has arrived."

The soldier made his leisurely way into the palace, and the horsemen sat waiting in their saddles. They had to wait a long time; there seemed to be no great hurry to welcome the Captain-General of Leon or to offer him the subservience which his rank demanded. It was only after a considerable pause that the doors opened and O'Neill emerged. He was still wearing his shabby artillery uniform, but he bore himself very erect. His black eyebrows nearly met above his blue eyes—a danger signal to any who knew him. He took time to walk down the steps and out to where the Duke of Menjibar fumed in his saddle.

"There is some mistake," said O'Neill slowly. "Perhaps the message was delivered to me incorrectly. I know of no Captain-General of Leon."

The Duke of Menjibar was a stout little man with fierce

black moustaches. He beat impatiently on the pommel of his saddle.

"I am Captain-General of Leon," he said. "Do you doubt my word?"

"I doubt either your word or your sense," said O'Neill.

"I hold the commission of the Junta," said the duke. "Must I show it to you to be believed? It will go hard with you if you compel me to."

"From the Junta of Galicia?" asked O'Neill. "There is no Junta of Leon, nor has been for two years back."

"The Junta of Galicia represents Leon as well," said the duke.

"Oh," said O'Neill. "So that discredited gang, loitering at Ferrol a hundred miles from the enemy, presume to nominate a captain-general for a province it has never set eyes on? I suppose it wants some of the gold we have captured? Or it wants to filch the credit for the conquest of Leon?"

"That is not the way to speak to me, Captain O'Neill. Remember, there are grave charges against you already. Do not add to them."

"Charges?" repeated O'Neill, innocently. "Against me?"

"Don't try to fool me any longer," said the duke, testily. "Leave——"

O'Neill's gesture interrupted him. He glanced up at the windows of the palace whither a wave of O'Neill's hand had directed his gaze, and his words died on his lips. At every window there were soldiers, and every soldier had a musket, and every musket was pointed at the duke and his followers.

"I have a further message for you from the Junta," said the duke hastily, playing the last card of his instructions. "In recognition of your services the Junta is pleased to ignore the charges of mutiny preferred against you by Colonel Casa Riego. They will be glad to promote you to the rank of major-general, and they will solicit for you from the Central Junta at Cadiz the Order of Carlos III and the title of Conde de la Merced. That is, if I am able to report to them your willingness to act under my orders."

O'Neill's smouldering anger burst into a blaze.

"You try to threaten, and you try to bribe," he blared out. "I won't hear another word! Come down from your horse, you poor thing. Come down, or by God——! And you others, come off your horses! Here, Jorge, take them away. Put them in the dungeons under the prison. Set Vadilla and fifty men on guard over them. By God, you fools, I have it in mind to cut off your noses and ears and send you back to your Junta to tell them what I think of them. Perhaps tomorrow I shall do so—you can wait till then. With your stars and your epaulets, and you've never set eyes on an enemy in your lives. Jorge, take the horses away, too. We need remounts."

This was treason of the wildest sort. The news that their Captain-General had been clapped into a dungeon would rouse the Galician Junta to transports of rage beyond even those caused by the defection of the Princesa Regiment. Yet O'Neill did not stop there. Even before the keys were turned upon the raging Duke of Menjibar and his suite he sent messengers to summon the great men of the city. Coldly, he invited them to elect a Captain-General for

Leon, and coldly he accepted the office which they hastened to proffer him. With rolling of drums and blaring of trumpets the city bailiff proclaimed him Captain-General of Leon, and the printing presses were set to work reproducing his decrees.

That was not the only function which Plaza Major witnessed during the hectic five days following the fall of the citadel of Leon. There were more Josefinos routed out from their hiding places, to be garotted with great ceremony on the scaffold in the centre of the square—scaffold and garotte stood there permanently now. From the surrounding country others were sent in, too. The peasants of the plains turned fiercely upon all who had shown any sign of approval of the French occupation. Day after day little groups of prisoners were brought into the city, and a word from O'Neill sent them to death in the square.

He never thought of trying them, of hearing what defence they might advance. The mere fact that they were brought to his notice, that they crossed his path, made them worthy of death. His pride, his sense of power and of his own importance, were swelled to monstrous proportions. He held the unquestioned power of life and death over a wide province, and the knowledge maddened the young man like a drug. His cruelty grew with its indulgence. That threat of his to the Duke of Menjibar about cutting off noses and ears was the smoke which indicated the fire beneath. His imagination was dark with mental pictures of horrible public tortures. It was only for five days that the carnival of death went on in Leon, but those five days are still spoken of with lowered breath in the city, and are remembered even though the

F*

cruelties of the Carlist wars and of the revolutions are forgotten.

Perhaps this knowledge of the impermanence of his position helped to madden him. It could only be a question of days before the French could collect an army which would sweep him back into the mountains, where his army would break up again perforce into fragments, where he would be relegated to the humble position of guerillero chief with perhaps a hundred followers—and they none too loyal—and where the Junta of Galicia could call him to account for his actions. The thought of it brought the blood to his skin and set him vibrating with rage, so that he wished, like Caligula (of whom he had never heard) that all the world had but one neck, which he could sever at a stroke.

The other garrisons of the province had to be reduced, and that was clearly the work of the Captain-General. Especially so, seeing that to do this called for the use of the big gun, and the possession of that gun was the outward sign of the lordship of Leon, like a king's sceptre. After five days in Leon, five days of executions and confiscations and requisitions, O'Neill marched out again. He took his army with him, and his big gun. He left behind him his puppet council; for he could not trust his army save under his own eye, while he knew there was not the slightest chance of those terrified civilians doing anything to thwart him.

There were only six small places which held out against the Spaniards in Leon, small fortresses guarding strategical points, after the fashion of La Merced and Santa Maria. The garrisons knew the details of the revolt; they had been brought by terrified Josefinos flying to them to take refuge. They knew how every soul in La Merced had been killed, and how the citadel of Leon had fallen, and how every man for miles round was in arms against their dominion again, and how O'Neill was a devil in human form, with an insatiable thirst for blood, and with a siege gun of unbelievable power and accuracy. They were cowed by the news before ever O'Neill came up against them. Santa Eulalia surrendered the moment that O'Neill appeared before it, and Mansilla and Saldaña and Carrion as soon as the big gun began to pound their flimsy defences to pieces. Each place was sacked in turn, and the French prisoners were sent back to Galicia—Heaven knew what chance they had of ever reaching it, and of being sent across the sea to the sybaritic comfort of the English hulks and of Dartmoor Prison.

Old General Dufour held out in Benavente for two whole days; he had a garrison of five hundred men and two concentric rings of defence. But he had no luck. If he had succeeded in beating back an assault he might have taken the heart out of the besiegers, but the wild attack of the peasantry and of the guerilleros lapped over his walls and up through the narrow breach. Dufour died sword in hand at the last breach, as Jonquier did, and his men died in holes and corners as the attackers raged through the place.

O'Neill left the place behind, silent, peopled only by the dead, and passed on with the big gun lumbering behind and the peasants flocking to join him. His circular tour had consumed less than a fortnight. In thirteen days he was back in Leon, marching his army in triumph through the cheering streets, and dragging behind him the wretched

Spaniards who had been found in the captured places; men
and women, peasants and landowners, tailors and cobblers,
prostitutes, mistresses, and wives. Leon gave itself up to a
fresh orgy of blood and pleasure.

When they forgot to rejoice the Leonese found plenty
at which to grumble. O'Neill had ten thousand men at his
command now that he had swept the countryside. These
ten thousand men had all to be fed and clothed and paid.
O'Neill considered that the well-being of his soldiers
weighed far heavier in the scale than the suffering of the
civilians. Only the best—if there was enough of it—would
do for his men; the best boots, the best clothing, meat
every day although before they became soldiers they had
rarely eaten meat oftener than once a fortnight. Anyone
with a little hoard of money or silver plate was compelled
to make a free gift of it to the State, which meant to
General O'Neill. There was some to be found despite the
exactions of the French, and O'Neill had little difficulty in
discovering it, for his reign of terror produced the inevitable
crop of informers. Even the French had not thought of
garotting the man who buried his spoons, but then the
French could not call such an act 'treason', as O'Neill
did.

In the forcing heat of present conditions all the charac-
teristics of a military autocracy developed instantly; the
inevitable bloodthirsty leader, trusting no one, with an eye
on every department of state and a toadying mob of
informers to help him; the usual inner ring of personal
guards—lately the bands of Hugh O'Neill and el Bilbanito;
the usual soldiery, rapidly learning their power and steadily
increasing their demands; the usual ruined civilians, too

terrified to murmur openly. In three weeks the government of Carlos O'Neill had reached the pitch which it took Imperial Rome a century to attain.

Possibly O'Neill was the only one of his army with an acute sense of the impermanence of it all. He was aware every minute that by now the French armies would be making a convulsive effort to gather together enough troops to strike him down. Wellington might be loose in the south, hot in pursuit of Massena's army reeling back from the lines of Torres Vedras, Soult might be staggering under the fearful blow dealt him at Albuera, King Joseph at Madrid might be trembling on his throne, but all the same they would spare no effort to dispose first of this menace to their communications. Every man that could be collected would be hurled upon him soon, and O'Neill, unlike his men, had not the slighest doubt as to the result.

Characteristically, he went forward to meet his fate, instead of waiting for it to come to him. Moreover, his best policy was to advance. A rebellion on the defensive is doomed for certain, as his military instinct assured him. Perhaps if he were enormously lucky and enormously active, if he rushed upon the great royal road which ran through Burgos and Valladolid, he might burst in among his enemies and prolong the struggle long enough for something unexpected to turn up and save him. Any other policy, whether he chose to wait round about Leon or to try to lead his forces back over the Cantabrian mountains to reduce the French garrisons along the Biscay coast, meant ultimate certain ruin.

There is room to doubt whether it was these considerations which influenced him in his decision to advance. O'Neill was a fighting man. His whole instinct called upon him to rush upon his enemies, to meet his fate half-way, to go down, if go down he must, with his face to the foe rather than his back.

CHAPTER XV

TEN THOUSAND men were on the march towards the
Royal Road. O'Neill's messengers had summoned them from
their billets in the town, and from their cantonments in
the villages round about. Not even O'Neill, fount of
dynamic energy though he was, had been able to make an
army out of them. There was some faint trace of organization; there were the batallions of Mansilla and Saldaña;
there were the first and second and third of Leon, officered
somehow by untrained local magnates. Alvarez' band and
el Platero's band and O'Neill's band had absorbed all the
recruits they could, and more. Don Cesar Urquiola had
five hundred cavalry now under his command, mounted
on horses captured or requisitioned. But it was much more
of a mob than an army.

The very act of concentrating on a single road had led
to incredible muddle. Units approaching by by-roads had
found their paths blocked by others marching across them,
and, sooner than wait, had casually intermingled with the
other stream. Some had been late and some had been early.
The mass that poured down the road displayed no trace
of military organization, despite the cavalry out ahead and
the train of artillery in the rear, the six field guns, and the
one big siege gun, and the long files of baggage mules.
Handling ten thousand men is a very different matter from
handling two thousand, and when the greater part of the
ten thousand is a mere undisciplined rabble the task calls

for a genius, which was exactly what O'Neill was not.

The fates turned against him. The pleasant spring weather which had prevailed for some time now changed on the very day that the march began. It seemed as if winter had come back again. A cold wind blew from out of the mountains, and it brought with it torrents of icy rain—the kind of rain which only can be experienced in Spain. The road was churned into mud, the ditches overflowed, the wretched soldiers were soaked to the skin. The end of the day's march found them only ten miles from the city, and many of the men went off in the night to seek the comfort of their homes. Of the remainder few were fortunate enough to have a roof over their heads, and spent a comfortless night lying out in the drenching rain.

And the next day it rained, and all night too, and all the day after; and by this time the eternal commissariat difficulty had arisen again. O'Neill had depended—for lack of any better system—upon supplies gleaned from the district over which they were marching, but it had been plundered and re-plundered, and when the news of the approach of the vast column was passed round, every one fled from its path as if it bore the plague with it. Three days of rain and two of half rations made even that contingency not unlikely. The effect upon O'Neill was bad indeed. He raged against the delays and the desertions. The evil temper which the blinding of his brother and the responsibilities of his position brought him vented itself in unpleasant ways. He rode his big grey horse up and down the column and struck at the men with his whip, and they did not love him for it. The townsmen among them, and even the long-suffering peasants, did not take kindly to blows. But with the rain soaking his clothes and the icy wind whistling round him he could not control his temper, even if it had been possible after his weeks of enjoyment of unfettered power.

A mile behind the rear of the column he found the big gun stuck in the mud, buried up to the axles of its five-foot wheels, and Jorge and the rest of el Bilbanito's band toiling to free it. They were all free to work on this one gun, because the others had already been abandoned. It might have been more sensible to leave the heaviest behind and press on with the lightest, but it would not have been in accordance with the tradition of this army. Moreover, with further sieges in prospect, it really would not have been wise to abandon the big gun; they could manage without field guns, but not without the big eighteen-pounder. That was only an academic argument, all the same. No one would have dreamed of abandoning the gun which was the emblem of their new power and future hopes.

Yet they were having a difficult time; the draught mules floundered in the mud unable to gain a foothold, with the steam of their exertions rising from them in clouds, while Jorge and his men slaved with levers and drag-ropes to get the gun on the move again. They countered O'Neill's imprecations with dumb insolence and with angry mutterings, according to their several constitutions. Jorge wiped the blood from his neck where O'Neill struck him, but said no word. His mouth still smiled—his mouth was made for smiling—but his brow was black with anger. Someone shouted a curse after O'Neill when he wheeled the grey horse round again and galloped off amid a spatter of mud, but the wind and the rain deafened O'Neill's ears and his senses so that the curse passed unheard and the man's life was not imperilled.

At midnight that night O'Neill in his headquarters in an inn shouted for the guard, and Jorge came in—circumstances and recent history had imposed upon the combined bands of el Bilbanito and O'Neill the two rôles of siege artillerymen and headquarters guard, with Jorge as general factotum. Jorge, looking round the room, was able to amplify from observation what he had guessed from the loud quarrellings he had heard through the door. O'Neill, white with rage, was seated at a small table at one end of the room; the candlelight lit up his face and revealed the ungovernable rage which distorted it. The other officers were standing here and there about the room, some of them sullen, some of them uneasy, but all of them obviously as angry as O'Neill himself, even if through fear or caution they could not show it. Clearly O'Neill had been dealing out reprimands regarding the marching, and clearly they had been resented.

"Arrest that man!" said O'Neill in a high-pitched voice.

The wild gesture of his arm indicated el Platero, standing mute and solitary in the middle of the room, with his usual four days' beard disfiguring his cheeks. There was a cornered look in his eyes, and he looked here and there sidelong, his hand on his knife. The other officers moved restlessly.

"Arrest him!" repeated O'Neill, his voice rising even higher in the scale. "Lock him up. I shall have him shot."

Jorge stood fast. With one hand he felt the weal on his neck where O'Neill's whip had drawn blood that afternoon. He was slow of thought, was this big-limbed boy, and when he thought his lips pouted in a rather inane grin.

"Don't stand grinning there," snapped O'Neill. "Take him and put him under guard until morning."

Jorge still stroked his neck. He had arrested many people already at O'Neill's bidding, and sometimes he had made history thereby—the Duke of Menjibar, and the pitiful men who had come out from Leon the day after La Merced fell, and men in Leon whom O'Neill had deemed to be traitors; men who had struggled and men who had wept, and women, too. He had obeyed because it had never occurred to him to do anything else. But now something else had occurred to him, and the pleasure of reaching a decision broadened his grin.

The others saw his face, and their attitudes changed suddenly. They all seemed to draw in a little, ringing O'Neill round like dogs round a wolf. Still no word was spoken until O'Neill broke the silence.

"Why, what is this, gentlemen?" he asked. Bewilderment was taking the place of rage. His voice rang flat now instead of sharp.

El Platero laughed with the relief of tension, but it was left to Urquiola to express the changed views of the assembly. He stepped forward towards O'Neill, resting his finger-tips on the table. His spurs rang in the silence. They even heard the creaking of his long gaiters of soft leather reaching up to mid-thigh.

"El Platero will *not* be shot," he said. "He will not be arrested."

Now, too late, O'Neill tried to reassert his authority.

"Is this mutiny?" he roared, glaring round the room.

But in those few seconds the baseless fabric of his omnipotence had fallen to the ground, and nothing could build it up again. Everyone had realized that there was no need for anyone to obey him—at least as long as Jorge commanded the guard and Jorge was unfaithful to him. His choice of words, even, was unfortunate, for it put into the mouths of the others words which they might have flinched from using.

"Yes, it is mutiny," said el Platero, and that clinched the matter.

Captain Elizalde sidled up alongside O'Neill and took his sword from his sheath, and the two pistols where they had lain handily on a shelf behind him, O'Neill offering no resistance in his surprise. Only when they were out of his reach did he think of falling sword in hand upon these mutineers and slaying them where they stood; now it was too late.

"Well, gentlemen, what shall we do with him now?" asked Urquiola.

"Keep him to work the gun," said Alvarez—a surprisingly rash suggestion from one so experienced and cautious.

"Never!" said el Platero. "You'll not risk my neck like that. Hang him and save trouble."

"Hang him," said one of the infantry majors, whom O'Neill had insulted before his men yesterday.

The candles flickered in a draught, casting strange shadows on O'Neill's face as he stood there, stock still, listening to this debate over his life or death.

Don Cesar pulled at his thin, old-fashioned beard, looking from one to the other.

"Can he hurt us if we set him free? " he asked mildly.

"Certainly he might," said el Platero. "I'll not trust him. Remember how his brother brought Princesa over to him. He might get us in his power again. Think what he would do to us then—look at his face."

At el Platero's gesture they looked at O'Neill's face as none of them had dared up to that moment, and all of them caught the end of the expression which had flickered over it. At the thought of the treatment he would like to deal out to them O'Neill had been unable to keep his face immobile; the mental picture had swept away his stunned apathy.

"Hang him, I say," said el Platero, rubbing in his lesson.

"Send him back to Leon," suggested Major Volpe. "They know how to use the garotte there."

Several people brightened at that suggestion, because the majority were not at all anxious to risk the obloquy which might reasonably follow the execution of the man who set Leon free.

"You cannot be sure they would use it on *him*," persisted el Platero. " Though there would be a few who would be glad to."

"To Ferrol, then," said Volpe. "The Junta wouldn't hesitate."

El Platero shook his head.

"Too far," he said. "Too risky."

Don Cesar interposed again, mildly:

"What about the gun, gentlemen? Artillerymen are scarce."

"I can work the gun," said Jorge. Those were actually the first words he had spoken since O'Neill had called him in; up to that time his silence had made history, and now this brief speech of his obviously threw much weight into the scale.

The others looked at Jorge; they were trying to decide if here was another O'Neill, if by entrusting the gun to him they would be setting a new yoke on their necks all impatient of authority. They could not believe it of this thick-limbed, stupid boy who had forgotten his own surname.

"Of one thing I am sure," said el Platero. "I have never yet wanted to bring back to life any man I have hanged, but twice at least I have regretted allowing a man to live. I don't want this to be the third time."

El Platero was clearly of a more thoughtful and philosophic turn of mind than his appearance would lend one to expect, but then he was older than most of them, and had worked at a highly skilled trade before ever he had become a guerillero.

"What would the men say?" asked Alvarez.

"Mine would not ask questions. You know best about your own. As for the others—if O'Neill is dead before we leave this room what would they care? What could they do? But if we let him go out from here alive, by this time tomorrow we may all be rotting on trees—if there are enough trees in this God-forgotten plain."

"He would have to answer for my life to Mina," said Alvarez.

"Mina? Do you think he cares about Mina? Mina is in Navarre, and we are on the borders of Castile."

"Why not ask O'Neill what he has to say?" put in Delgado, the junior major of the Princesa Regiment.

"Yes," said Elizalde eagerly.

All eyes turned towards O'Neill again, where he still stood at the table. He had listened almost unbelievingly while they bandied back and forth the pros and cons which would decide whether he should live or die. It was hard for a man to realize that one minute after being undisputed Captain-General of Leon he was in the most pressing imminent danger of dying a criminal's death. But Jorge had never taken his eyes of him, nor his hand from his knife.

O'Neill could only stammer at first. He may have wanted to plead for his life, but he could not do so. It was difficult to find his tongue in the face of this startling change in his position. It was Hugh O'Neill who ought to have met this situation, not Carlos—but Hugh would never have allowed matters to reach this pitch.

"He has little enough to say, you see," sneered el Platero, "this Captain-General."

Jorge took a step forward.

With a huge effort O'Neill pulled himself together. He glanced like a hunted animal from one face to the next, and he found small comfort there. It was their lives or his, and O'Neill knew it too well. He could not gloss over that obvious fact in a ready speech for he was a man of no words. He could not promise amnesty and forgiveness so as to get himself out of that room to where he could change his mind safely, although possibly a man of glib tongue and no scruples might have persuaded the assembly to agree. He was a man of action, not of words. Finding himself in a trap, his whole instinct was to struggle madly, hopelessly even, like an animal. His fingers closed upon the top of the table in front of him; it was a small, massive piece of furniture, clumsily made out of thick slabs of wood. With it he could dash out brains, smash bones, hack his way to the door. At the prospect of action the fighting madness inflamed in his veins. He tightened his grip on the table, tautened his muscles, made ready to spring.

Jorge uttered an inarticulate shout of warning just as O'Neill charged. Like the fighting animal he was, O'Neill was guided by his instincts to launch himself upon the decisive point. Whirling the table horizontally to save time, he struck Jorge to the floor before the knife was well out of Jorge's belt. Then with incredible agility and strength he shifted his grip upon the clumsy weapon so that he held it by the legs and could make use of its heavy top. Don Cesar Urquiola caught him by the belt from behind as he went by; he tore himself loose and plunged for the door. Someone fired a pistol and missed; in the low narrow room the report sounded like a cannon. Elizalde barred his way; the table top crashed down on his shoulder and felled him. Delgado was before the door with his sword in his hand. O'Neill struck at him, but the table caught on one of the low beams of the ceiling. He struck again and dashed him out of his path. He was reaching for the door-handle, when Jorge flung himself along the floor like a snake and gripped his ankle. O'Neill and the table fell together to the floor on top of Delgado and Jorge and Elizalde. Their bodies tossed and heaved in a wild wrestling match. El Platero rushed in with knife drawn, but before he could strike effectively a fresh upheaval engulfed him and he, too, fell to the ground entangled in the struggling bodies. First here and then there the mass of undignified

humanity thrashed across the floor. Some prodded at it
ineffectively with their swords. Don Cesar held himself
aloof from a rough and tumble which consorted ill with
his Castilian dignity. Someone else saw O'Neill's head
emerge from the muddle and kicked it shrewdly with a
heavy boot. Others saw their opportunity and, falling on
their knees, struck with their knives, over and over again.

And there, on the earthen floor of an inn, the Captain-
General of Leon—self-appointed—died. The military
despotism he had set up was thus marked, in the best
traditions of such a form of rule, by a palace revolution
initiated by the defection of the captain of the bodyguards.

It had taken much to kill an unarmed man. O'Neill's
body bore as many wounds as any Cæsar's, as he lay there
in a wide pool of blood in the semi-darkness. Only one
candle had survived the struggle, and this stood in its
candlestick with a long sooted wick protruding from its
flame, stinking abominably. El Platero snuffed it carefully,
and then relit the other candles from it. The other men
were recovering from the struggle, breathing hard. Volpe
was trying to adjust his tunic, which had been torn right
across the breast. Elizalde, gasping with pain, was sitting
in the blood on the floor nursing his shattered shoulder.
Don Cesar bent over the body sprawled upon the ground.

"He solved the problem for us," said Don Cesar.

It was perhaps a more kindly epitaph than a dead despot
deserved.

CHAPTER XVI

As though the very elements wished to mark their approval of recent events, the next morning dawned bright and promising. The icy wind had dropped, the rain had ceased, and the sun broke early through the mist to warm the aching limbs of the marching soldiers, and to harden the miry roads, and to comfort the hearts of all. The army of Leon was on the march just as if its general had not died during the night. It continued to sprawl forward across the plains like some shapeless monster—an acephalous monster, now—like some vast amœboid organism trickling over the plains towards the great road from France to Madrid along which ran the life blood of the French army.

The many leaders had been wise to keep their several sections on the move. No one was likely to ask questions about a dead general in the course of a long and sultry march, or while recovering from it afterwards—and while the prospect still dangled before them of new conquests to be achieved. Not the stupidest man in the whole army could be unaware of the existence of that road, and of its supreme importance in the war; nor could he fail to thrill at the prospect of closing it to French supplies and messages.

Besides, there was little motive for asking questions. El Platero's men obeyed el Platero's orders, and Urquiola's men Urquiola's. No one was specially interested in O'Neill's continued existence. The men who had once formed

O'Neill's band, and those who had once formed el Bil-banito's, had grown accustomed to their combined duties as headquarters guard and men of the artillery train, and in consequence to obedience to Jorge. Their experiences as guerilleros had taught them that too great an interest in the doings of their superiors was unhealthy. Some men had opened their eyes wide at sight of Jorge astride the big grey horse which O'Neill had ridden, but they knew better than to open their mouths as well. There had been no love for O'Neill.

As for Jorge, he was as happy as a king. The sun shone, and he had a good horse under him, and he was undisputed master of the gun. He had come to love that big eighteen-pounder. There seemed to be some fraternal bond between him and it. There was an odd physical resemblance, cer-tainly. Although Jorge, at eighteen, had hardly come yet to his full strength, his figure was immense and square, with vast thews, and on foot there was a roll in his gait queerly like the gun's motion on a rocky road. He loved the gun for its deadly precision, for its crushing power. Its pig-headed obstinacy when being pulled over broken country was to Jorge's mind (which was also somewhat inclined to obstinacy) much more of a virtue than a vice.

As Jorge rode along beside the gun team he felt—even if he was not yet conscious of them—unwonted prickings of ambition within him. He hoped—he even nearly believed —that he was on the high road to eminence as a soldier. Certainly the council of war which had been held the night before over O'Neill's dead body included him in it as a matter of course. It was assumed without question that he was to be responsible for the artillery; as chief of a detachment he could rate himself on an equality with Don Cesar Urquiloa, a gentleman of the bluest blood of Castile, or with Alvarez, the most famous of Mina's lieutenants. He could even look down upon the inexperienced country gentlemen who found themselves in command of the battalions of local levies. At a conservative estimate he was not lower than fifth or sixth in the unstated hierarchy of the army. With a little good fortune he might find himself soon in command of all the ten thousand men of the army of Leon, able to proclaim himself Captain-General if he wished, and with a long future of military glory before him. The prospect more than compensated him for the saddle soreness and stiffness which almost prevented him from walking at the end of the day.

These physical disabilities did not deter him at all from limping round among the men that evening. The mercurial temperament of the mountaineers had risen with the improvement in the weather; perhaps also with the unexplained disappearance of O'Neill; and the mountaineers' light spirits infected the graver men of the plains. The guitars of the south and the bagpipes of the north blended in a raucous discord as the men danced in their bivouacs and billets. There was laughter and merriment, and, perhaps because there was food in plenty in this halting-place, perhaps because—as seems barely possible—Jorge's newborn pride communicated itself to the others, everyone was newly filled with confidence. On the next day's march the men roared out songs as they tramped along, and the drums rattled and roared with a gaiety they might almost have learned from the French, and Jorge rode along among them, shrinking from contact with the saddle, but rapt in

blissful dreams of future triumphs and glory, as unwarrant-
able as they were ill-defined.

Now they came to the road at last. El Bilbanito had
hardly dared to think of reaching the road. O'Neill, before
his megalomania overmastered him, had thought of it as a
very desirable but hardly attainable ideal. It was Jorge who
had finally brought the gun there. It ran as straight as a
bullet flies, as far as the eye could reach in either direction
across the plain. Fifty miles to the north it had quitted the
mountains of the Basque provinces, where Mina and Longa
and el Marquesito threatened it; fifty miles to the south it
charged the slopes of the Guadarrama, where el Empecinado
lurked. For two years no Spanish force had ventured to
approach it here, in the heart of Old Castile.

The great roadmakers of the world would not consider it
to be a very remarkable road. It was narrow, it was not too
durably paved; its gradients were not engineered with
particular skill. But for all that, it was a very remarkable
road for Spain; if only for the fact that it was the one
beneficial public work undertaken during two centuries by
the dynasty for which Spain was at that moment so
lavishly pouring out her blood. It was the link which
joined Spain to Europe; the stages along it, Vittoria, Burgos, Madrid and the rest marked the flow and the ebb of
the Moorish conquest just as they were to mark later on
the ebb and the flow of the French conquest. It was at
once the main artery and the main nerve of the French
army of occupation. Along it came the recruits, the stores,
the money, and the information which enabled King
Joseph to rule in Madrid, and Massena to confront Wellington in Portugal, and Soult to hold down the opulent south.

In the mountains to the north and south experience and necessity had taught the French to fortify almost every yard of its course; here in the plains there had been no need so far and small indication of any eventual necessity. But at this vital strategic point, where the road was joined by the by-road from Leon, and where it crossed the Salas River by a long stone bridge, Bessières had taken the precaution of building a fortress. Here convoys could rest in security, and here was a convenient depot wherein could be concentrated the tribute and the supplies wrung from the surrounding country.

It proved its value now; when the news had come that Leon had risen in revolt, that the garrison had been massacred, and that a new Spanish army was pouring down towards the road, the little garrisons of Old Castile had gathered here for protection; the convoys bound south and the convoys bound north had halted here, and measures had been taken to offer a desperate defence while messengers had sped north and south with the alarm, to summon the inevitable armies of relief.

Jorge, filled with a most delicious sense of his own importance, trotted forward on the big grey horse, Urquiola and Alvarez at his side, to reconnoitre this new object of attack. The army stopped to rest, higgledy-piggledy along five miles of road, save for Urquiola's lancers, who were riding in groups over the plain. The fort did not look as formidable as La Merced, because it did not stand on such a dominating height, nor as the citadel of Leon, because it could be inspected from a much greater distance. Jorge could see long walls of grey stone, and storehouses within and a central citadel. At the foot of the walls might be a dry ditch, and in the bottom of the ditch might be palisades. Jorge rode forward to confirm these suspicions, Urquiola and Alvarez jingling beside him. There came a puff of smoke from the wall; a cannon ball pitched close to them in a cloud of dust and bounced onward over the plain.

"That was heavy metal," said Alvarez, eyeing the length of the range.

Jorge said nothing. He was so interested in this business of reconnaissance that the fact that he was under fire made no impression on him. He rode on through the sparse corn. Another jet of smoke showed on the wall. This time the ball pitched almost in front of them and ricochetted past them.

"Garcia told us that they have eighteen-pounders mounted on the wall," said Alvarez.

Jorge pressed on through the dust cloud which obscured his view. It was from this side he must make his attack; the other was guarded by the river. As far as he could see, apart from that, one starting point was as good as another on this naked plain. But there might be something, some fold in the ground, some dry water course, which might facilitate the attack.

A third shot from the fort screamed closer over their heads; they felt the wind of its passage.

"Haven't you seen enough yet?" growled Alvarez anxiously. "There's no sense in being shot at without an object."

He quieted down his plunging horse and addressed himself to Jorge more directly than ever.

"Come back now," he said. "They'll hit us next round."

Jorge shook his hand from his arm and rode diagonally forward still, his attention all concentrated in the unwonted stream of thoughts passing through his mind.

" Then go on if you want to," said Alvarez. " I shall not come; my men have still need of me. Shall we go back, Don Cesar? "

Urquiola turned his horse without another word, and the two trotted back. Jorge rode on. He approached the river bank on one side of the fort, wheeled the grey horse about and rode round the fort till he neared the river on the other side. They gave up firing eighteen-pounders at him as he came nearer, and opened instead with handier field guns. Several enthusiasts on the wall took their muskets and tried long shots with them; even at three hundred yards it was just possible to hit a man on a horse with a musket if one fired enough times. Bullets kicked up the dust round his horse's feet. They roused him from his abstraction in the end by wheeling an eighteen-pounder round again and firing at him with grape. It was long range for grape shot, but the aim was good. The bullets tore up the ground all round him; it seemed for a second as if the grey horse was wading knee-deep in a river of grape.

Jorge woke like a man from a dream. Miraculously he had not been hit, nor his horse. He shook his reins and cantered away, to where half the army had gathered to watch the performance.

" Well? " asked Alvarez, anxiety in his narrow eyes. " Can you take the place? "

Alvarez and Urquiola had decided that they neither of them liked the look of the fortress of Salas at all, and they

were anxious to thrust the responsibility of a decision upon
Jorge's shoulders.

"Of course I can," said Jorge. It never occurred to him
that his marvellous eighteen-pounder could fail.

"Then get to work," said Alvarez. "I will take my men
northward up the road to cover you."

Alvarez had by no means sufficient trust in the eighteen-
pounder—or at least in Jorge's management of it—to
risk his men's lives and his own reputation in the
attempt.

Jorge found himself there on the road, just out of range
of the big guns, with the siege of a powerful second-class
fortress on his hands. He had never even seen a real fortress
before. But the other commanding officers gathered round
him for orders with pathetic confidence. They looked upon
him—as Alvarez and Urquiola did not—as O'Neill's successor. They were quick to toady to him, quick to defer to
authority, or quick to evade the responsibility which Jorge
assumed without a thought.

Jorge peered down the road under his hand. He was
under the necessity of working out for himself the highly
technical art of siegecraft from first principles. 'Parallels'
and 'approaches' meant nothing to him at all, but he
knew that no troops could advance against that fortress
over that naked plain under the fire which would be turned
on them. But he had heard of trenches—he had even seen
one or two minor trenches dug during the sieges O'Neill
had conducted. By a trench the man could approach the
fort; but naturally the trench must not point directly at
it, or the artillery would play straight down it. The trench
must point towards some point just outside the fortress,

and then at a convenient distance must change direction and point towards the opposite side, and so on, approaching the fort in zigzags. Then, when the trench was close to the fort, the big gun must break the walls, and the infantry rise up out of the trench and storm the breach. A very technical art seems simple when stated in simple terms.

Jorge, positively inspired, rose to greater heights still. If the trenches were to be begun out of cannon range—a mile and a half from the fort, say—and carried forward in zigzags by work at one end only, it would be months before the approaches neared the walls. But Jorge had not been a guerillero all these years for nothing. He had acquired an eye for ground. There were two successive, almost imperceptible undulations in the plain; the crest of either would shelter men from fire. The nearer one was no more than half a mile from the walls. If the trench were to begin there on a long front much time and trouble would be saved. True, men coming to and going from it would be under fire, but what was night for if not to conceal besiegers? And when circumstances permitted they might dig a communication trench for use in daylight.

The first trench would have to be dug at night, too, and Jorge had had a fair experience of military operations at night—trust a guerillero for that. He knew how incredibly easy it was for them to go wrong in the darkness, and he was keenly appreciative of the necessity of making every possible preparation beforehand. If the trench was to be dug at night it must be planned and marked in the daytime. Jorge abruptly issued orders for the cutting of a number of pointed stakes, and for strips of white cloth to be tied to them. As night fell, in the last feeble glimmering of daylight, he went out himself to the second fold in the ground and drove those stakes in a long line beneath the tiny crest of the insignificant ridge.

CHAPTER XVII

A TALENTED engineer officer, set to besiege the fortress
of Salas, would have acted just like Jorge. The only difference would have been that the engineer would have had
a vocabulary with which to describe his actions. On the
first night of the siege, his report would have stated, he
would have 'broken ground' and 'thrown up his first
parallel' in 'dead ground' half a mile from the fortress.
But, just like Jorge, he would have sent forward a 'covering party' in skirmishing order to guard against a sortie,
and, having lined up his 'working party' along the stakes
previously driven in, he would have bade them dig like
devils, throwing the earth forward in a 'parapet' along
the very line which Jorge's untutored eye had selected as
most suitable.

Perhaps because Jorge's methods were so strictly orthodox the besieged discovered his nocturnal activities at
once. They fired a few cannon balls at his workmen, but,
not being sure of their aim in the dark, they took to a much
more effective weapon. There were four big howitzers
within the place, and with these they began dropping shells
just over the line of the ridge, whose range was naturally
known to them to a yard. They did a good deal of damage.
They blew down parapets, they killed workmen half a
dozen at a time.

But Jorge's men stuck to it. Some of them were miners,
and most of the rest of them had been tillers of the soil

until recently. They were accustomed and hardened to digging; more important still, they had never so far besieged a place without taking it. They, in their ignorance, were far from sharing the doubts of Alvarez or Urquiola. They dug with enthusiasm. They dragged their dead comrades out of the way and went on digging. It was not long before the howitzers lost the range so that the shells only rarely interfered with the work. By dawn there was a long narrow seam of trench all along the fold of the ground, and six hundred men were comfortably settled into it. They were in a state of siege as long as daylight lasted as much as the garrison of the fortress was, because the artillery fire cut them off from supplies from the rear, but they did not mind that today. They rested content, and began to reduce the trench to that happy state of filth which made things home-like, while two small working parties began the one to push a communication trench slowly to the rear and the other to sap forward towards the fortress from one flank of the trench.

On this advancing trench the garrison turned all their guns, big guns, field guns, and howitzers. They knocked down big sections of the parapet, and killed a good many of the working party. Even Jorge saw that what the besiegers ought to do was to build a battery somewhere along the line of their 'first parallel', arm it with big guns, and so keep down the fire of the fortress. But Jorge had only one eighteen-pounder, and he was not going to risk it in a duel so unequal; he had to reserve it for breaching the wall when the approaches were completed. Perhaps when the field guns struggled up from the rear he might use those, although they would be too small to do much damage. Meanwhile men's lives must be sacrificed in the absence of artillery. The murderous work at the sap-head proceeded steadily. The sturdy miners dug furiously despite their losses.

Partly their enthusiasm was kindled by Jorge's example. He worked as hard as any; he seemed to be quite indifferent to danger. As a matter of fact, he actually was indifferent. He was so intensely interested in this new enterprise that he quite forgot about the danger he was running. It was something new to him to hold this high command, to bear this great responsibility. It was peculiarly gratifying to see his siege works growing under his eyes. It satisfied his creative impulses.

But while he was so engrossed in the bustle and toil at the sap-head he was suddenly interrupted by a messenger who came pushing his way down the trench to him. The other officers urgently requested his attendance at head-quarters. Jorge cursed aloud, but comically, somehow, so that the men digging beside him laughed. With a parting incitement to work harder still he left them, and they cheered him as he went—so much had his popularity grown overnight.

Jorge made his way along the trench, scrambled out over the back, and ran the gauntlet of the enemy's fire as he hastened across the open country. But nobody bothered to fire guns at a single man on foot. At the roadside where Urquiola and Alvarez and Delgado, with half a dozen of Urquiola's lancers; and a man in peasant's clothes was sitting on the ground, his face grey with fatigue. Behind him his small horse, grey with dust, hung his head in exhaustion. Urquiola handed Jorge the note the man had brought, and Jorge looked at it upside down and handed it back.

"What does it say?" asked Jorge, who naturally could not read.

"It is from Brother Bernard," said Urquiola, "the man who put the arsenic in the flour at Leon."

"I am glad to hear from him again," said Jorge. It was wonderful how his new activity was bringing him out of his previous dumbness.

"There is a regiment of the French Guard marching down from Biscay, he says," said Urquiola. "He is out with all the peasants he can raise—which are not very many."

"Nor likely to be," said Jorge. O'Neill had swept every man he could catch into the ranks of this army now gathered before Salas. "And how many Frenchmen did you say?"

"A regiment," said Urquiola, testily.

Jorge, groping in his mind, was just able to recapture his recollection of what a regiment was—two or three battalions; altogether from one or two thousand men.

"Of the Guard," added Alvarez, sombrely.

"Yes," said Jorge, "I expect Brother Bernard finds his hands full."

Jorge in his guerillero days had come up against the Guard once or twice, and he knew what kind of soldiers they were.

"Brother Bernard says there is no stopping them. They march where they will. He asks for help. He asks us for cannons."

"Cannons?" said Jorge. In his mind's eye he saw the

army's field guns embogged and deserted, left without teams fifty miles away. It would be a week before they came up.

"It must be guns," said Alvarez. "What can we do against a regiment of the Guard here on this cursed plain?"

Alvarez could never mention the plains without bitterness. He had learned his soldier's trade under Mina in the mountains of Navarre. But Jorge, just as well as Alvarez, could picture the attempt to engage the Guard on the plains. No Spanish troops, however numerous, could face them. They would shatter any infantry force opposing them; they would beat off any cavalry. They might march unchecked even into Salas, and the addition of their strength to that of the garrison would render a siege impossible; it would in fact imperil the whole army.

"How far are they off now?" asked Jorge.

"They were thirty miles away at dawn this morning, when this man left Brother Bernard," said Urquiola.

"Thirty miles? Then they may be here at nightfall. And we must meet them as far from here as we can."

"We know that," snapped Alvarez. "Can you move your gun at once?"

"Yes."

"Then for God's sake come now. Don Cesar, are your men ready?"

"Bring my horse!" shouted Jorge to his orderly. Within three days it had grown to be perfectly natural to Jorge to call to a man to bring his horse. The thrill of pleasure which the giving of the order had originally caused him, already growing stale, was quite unnoticed now in the excitement of the moment.

The evils of a divided command were not at all apparent at this crisis. The situation was too simple, the need was too urgent, everyone was too enthusiastic in the cause for opinion to be divided or for irresolution to display itself. Soon, drawn by thirty mules, yoked two by two, the big gun was off up the great paved road. On this admirable surface, and under the goadings of the excited muleteers, the mules made prodigious speed. At quite three miles an hour the big gun was dragged along; it crashed and rattled over the inequalities of the *pavé*, rolling about like a ship at sea. After it came thirty mules of the pack train, plodding stolidly along under their vast burdens of cannon balls and powder—some of them (those with careful drivers) bearing a net of forage as well.

Don Cesar's lancers were already clattering up the road far ahead, and hot on their tracks marched Alvarez' Navarrese. The garrison of the fort saw them go, but it was only a detachment after all. There were still several thousand men in loose formation round the place. A sally at present would be objectless and dangerous.

G*

CHAPTER XVIII

THE FOURTH REGIMENT of the Fusiliers of the Imperial Guard—the premier regiment of what was colloquially termed the Young Guard—had had a disturbing march. They had been sent over the mountains from Biscay in consequence of the wild rumours which had drifted into that province regarding the situation in Leon. Even the men in the ranks had heard the fantastic stories; they had heard whispers of universal revolt, of huge Spanish armies, miraculously sprung from the ground, of fortresses taken, and even unbelievable tales of the poisoning of the whole garrison of the citadel of Leon.

The fact that no messengers came in from Leon did not do much towards confirming these rumours. The French garrison of every Spanish province was accustomed to being quite isolated from every other province for weeks at a time, thanks to the activities of the guerilleros who lurked in the mountains. It was a usual assumption that no message was safe unless four hundred men at least escorted it. But the rumours had grown insistent, and at last the Military Governor of Biscay had felt compelled to act upon them. Only by pinching and scraping, and by careful redistribution of his garrisons, had he been able to set free a single regiment and launch it over the passes with orders to get into touch at all costs with the troops guarding the main line of communications. Wellington was loose in the south, he knew, and the knowledge was enough to make any French general nervous; moreover, when every available man had already been drawn off to oppose him there was always this difficulty about finding a sufficient force to reopen communications.

The march of the Fusiliers had all the nightmare quality which characterized the march of small bodies of French troops in Spain. There had been the usual sniping from hillsides, and the usual number of sentries found in the morning with their throats cut. They marched along roads without a soul being seen; they entered villages without a single inhabitant—everything was left deserted at their approach. The hard-bitten veterans of the Guard took care in every village to see that nothing of value was left behind when they quitted the place, although the loot was poor because every village had been plundered half a dozen times already. It usually happened from carelessness or malice that the villages were set on fire as they marched out.

Down in the plains the conditions seemed more ominous than ever. The number of irregulars hanging round their flanks as they marched apparently increased. They could see gangs of fifty or so marching parallel to them, ready to run at the first attack, but equally ready to cut a straggler's throat or to cut off a small body of marauders, and much too fleet of foot for the heavily laden infantry men to catch them. The march seemed to the men in the ranks like the passage of a swimmer in the sea. No individual droplet of water could offer him any measurable resistance; but the water would close behind him as readily as he cleft it in front, and if he tried to swim too far the water would overpower him in the end.

Then they reached Saldaña, and they knew matters were

serious, for where the tricolour had once waved they now saw the red and gold of Spain, and where they had anticipated welcome they now received musket shots and yells of defiance from the fanatics who had shut themselves up in the place. There was no retaking the place; as the Spaniards had discovered long before, these little fortresses were impregnable to infantry without artillery. The Fusiliers swerved aside and marched to Santa Eulalia, and Santa Eulalia was in the hands of Spaniards, too. Surely Leon, the capital, with its garrison of a thousand men and its formidable commandant would still be holding out? But when they marched up the road to Leon they found the gates shut against them, and the walls manned by excited mobs who fired off muskets at them at impossible ranges but who could still be relied upon to beat off any attack unsupported by big guns. That impression as if a sea was closing about them was intensified. Already the sea had engulfed many of the refuges where they had hoped to rest awhile.

On their march back to Carrion they met the first real opposition in the field. A few score misguided peasants tried to hold the crossing where the road passed one of the ravines which seam the plain. But it had been folly to suppose that a mere ravine and a few brave men could stop two battalions of the Guard. The Fusiliers rejoiced at the prospect of action. In front one battalion threatened the crossing. Half a mile away the other battalion swarmed down the side of the ravine, fought their way waist deep across the raging water, up the other side, and came down on the flank of the opposition almost before the poor fools realized that their flank might be turned. Some they caught

and bayoneted, and the rest ran like hares across the plain
—half a squadron of dragoons would have cut them all to
pieces, but with Wellington loose in the south there was
not even half a squadron of dragoons to spare in the north.

It was only by the greatest exertions that the officers
could prevail on the maddened soldiers to spare two or
three of the men they caught. It was of the utmost importance that information should be gathered, and it was only
from prisoners that information could be got. The prisoners
did not tell willingly, but they talked after a time, after
'the question' had been applied to them—a most significant expression. Kept rigidly apart, and questioned by men
who had learned how to extract information from recal-
citrant Spaniards, and then requestioned on points in
which their tales differed, they told all they knew.

Pieced together as far as might be—for the wretched
men had only fragmentary knowledge themselves—the
story they told was like some fantastic romance of the old
chivalry in which the supernatural was inextricably
blended with the truth. They told of a marvellous man
called O'Neill, who had marched down from the mountains with a great army, and with a new sort of gun which
had blown in the gates of the city of Leon from five miles
away. He had ranged the length and breadth of Leon,
killing all who had offered him opposition, Spaniards and
Frenchmen alike. The peasant's hearsay account of the
executions in the Plaza Mayor took on the aspect of the
multiple human sacrifices of a King of Dahomey. They
knew something of the killing of the garrison of La Merced,
and a little of the more prolonged, processional massacres
of the garrisons which had capitulated and had been

marched to the rear. Along with all this, and recurring like a refrain in their account of slaughter and destruction, they kept referring to someone else, vaguely identified as Brother Bernard, who apparently achieved by magic and prayer what was necessary to complete the work which O'Neill's strength had begun. It was from what they told that the Fusiliers were able to guess, with sickening hearts, at the poisoning of the garrison of Leon. And the peasants agreed that it was on account of orders issued by Brother Bernard that the peasantry were out in opposition to the Fusiliers. He had passed over the country with magic speed, and where he passed the men took arms and stood to fight the French. Finally, as to O'Neill, he had gone on with a great army—so said the peasants, whose eye had not been trained to appreciate the difference between a force of ten thousand men and one of a hundred thousand. He was gone to Madrid to hang King Joseph, and he would take King Ferdinand out of his dungeon and set him on the throne again.

Colonel Baron Laferrière, listening to all this muddle of fact and fiction, had to decide what to make of it. He had to discount some proportion of the obvious exaggeration about the size of O'Neill's army; he had to guess where its next blow might be struck; he had to make up his mind as to what was his duty to do next. Not without reason he was convinced that his men could march through any mass of hastily raised Spanish levies. He made up his mind that the best thing he could do would be to march by cross-roads over the plain to the great road. There he would at least be at the place where his troops would do most good; he would complete the circle and march back to Biscay if he were wanted there, and, most important of all, he would carry the news of the rising and some facts about it to Burgos on his way.

After a few months of warfare in Spain every French officer learnt how necessary it was to take every opportunity to carry news—news in those isolated provinces where guerilleros haunted every road was the most precious military requirement that existed; the march of every column had to be modified so that it could escort despatches as well as carry out whatever other function was allotted it.

So the Fusiliers of the Guard turned eastward, and marched along the country tracks over the plains. They were a very fine spectacle, in their smart blue tunics and their white breeches and black gaiters. The stream of tall black bearskins ornamented each with a long, gaudy red feather poured along the rough tracks; in the centre of the column between the two battalions the band blared away nobly, and the drums thundered and rolled, and overhead on its long staff the silver regimental eagle flashed as it caught the sun. These were the men who had marched into every capital in Europe, the men who had decided the fate of Europe at Wagram. Colonel Baron Laferrière was the man who had headed the charge at Jena which brought down in ruins the greatest military monarchy in the world.

It was ironical that they should now be ringed in by armed peasants. The men of whom the kings of the world went in terror were glad to halt for the night in mud-built villages, where they made their meagre supper of corn looted from the barns, pounded between stones, and toasted into tasteless girdle cakes. And a knife between the ribs killed a sentry of the Guards just as surely as it would the youngest conscript in the Imperial army.

They were thirteen hundred strong, and the men who scrambled through the fields beside them, who took long shots at intervals into the column, who pestered and worried them so remorselessly, were perhaps less than two hundred. If there had been ten times as many they would have effected no more, and perhaps their numbers would have tempted them to attempt more and fail; but that was cold comfort to Colonel Baron Laferrière when he saw his sunburnt men, veterans of Marengo and Austerlitz, tumble over when the muskets squibbed off in a distant ditch.

It was near evening at the end of one of these nightmare days when they reached the great road at last. Southward it went like a bullet across the dreary plain towards Madrid; northward it plunged into the mountains, blue in the distant horizon, where lay Burgos. and their friends, and a meat ration, and a rest from this continual sniping. While the men were cooking their evening meal—tearing out doors and window frames for fuel—Colonel Baron Laferrière thought he heard a significant sound to the southward. It was gunfire, he thought, and a man who had heard artillery firing on fifty battle-fields over Europe could not be mistaken. But when he called the other officers' attention to it they could hear nothing, nor could the sergeant-major when he was consulted. Even the colonel could hear nothing again now. He felt he must have been mistaken, although he could not really believe it. Truly he could hear nothing now. Jorge had by now turned his horse away from the fortress of Salas and the garrison had ceased trying to hit with grape the fool on the grey horse who had ridden so close up to their walls.

Yet in the night the adjutant came and woke the colonel where he lay wrapped in his cloak in the flea-ridden inn. Out in the courtyard several officers and men were listening intently. As the colonel joined them he was quite certain that he heard the distant thud-thud of guns. A chorus of exclamations from the listeners confirmed him in his belief. The sergeant-major lifted his head from the drum on which he had laid it and announced positively that there was firing somewhere to the south. Everyone listened again. In the still night the sound came to them clearly enough— the garrison of Salas was firing at the first parallel which was being thrown up under Jorge's direction.

Colonel Baron Laferrière had no difficulty next morning in deciding what he ought to do. Thirty miles down the road was the fortress of Salas, one of the most important posts on all the Royal Road. The gunfire—men still affirmed that they heard it, despite the bustle of the regiment's getting under arms—showed that Salas was beleaguered, presumably by the Leonese rabble which this unknown O'Neill had organized. Salas, Laferrière knew, was well provisioned—many were the convoys he had helped to escort thither—and with an adequate garrison ought to hold out indefinitely. Yet he could not be sure that the garrison was adequate. It was of the first importance that he should march there to reinforce it, breaking through the mob of besiegers. Then Salas would be safe until a real relieving force came up from the south.

The orders that Colonel Baron Laferrière gave on parade that morning turned the head of the column down the road towards Salas, instead of up it towards Burgos. It was then that Brother Bernard sent off his only horseman with the news to the Leonese army, while he himself mounted on his little white mule—his feet almost touched the ground on either side—to stimulate his peasantry into delaying the march of the French. Brother Bernard was quite as well aware of the importance of Salas as was Colonel Baron Laferrière.

The Fusiliers of the Guard marched southward down the great road. Still the pestilent irregulars pursued them. They acted more recklessly than usual, all the same. Several of them stayed firing until too late from the ditches and dry watercourses in which they had hidden themselves, and were caught by the advanced guard and killed. All through the morning the Fusiliers saw in full view the leader of these pests—a monk in greyish brown robe astride a white mule. Once he approached so close that the colonel departed from his rigid rule of paying no attention to irregulars, and, halting the column, had the leading platoon fire a volley at him. But he trotted off quite unharmed through the gust of bullets; it was a waste of five minutes and fifty rounds.

Then, as the weary morning wore on, and the heat of the sun grew more crushing, a new enemy appeared. A long column of horsemen came trotting up the road towards them, and, as they grew near, they spread out over the plain in little squadrons, ringing in the marching column from a safe distance. The colonel cared nothing for them; they were no danger, but merely an additional nuisance. There were no Spanish cavalry in existence which could charge five hundred men together, and these poor levies, on their Lilliputian horses, could do his regiment no harm as long as it kept closed and ready to form square in the event of a rush. But they were undoubtedly a nuisance. The Fusiliers had to abandon their comfortable marching order in column of sixes and form quarter column of companies astride the road, slowing their rate of march and worrying the men with the need for careful dressing and distancing. And the endangered flank guards and advanced guard having been called in, the irregulars on foot could creep in close to the column and fire into the vulnerable masses.

CHAPTER XIX

JORGE LEFT the gun and the ammunition train making its slow way up the road, and, digging his heels into the grey horse's sides, galloped on ahead whither Urquiola and Alvarez had vanished over the grey-green plain. Thoughts and ideas were pouring through his mind like a millstream. He knew nothing of text book principles of war; he had never heard of 'the intelligent combination of the three arms' or any of the other ideals held up before aspiring generals. But he knew that ahead of him was an enemy whom the cavalry could not break, whom the infantry could not face, but who would be quite helpless before a skilful employment of the big gun which he so dearly loved. So engrossed was he with the plan of action which he was evolving in his slow brain that he never noticed the agony which riding caused his skinned and blistered body.

He was looking for a safe ambush for the gun—a place from which he could open fire unexpectedly and at close range, and yet have time to fire a dozen rounds without having to fight for his life. As he urged the big grey horse up the road his eyes swept the plain to left and to right in search of the sort of place he had in mind. He found it a couple of miles higher up.

Here a steep banked ravine seamed the plain, crossing the road at an acute angle. It was not in the least impassable to infantry, but it would be an awkward obstacle, causing delay and disorder. The massive stone bridge by

178

which the road crossed it was far too solid a structure for him to think of destroying it in the hour which was all he had to spare; but the destruction of the bridge was not essential to his plan. For on the near side of the ravine, where it flanked the road beyond the bridge, stood a solitary cottage, of the usual sun-dried brick, with beside it some sort of cow-house of the same material.

Jorge urged the big horse through the crops towards the cottage, clattering up to the door. There were two young women working in the field near at hand who looked up, and an old bent woman came out through the door at the sound of his approach, with two small children clinging to her skirts. Jorge gave them neither word nor look—possibly he did not even see them—and the children looked at him wondering as he wheeled the big grey horse here and there, riding round the cowshed and the dung heap, taking in the details of the position before he turned his horse's head back to the road like the wind to set his plan in motion.

Alvarez, wondering how he could use his Navarrese infantry with their untrustworthy leaven of Leonese levies in this featureless plain against this solid mass of disciplined troops, heard the hoofbeats of the grey horse as it came up to him at frantic speed. Jorge reined the sweating animal up beside him; his eyes blazed strangely out of his face caked with dust and sweat. He poured out his plan. Excitement lent him unwonted eloquence. Even Alvarez the sceptical and cautious took fire. It was at least a plan, while Alvarez had none to offer. Within five minutes four hundred of Alvarez' men were marching back down the road again as fast as they could set foot to the ground, under the burning sun, to the bridge they had crossed an hour before.

Jorge gave no thought to the scene before him. He did not spare the Fusiliers of the Guard the grace of a glance. The visual imagination which excitement and action had roused in him had pictured the whole scene before he set eyes on it—the long beautiful lines of bearskins and plumes moving regularly across the plain, the eagle flashing overhead, the bayonets gleaming through the dust; and the knots of horsemen prowling round out of range, helpless and disconsolate.

He found Urquiola riding with a hundred of his Castilians, grimy pennons fluttering from the lance points. Two years before, Urquiola would have charged them, to red ruin and certain death, but in two years of war Urquiola had learned that it was folly to charge on these weakly horses against unshaken infantry. But it was a bitter pill to swallow, to follow these French like jackals, picking up the stragglers who fell out with sunstroke, and apart from that acting more like an escort of honour than like an enemy as they made their triumphant way to Salas.

To Urquiola Jorge poured out his plan again. With a sweep of his arm he pointed out the features of the land—it was strange how quickly Jorge had acquired the general's eye for country—and next minute another detachment of lancers was trotting off along the route Jorge had pointed out, turning the end of the ravine so as to be on the further side before the French could reach it. Then Jorge galloped back down the road again to where the gun was lumbering up towards him; he was wild with panic lest he had not time to get all things ordered before the French should reach the ravine.

The children at the cottage had not yet ceased from asking questions about the man on the big grey horse who had galloped up and galloped away again—questions which their grandmother could not answer—when things began to happen which ended their questions. A long double line of mules came tugging and straining over the field to the cottage, drawing after them an immense cannon. The sweating men who goaded the mules said something to their grandmother which set the poor old lady into a terrible panic. Their mother and their aunt came running in from the field, and began despairingly to bundle together pots and pans and the treasures of the household, but when the man on the grey horse came up they had to leave off doing this and hurry out of the cottage with the children, aimlessly out across the fields. The children whimpered, and struggled vainly as they were dragged away. They wanted to stay and see what was going to happen, and to hear the big cannon fired; already, with shouts and gaspings for breath, it had been hauled through the yard and wheeled round beside the cottage wall so that its long grim muzzle pointed out round the corner. There were other men, too, who came clattering into the cottage, and broke holes in the walls, and who loaded their guns with long ram-rods, and who turned the precious goats loose, and who yet had time and thought to spare to wring the chickens' necks and hang the bodies to their belts.

Jorge had found time for everything. The gun was well concealed between the cottage and the dung heap. The cottage was garrisoned; the banks of the ravine were lined with skirmishers. Urquiola and his lancers were waiting ready in line two hundred yards away. Jorge loaded the gun with care. He was meticulous about the ladleful of gunpowder which was scooped into the gun muzzle and rammed carefully down. He saw that the touch-hole was filled with loose powder. He rammed down with his own hands one of the long cylindrical tin boxes filled with musket balls which constituted the projectile known as 'canister'—Jorge had never seen canister used in action before. Close beside the gun stood a further dozen rounds of canister, a dozen of grape, a dozen of roundshot. A ladleful of powder was ready for instant reloading. There were two slow-matches ready burning—Spanish slow-match was unreliable material with a distressing habit of going out at a crucial moment. The mules had all been sent half a mile away so that in the event of disaster they would not be captured, and the French would have no means of dragging away the big gun. For the last time Jorge looked along the sights of the gun and saw that it bore exactly on the point of the road nearest the cottage.

The Fourth Regiment of the Fusiliers of the Guard came marching steadily over the plain. The afternoon was well advanced now, and they had been marching since dawn under a burning sun. They had eaten nothing since morning, and all they had drunk had been the contents of their water bottles. One or two men had collapsed under the strain. One or two men had been killed by long shots. One or two wounded were being carried on the officers' horses—no wounded could possibly be abandoned to the mercy of Spanish irregulars.

But the honour of the Imperial Guard was involved. At

the thought of that the big, sunburnt, moustached soldiers pulled themselves erect again under their heavy burdens, as a child will wipe his eyes when told that no really big boy ever cries. Their officers told them that their troubles were nearly over, that Salas lay only six miles ahead, and that in Salas they would find rest, and security, and food, and a bottle of wine for every man. They marched on hopefully.

At the sight of the ravine, and the bridge, and the cottage, with the enemy drawing in closely at this point, Colonel Laferrière realized that it was here that the enemy had decided to make his decisive stand; and the colonel's heart grew proportionately lighter. The ravine was not the sort of obstacle which would stop his hardbitten men. They would shatter the enemy's line at the bridge, and with any sort of good fortune they would deal the enemy such a blow that they would not be molested again that day. He would have to guard his rear while attacking in front, and it might be better to give his men ten minutes' rest before sending them forward, but his troubles were over, he thought. At his word the long lines of plumes stood fast, and the men wiped their sweating faces, and saw to the priming of their muskets, and looked forward expectantly to taking their revenge on the Spaniards.

Then the drums rolled, wilder and wilder in the *pas de charge*. The officers moved out to the front, with their swords flashing in the sun. The long lines came forward like walls. The company of voltigeurs ran out ahead, the green plumes waving gallantly, to the edge of the ravine, and the solid lines followed them. Jorge squinted along the sights of the gun. He blew the smouldering slow-match into a brisker glow, and pressed it into the touch-hole.

An eighteen-pounder round of canister contained four hundred musket balls. The thin tin box which held them served to lessen their spread just a little, like the choke bore of a shot gun. Four hundred bullets were flung at once with precision into the flank of the advancing lines. No infantry battalion—not even an English one—could have fired a volley of such deadliness. The Guards staggered with the shock.

The gunners tried to peer through the billowing smoke to see the effect of the shot, and those who could see raised a cheer at the destruction it had caused, but Jorge, cursing at the top of his voice, recalled them to their duty. Already he had wiped out the gun. He ladled the powder into the muzzle, and forced it down with the rammer and the wad. He swung a new canister into the gun and rammed that. He flung his weight upon the breech as if by his own unaided exertions he would run the gun up into position again. They helped him wildly. The muzzle of the gun peered forward round the corner of the cottage again. Jorge looked along the sights, turned the lateral adjusting screw half a turn, looked again, and then, grabbing a handful of powder, scattered it over the touch-hole. He caught up the slow-match and fired the gun. It roared out deafeningly, with the smoke pouring over them all. One born fool had forgotten to get out of the way of the recoil and lay shriek-ing with his leg under the wheel, but no one minded about that. Their business was to load and fire the gun as fast as it could be done.

The massed Fusiliers reeled as though every single man

had been hit. Jorge had made 'intelligent use' not merely
of the 'three arms' but of the general's fourth great
weapon, surprise. No one had anticipated that blast of gunfire from the edge of that cottage. Not for the last year had
the French in northern Spain encountered artillery in
Spanish hands in the field. An eighteen-pounder firing
canister can tear fearful gaps in massed infantry; and
canister fired in from behind a flank when an attack is
about to be made to the front is the most staggering of
all.

There were a few young soldiers among the Guard; they
tried to edge away from the merciless fire. The stoutest
hearts—and the thickest heads—were bent on pursuing the
attack, and pressing forward to the ravine across which
the voltigeurs were already exchanging shots with the
Spaniards. The more intelligent and less disciplined tried
to alter the direction of the attack so as to rush the gun
which was doing the damage. Into this wavering confusion
came the fourth discharge to complete it. The colonel fell
dead from his horse. The eagle fell in a wide arc as the
standard bearer collapsed riddled with bullets. Someone else
—one of the men who can be found to display Quixotic
gallantry in any regiment—raised it up again.

But the mischief was done. After lurching in indecision
the Guard began to move slowly away, along the ravine,
away from the gun. No one directed the movement, no
one ordered it, but all followed it. The old formation had
disappeared. There were no more rigid lines. Even the two
battalions were hopelessly intermingled. It was only a vast
mob which stumbled over the plain.

The Spaniards yelled with triumph. They closed round

the shattered regiment like jackals round a wounded lion, firing at close range into the clumsy mass.

Jorge eyed the lengthening distance between his gun and the target and called for grapeshot. An eighteen-pound round of grape contains only thirty balls, each a little more than half a pound each, but thirty balls, each claiming its two or three victims, can smash a hole in a mass of human bodies. Jorge felt the inspiration of warfare boiling up inside him more furiously even than before. He called to his gun's crew to go on firing, rushed round the cottage to where the grey horse was tethered, and hauled himself into the saddle. Next moment he was galloping to the ravine. The good horse steadied himself at the obstacle and then leaped it like a stag. Jorge lost stirrups and reins and all, but he grabbed the saddle, regained his seat by a miracle and came flying up to where fifty of Urquiola's lancers were trotting cautiously after the French. Jorge shrieked "Come on!" to them as he tore by, and they followed him. The lances came down to the horizontal, the sound of the hoofbeats rose to a roar through which the sound of the wind in the lance pennons could be distinctly heard.

A fresh blast of grape crashed into the mass of men and Jorge rode for the gap. Some of the Frenchmen—men who had beaten off the charge of the Russian Imperial cavalry at Austerlitz—faced about and raised their muskets, but it was only a few spattering shots which met the charge. The grey horse, badly wounded, rose on its hind legs and then came down among the Fusiliers kicking and struggling. Jorge, dazed, stupefied, without even a weapon, rolled in among them. But the lancers with that example before them charged home for the first time in their lives. The very pennons were soaked in the blood of Frenchmen. The impact of fifty galloping horses clove the mob in two parts, and each part disintegrated into smaller parts, into little groups that surrendered, into little groups that closed back to back and fought to the last, into isolated men stricken with panic who tried to run away over the plain through the victory-maddened Spaniards.

It was a pitiful sight to see the fine tall guardsmen in all the glory of bearskins and scarlet plumes and manly moustaches asking for their lives from the tatterdemalion semi-savages who seized them, but it was just as pitiful to see the others who scorned to ask for mercy being shot down one by one by the prowling guerilleros who would not close.

CHAPTER XX

THE GUN had won another victory. Previously it had only beaten down walls; but now it had beaten down discipline, organization, esprit de corps. It was a most resounding achievement. A whole regiment of the Imperial Guard had been destroyed. There would be a gap in the next army list to be issued in Paris. In the Almanac Imperial the name of Colonel Laferrière would have to be erased from the list of wearers of the Grand Cross of the Legion of Honour—his star was now borne upon the breast of a woman of the fields, who had received it from her lover who told a great tale of how he had won it in single combat hand to hand with the colonel himself. The eagle itself was in the hands of the victors, and was borne in triumph at the head of Alvarez' men when they marched back to Salas.

Despite all this Jorge did not seem to be spoilt by success. He was the same grinning giant, cracking the same jokes with the men who cheered him as the author of their triumph. For Jorge, although he might yearn for military distinction, could not visualize himself as a great man and had no touchy sense of his own dignity. When some enthusiast offered him a captured horse—most valuable personal plunder—to replace the dead grey he was actually embarrassed by the magnitude of the gift, but unfortunately he remembered he had in his pocket the purse which he had taken from O'Neill's body, and he filled the man's hands with gold; he had never seen gold, save in the

188

Cathedral of Santiago, until the war began, and he was conscious of a feeling of strangeness as he made the gesture. He shook off the awkwardness by a couple of jokes about those parts of his body which had no skin left on them, as he climbed up into the saddle.

It was only ten hours since he had set the gun in motion up the road from Salas, but it seemed like a week. The fields were littered with dead men, and there were heaps of wounded to mark the place where the blasts of canister had reached their mark. Some of them were still able to call for help; they had been thirsty before they had been wounded, and only God knew how they felt now. But they would not be thirsty long. The irregulars were going over the plain systematically, stripping the bodies, emptying pockets, and bringing rest to the wounded. Brother Bernard was among them. He took his spiritual duties seriously. As far as Latin and the wounded men's Spanish would permit, he confessed the wounded, and performed all the necessary offices before he cut their throats.

No one saw anything odd about that; irreligion had never been fashionable in Spain, and it was important to save souls, while as Brother Bernard's followers had never heard that there were such things as customs and usages of war they assumed that it was purely a matter of taste whether a helpless enemy's life should be spared or not. That Brother Bernard should cut a man's throat—in warfare, of course, not in civil life—meant no more and no less to their opinion of him than that he should wring a chicken's neck.

And Jorge was only eighteen, and he had been fighting since he was sixteen. Death was a commonplace to him, and he did not set the value on life which old age does. It did not move him in the least to pity to think of all those splendid men dead by his own act, and the huddled mass of prisoners doomed to a lingering death on the long march back to Leon and the mountains. He was merely elated at his own success, and he was still more pleased when he found that the whole force—Alvarez and Urquiola included—were waiting his decision as to what should be done next. He had no hesitation in deciding to move back at once to continue the siege.

Alvarez and Urquiola had enough consideration for their own dignity not to come and ask for orders; but when Jorge gave the word for the gun to be got back on to the road for Salas they went off hastily to their own contingents and issued similar orders. They knew that their men knew who had won the victory, and, at least until the glamour wore off, they knew that it would be as well to conform to his movements.

The victors rejoined the besiegers of Salas before the one survivor of the vanquished joined the besieged. Lieutenant Aubard, assistant adjutant of the Fourth Fusiliers of the Guard, had not meant to desert his regiment. He had wanted to die with them, although it was dreadful to die in such a fashion in an obscure skirmish in Spain with the Emperor eight hundred miles away. There had indeed been occasions when young Aubard had imagined himself being killed in action, but it had always involved a charge under the Emperor's own eye, on a field which would decide the fate of the world, with half a column devoted to his exploit in the Moniteur afterwards.

Aubard was the only man of the Fusiliers left mounted

when the square broke. A rush of the Spanish lancers
carried him away. He fought his way clear and rode to
join the nearest rallying-group, but it surrendered before
he reached it. He rode to join another, and was chased by
a dozen yelling lancers. His splendid thoroughbred soon
outdistanced their Lilliputian mounts, but he found himself a long way from the nearest French infantry by the
time he had shaken off his pursuers. Then some irregular
infantry began firing long shots at him, and he had to
make a wide detour round them. Then more of the lancers
crossed his path and headed him off. He saw the silver
eagle which towered above one group of the Guard fall a
second time, and it did not rise again.

He sat his horse disconsolate, the sword he was so proud
of dangling idly in his hand, as he saw the last flurry of
the battle under the scorching sun across the grey-green
plain. Presumably he still could, had he chosen, have ridden into the Spanish ranks and hacked away with his
sword until someone killed him, but it was not easy to
decide to do it. No one could blame Aubard—he did not
even blame himself—for wheeling his horse round and riding away from the scene of the defeat.

He was only twenty, and he wept as he rode away. The
tears rolled down his cheeks. All that he had once been so
proud of now seemed to be a mockery. His nodding bear-
skin and its scarlet plume, his blue uniform with its silver
lace, his little scrubby moustache, so carefully tended—for
no one might disfigure the ranks of the Guard with a bare
upper lip—were all hateful to him now. It was not until
an hour later, when his life was in danger again, that he
forgot his unhappiness.

H

Aubard found a place where he could get his horse across the ravine. He rode hard for Salas; he nearly rode straight into a party of foragers from the besieging force, and was chased away along the Salas river. Forcing himself to be calm, he reined in his horse when he was once more safe and looked back at the distant fortress. The dust along the high road indicated the spot where the covering force— the force which had destroyed the Fusiliers—was marching back to join in the siege again. Besides them, there seemed to be several thousand men still round the fortress.

But to reach Salas was his only hope. Alone, and wearing his conspicuous uniform, he could not dream of riding back across Leon, or of riding forward over forty miles of unknown country to Valladolid. His one chance was that there was no strong force of the enemy on the other side of the Salas River opposite the fort.

Aubard reached Salas in safety in the end. He had to ride a long way up one bank of the river before he found a place to cross, and then he had to ride a long way back down the other side. Then at nightfall he had to turn his horse loose and scramble down the ravine to the rushing water in its rocky bed, and in the darkness he had to make his way, stumbling and slipping in his heavy boots, along the stream to where the fortress towered above the bank. Then he climbed the bank with fearful difficulty—expecting every second to be observed and shot from the other side—and then cowering at the foot of the wall, he had to call quietly until he attracted a sentry's attention, taking his chance lest the sentry should be one of the kind that fires first and challenges afterwards. He was nearly weeping again, with hunger and fatigue and cold, before they opened a postern to him and led him in to where General Meyronnet was waiting for news.

For Aubard had achieved something at least that day. He had brought the first authentic news out of Leon, the first real information which for three weeks or more had been able to trickle through the cordon of irregulars which the rebellion had called into being.

CHAPTER XXI

GENERAL COUNT DARPHIN woke with difficulty and realized that some one was pounding on his bedroom door.

"Who the devil's that?" he shouted, inhospitably.

"It's me, Guillermin," said someone on the other side of the door.

"Oh, to hell with you," said Count Darphin to himself, closing his eyes and promptly forgetting that Colonel Guillermin was anywhere near.

"Can't I come in? It's important," persisted the pestilent Guillermin.

"Er—what?" asked Darphin, waking up again with a jerk.

"I want to come in," said Guillermin.

"Confound these enthusiasts," said Darphin to himself. He heaved himself out of bed, scuttled in his shirt across the floor and unlocked the door, and scuttled promptly back again and dived back into the warm comfort of the bed. It was still some time before dawn; only the faintest light was creeping in through the windows, and it was most savagely cold.

Colonel Guillermin came in slowly; although it was at such a ridiculous hour of the day he was dressed in the full uniform of the Imperial staff—the blue breeches with the gold stripe, the blue tunic covered with gold lace, the cloak trimmed with grey astrakhan; under his arm was the smart

grey busby with its panache, and trailing at his side was
the heavy oriental sabre which fashion had just decreed
should be worn by staff officers.

"Take a chair," said Darphin, shutting his eyes again.
"Make yourself quite comfortable, and then tell me what
it is all about. More wails from the Army of Portgual
again?"

"There are some complaints from the Prince of Essling,"
agreed Colonel Guillermin, "and something must be done
about them. But I have something much more important to
tell you."

"Well, what is it?" said General Darphin, quite
resigned.

"The news is from Leon," said Guillermin; something in
the quality of his voice would have told the general that
the matter was of burning importance, pregnant with
disaster, except that the general was still too sleepy to be
receptive of minor details.

"News from Leon at last?" he said. "What is it?"

"Leon is taken. Paris is dead—poisoned—and all the
garrison with him. La Merced is taken. So are Mansilla and
Saldaña. And the Fourth Fusiliers of the Guard were cut
off in the plain and every man except one killed or taken.
And there are ten thousand Spaniards besieging Salas at
this moment."

By the time the recital was finished Guillermin could
have no cause for complaint regarding Darphin's lack of
interest in what he was saying. Darphin was sitting bolt
upright, having gradually pulled himself up to that position while Guillermin was adding horror to horror. And
simultaneously with the rising of his body his jaw had

fallen until his mouth was wide open. The natural disorder of his hair, of his heavy moustaches and whiskers, added to the ludicrous consternation of his expression.

"How do you know this is true? " demanded Darphin; but he showed his appreciation of the importance of the matter by flinging off the bedclothes and stepping out of bed.

"Meyronnet has sent the news from Salas. One of the Fusiliers got there after the regiment was destroyed—Salas is still open on the side of the river."

Darphin pulled on his breeches.

"Have you told the marshal yet? " he asked.

"No," said Guillermin with a trace of bitterness in his tone. One of the cast iron rules that General Darphin, as Chief of Staff to Marshal Bessières, had instituted, was that no one should dream of reporting direct to His Highness; it was significant that Darphin should have forgotten his own orders.

"I shall tell him at once," said Darphin. "Send to Dumoustier to tell him not to march this morning as last night's orders told him to. Send to Kellermann at Palencia to say he must be here with all his dragoons before nightfall tonight. Call Serras back too. The marshal will confirm in writing, but those messages must go in five minutes. Hurry ! "

General Count Darphin had been a staff officer during nineteen years of continuous warfare. In the old revolutionary days the guillotine, and after that the Emperor's own drastic methods, had winnowed out the incompetents. Darphin knew his trade from beginning to end. The news that five thousand Frenchmen had been lost, that the

communications were broken on which a quarter of a
million French soldiers depended, left him unshaken. He
might be growing old, careless, lazy, but there was nothing
wrong with his nerve. Now that the news had come
through at last which cleared up the mystery as to what
had been happening in Leon he took no longer than the
time necessary to button his tunic to issue the orders which
would set matters right. Yet he had to brace himself before
going into the marshal's room with the news. His Highness
Marshal Bessières, Duke of Istria, Commander-in-Chief of
the Army of the North of Spain, Colonel-General of
Cuirassiers, Grand Eagle of the Legion of Honour, was
not at all a sympathetic person in the matter of receiving
bad news before breakfast. And Darphin positively shud-
dered at the thought of the letters, wild with wrath, which
would come pouring in from Paris when communications
should be reopened and the news should reach there of
the destruction of one of the beloved regiments of the
Guard.

To make quite certain that no hint of the blow that was
intended should reach the Spaniards in the field he
sent orders to the guards at the gates. Until further orders
no Spaniard was to be allowed outside the walls. Any
citizen of Valladolid who wished to take the air must
breathe the insanitary odours of his own alleys; any
country man who wished to enter to sell his produce could
only do so by resigning himself to an indefinite stay in the
town.

With that settled, he went off to the barracks where
Dumoustier's division, on receipt of the orders conveyed by
Colonel Guillermin, had been dismissed from parade.

Dumoustier's division was the finest of all the French Army of Spain, eleven battalions of the Young Guard, Voltigeurs, Tirailleurs, and Fusiliers. Dumoustier himself was sitting down to a second breakfast when Darphin entered—until ten minutes ago he and his men had been under orders to march south to join Masséna's army opposing Wellington.

"You will march north, not south, general," said Darphin to Dumoustier. "And you will not be starting until tomorrow night, after Serras and Kellermann have come in."

"And why this change of plan?" asked Dumoustier.

"Leon has broken out, and wants taming all over again. You are just the man for the job, aren't you, general?"

"I have a reputation for taming provinces," said Dumoustier.

He nodded his head slightly as if he were remembering past achievements; his eyes narrowed, and his lips revealed cruel white teeth under his black moustache. If Darphin had had any doubts as to the suitability of Dumoustier and his Guard division for teaching Leon a lesson it would never forget they would have been instantly dispelled by the sight of the expression on Dumoustier's face. And when the Guard should hear of the annihilation of the Fourth Fusiliers . . . ! If there is any truth in the assertion that the contemplation of the sufferings of others helps us to bear more easily our own suffering, General Darphin must have found much relief in thinking about what was going to happen to Leon while he bent his steps back to that dreaded interview with his commander-in-chief.

The latter was already worried enough by the news that Wellington was loose in the south; to hear that the devil was unchained in the north would rouse him to paroxysms of rage. For the splendid army which Masséna had led into Portugal the year before had now come reeling back again, starving, naked, with a third of its men and two-thirds of its horses dead of exposure and starvation before the Lines of Torres Vedras. Wellington, whom everyone had thought to be out of the game for good, was back again on the frontier of Spain. He was starving Almeida into surrender; he was threatening Ciudad Rodrigo with the same fate, and without prompt help from Bessières Masséna could do nothing to stop him.

So that letters had come pouring in to the Duke of Istria from the Prince of Essling, demanding clothing, food, guns, horses, and, above all, men, so that the insolent islanders could be thrust back into the mountains again. Phrases from the letters ran through Darphin's mind— "You feed me only with promises"; "You have used all sorts of pretexts to evade my requests"; "Your letters are inconceivable"; "All the troops in Spain are of the same family"; "You are responsible for the defence of Almeida"; and so on interminably. And now at this very moment, when Dumoustier and Serras and Kellermann were all ready to march to Masséna's aid, and Masséna had been told to expect them, there came this news from the north.

There could be no hesitation about what to do. Every available man must be turned back to clear the communications. Not a man could be spared to help Masséna. What he would write when the news was broken to him Darphin could visualize with extreme clarity. Not so definite but

H*

even more dreaded was the thought of what he should write to Paris regarding the shortcomings of Bessières and —for the greater includes the less—his chief of staff. The thought of it made Darphin's blood run cold; and he knew, even as he walked jauntily across the palace courtyard, that his chief would be equally apprehensive and consequently irritable.

To Darphin's credit it should be added that his fears were not entirely selfish. There were vague apprehensions regarding the future of France which worried him just as much however unacknowledged they might be. He could not conceive of an end to the glorious Empire; that the French dominion of Spain, even, should ever be seriously threatened was beyond the limits of his imagination. He would have laughed to scorn anyone who should suggest that no more than two years from now Wellington would sweep the French from the entire Peninsula in one brief campaign and come pouring triumphantly over the Pyrénées to deal the death wound to the Empire on the soil of France itself. All that would have seemed the merest rubbish to Darphin. But at the same time the thought of Wellington steadily extending his conquests, laying hold first of Almeida and then of Rodrigo, with the French powerless to keep him back, seemed strangely ominous and depressing to Darphin.

In that, of course, Darphin's military instinct was correct. The fall of Almeida was the beginning of that ebb tide which was to continue until the Allies should reach Paris. And Almeida fell because of the success of the revolt in the north. And it was the gun which was the cause of that success.

CHAPTER XXII

JORGE WAS pressing forward the siege of Salas with all the vigour that was in him and which his example could rouse in his men. He was having to learn the craft from first principles, but his was just the sort of temperament to which first principles make most appeal, and his immutable courage and endless cheerfulness set an example which his men were not slow to follow. Under the steady, deadly fire from the fortress the 'approaches' crept out from the 'first parallel'; two nights after the defeat of the Fusiliers of the Guard the 'second parallel' was begun and nearly completed, despite the fire of the besieged, and after daylight had come it was finished at the cost of much blood— a long, well planned trench with a solid parapet, which established the besiegers no more than two hundred yards from the walls. The howitzers within the fortress dropped shells into it with monotonous regularity, and the eighteen-pounders battered the parapets into ruin, but the Spaniards were not discouraged. They had been victorious too often lately for that. They pitched the corpses out over the back of the trench, and they rebuilt the parapet as fast as it was pounded down.

During the course of the day Jorge laboured over mathematical problems—as mathematics were a complete mystery to him he had to solve them by rule of thumb methods. Yet he was successful in his endeavours, for he was a man of hard common sense, and his experiences of the last few days had inspired him. When darkness fell fifty men crept over the parapet of the advanced trench and began to dig furiously, throwing up a thick parapet to enclose a small square battery on the baselines which Jorge, at the risk of his life, had marked out with stakes and tapes during the daylight. Ten men were levelling a section of the trench behind it. Ten more were levelling a section of the first parallel, so as to provide a passage for the big gun—a hundred men were dragging that up with drag-ropes.

Jorge managed somehow to be at all these places at the same time. If when daylight came the gun had not reached the second parallel and the shelter of the battery, it would be pounded to pieces by the guns of the besieged as it stood exposed on the open ground. Similarly if it reached the second parallel and the battery was not ready for it the same thing would happen. Everything must be completed to schedule. Jorge hurried back and forward, from the road to the second parallel, from the second parallel to the road, to keep everyone at work.

The besieged heard all the bustle and did their best to interfere. They rained shot and shell on the place where the sounds indicated that the battery was being dug. They changed their target and fired at the place where they could hear the noise of the dragging up of the big gun— one lucky round shot killed ten men in a line at one of the drag-ropes. They pushed out a sortie across no-man's-land, but of course Jorge had foreseen that possibility and had had a 'covering party' lying out there since nightfall; the brisk musketry fire that promptly spattered up caused the attackers to be withdrawn lest a trap had been laid for them.

Jorge had simply excelled himself. The big gun reached the first parallel just as the gap which was being made for it was completed; it was dragged across, and the trench instantly redug. He brought up a burdened carrying party with the huge baulks of timber—the rafter beams of a house—which were to act as flooring beneath the gun's wheels just as the redoubt was nearing completion, and no sooner had he got these laid when the gun itself was dragged in and put into position.

It was time enough, for it was nearly morning. Sweating with exertion and excitement Jorge made sure all was well. The men digging outside continued to cast up final spade-fuls of earth on to the immense walls even when the grow-ing light and the furious fire opened on the battery by the fortress made the work terribly dangerous. The work was finished as far as was necessary. The battery could boast of earthen walls immensely thick. It was not a thing of neat geometrical symmetry—unskilled enthusiasts working in pitch darkness could not produce that—but it would suffice. The gun rested on its timber platform two feet below the level of the ground. For five feet above ground level rose the walls, progressively thinner from below upwards. The embrasure through which pointed the muzzle of the gun was very narrow—the merest slit. That was all that was necessary, for the gun was only destined to fire at one single portion of the wall, while the narrower the slit the less chance there was of lucky shots coming in through it.

Jorge had done well. An ordinary officer of engineers

would most probably have consumed two nights in the
construction of the battery, and a third in bringing up
the gun. Jorge had telescoped three nights into one and
had gained forty-eight hours. Already he was back on the
road starting a fresh carrying party up the trenches—men
carrying four roundshot apiece, slung over their shoulders,
and barrels of powder. Hurrying back to the battery, Jorge
issued instructions as to where this ammunition was to be
stored; it must be in little parcels here and there along the
trench near the battery but not too near; already a tornado
of fire was opening upon the battery, and men, crouching
in the bottom of the trench, were hurriedly filling sacks
with earth with which to rebuild the walls as they
crumbled beneath the cannon fire.

Then Jorge hurried off again and started men at work
upon the new approaches. Two more trenches were to be
run out from the second parallel, and then connected by
a 'third parallel' close to the ditch. Here the storming
party would assemble to attack the breach which the gun
was to make; breach and parallel would have to be completed simultaneously. Jorge knew nothing of the refinements of siegecraft; he was not aware of the fact that in a
properly conducted siege not only were the approaches
carried up to the ditch, but the sides of the ditch and the
obstacles in it should be levelled by mining, and the artillery
fire of the besieged quite subdued before the breach should
be stormed. These refinements were beyond Jorge's power,
if not beyond his imagination. All he aimed at was to get
a body of men near enough to a hole in the wall to have
a chance of penetrating. The storm would be a bloody busi-

ness—so would the approaching—but Jorge could not help
that.

So all day long the approaches crept forward over the
bare earth. Men were killed in them who had hardly had
time to throw up ten spadefuls of earth. Men were buried
under avalanches of earth and sandbags—the others only
stopped to dig them out if to do so carried forward the
work in hand. Dead bodies helped to give thickness to the
parapets. The approaches at least served the purpose of
multiplying the objectives of the besieged, so that the
battery was not under such concentrated fire. Here the
French were trying to drop shells into the work; but it was
not so easy to drop a shell with indirect aiming into an
area only ten feet square. French powder was not consistent
enough. French shells were not cast truly enough, to make
such accurate shooting likely—it was far otherwise with
the magnificent English powder and shot which Jorge had
at his disposal. Shells burst all round the battery; they
burst on the very parapet, but the only one which fell
inside failed to explode at once, and an imperturbable
Galician vaquero who found the thing at his feet cut off
the sizzling end of the fuse with a blow from his spade.

Meanwhile the gun had begun to fire back. Its bellowing roar, so well known to and so beloved by all the
Spanish army, punctuated the fighting at regular intervals.
Jorge was back with the gun again. It was he who squinted
along the sights before each shot. And his inventiveness
was developing hourly. Out of his own brain he had
devised a system to limit the force of the recoil and mini-
mize the labour of running up the gun each time. Behind
the gun he had built up the timber platform in an inclined

plane. At each shot the gun rolled backwards up it, hesitated, and then rolled forward again as gravity overcame
the force of the recoil until it was almost in its correct
firing position again. It almost doubled the speed of fire
and halved the labour of handling the big brute.

Jorge was half mad with exultation and excitement. His
face and hands were black with powder so that his eyes
were unnaturally noticeable. He roared out bits of songs
as he worked the gun. He slapped the big hot breech
caressingly after each discharge. He did not seem to be
fatigued, although he had fought a battle the day before
and spent two consecutive nights in the most exhausting
labour. He blazed away with the gun exultantly.

The effect of the battering upon the wall was small but
all that could be hoped for. The solid stone splintered but
little at each successive blow, but Jorge had thought out a
scheme of battering which, significantly, exactly corresponded with the methods employed by the best schools of
artillerymen. He was aiming at the foot of the wall, and he
hoped, traversing the gun a little to right and to left, to
undercut a section of it until the mass above it should
come tumbling down, presenting a slope that should be
easy of ascent; with luck the ruin should even fall into the
ditch and lessen the difficulties of passing it. He had no
idea how long this would take; all he knew was that he
had the gun in position to contrive it sooner or later, and
he was prepared to go on firing it until it happened.

He only left the gun at intervals to hurry along the
trenches to where the murderous work of continuing the
approaches was being carried on; he did this when he
feared that the breach would be achieved before the third

parallel could be completed. But sooner or later while he was at the approaches he became convinced that the third parallel would be completed before the wall should be breached, and so he hastened back to speed up the firing of the gun.

There were other interruptions. El Platero and Delgado and the others kept making their way up to the battery with complaints and requests. In the heat of all this fighting Jorge found himself beset with unending distractions. There were nearly ten thousand Spaniards grouped round Salas, and Jorge found himself in the semi-official position of commander-in-chief. He had to decide which sections of the army should man the trenches, and which portions of the trenches. He had to make arrangements for feeding them, sending out foraging parties on both sides of the road to bring in whatever provisions could be found. He had to see that provisions and water were carried up to the men in the trenches. He had to see that there was a sufficient force in support of the men in the trenches, lest the garrison should sally out and ruin everything. Jorge found himself not merely commander-in-chief, but his own chief of staff, his own artillery commander, his own chief engineer, his own chief commissary.

It was a matter of interest as to how long he would stand the strain. And it was a significant fact that in the sweltering heat of the battery, with the gun bellowing its loudest and with shells dropping all round, Jorge was able to devise far more complicated arrangements and issue far more practicable orders than ever he would have been able to do if he had been peacefully herding sheep in the way he had spent most of his short life.

When night came, and he could no longer see the impact of the shot against the wall, so that he reluctantly decided to cease firing, he suddenly realized how exhausted and hungry he was. He braced himself to make his way again to the approaches, to warn the men there to make the most of the hours of darkness to push the works forward and to send patrols out to cover them, and then he picked his way back to the road where makeshift tents had been put up for Alvarez and the others, and where the men not in the trenches were preparing for another night's uncomfortable bivouac.

He asked for food, and they brought him some, bread and meat and wine, but he fell asleep as he ate. The wine in his cup cascaded over his breeches as his head fell forward on his knees, but he did not notice it. He rolled over on his side snoring with a noise like a badly blown trumpet, and Alvarez, who had come to love him, took off his own cloak to cover him. He lay there, and neither his own snores nor the constant passage to and fro of men and animals close by his head could wake him.

Yet at midnight something else woke him, so that he sat up with a jerk, with all his attention at stretch, like a wild animal. There was musketry fire from the trenches. It was no mere idle firing either, as might be expected if two patrols had met or a sentry had allowed his imagination to be too much for him. It was a well maintained blaze of musketry, and Jorge guessed what was its import. He leaped to his feet and ran for the trenches, stumbling in the darkness over obstacles innumerable. He fell headlong into the first parallel where men were peering over the parapet at the flashes of the firing, but he was on his feet again and shouting loudly before anyone could put a bayonet through him.

"Come with me, Princesa," he yelled.

The men knew his voice. All along the trench in the darkness they followed the example of their neighbours and scrambled over the parapet and ran wildly forward, falling at length into the second parallel.

General Meyronnet in Salas had become really alarmed at the rapid advance of the siege works. At midnight he had sent out a strong sortie, which had overrun the patrols, had taken the approach trenches, where men were now busy shovelling down the parapets as fast as they could, and which had pushed a determined attack home upon the breaching battery intent upon capturing and disabling the one big gun which the besiegers possessed. Jorge and the Princesa Regiment arrived just as the attackers reached the second parallel. In the battery itself a grim fight was fought in pitch darkness, where no one could tell friend from foe but struck and spared not. Jorge had been weaponless when he reached the battery, but somehow a spade had come to his hand and with this he fought murderously, sobbing with excitement, until he suddenly realized that the clamour had abruptly ceased with the flight or death of every Frenchman who had broken in.

In the darkness he felt his way to the gun, and ran his fingers anxiously over it. It was uninjured; he found the touch-hole and made sure no one had driven a spike into it; he ran his fingers along the chase to the muzzle; there was no crack or sign of injury. The trunnions were intact.

Satisfied in this, he only wanted to sleep again. He cared nothing for the fact that in the approach trenches there

could still be heard shouts and shots as the last of the
raiders were driven out by the Spaniards swarming up
from the rear. He seated himself on the ground with his
back to the trail of the gun and his shoulder against the
wheel. He raised his head long enough to send an order
to Elizalde regarding the manning of the trenches, and
then he let it fall forward on to his breast again, and the
sound of his snores filled the battery. Daylight revealed
the extent of the damage. Great sections of the approach
trenches had been tumbled down, so that it was impossible
for men to reach the head of the sap under the fire of the
besieged. There were a good many corpses littered between
the trenches and the fort, and el Platero and several of his
band were missing—the patrol he had been leading had
been overwhelmed in the first rush, and el Platero was
now somewhere in a dungeon of the fortress. If the place
should be forced to surrender his life would be a valuable
counter in the negotiations; if the besiegers should be driven
off everyone knew what would happen to el Platero.

Jorge did not allow himself to be cast down; the sortie
could have done far more damage than it did. He started
the gun again at its work of battering, and went off to the
approach trenches where he set the example of beginning
the dangerous work of rebuilding the broken sections. The
besieged had gained half a day for themselves by their
sortie—it took that long before the sap heads could be
reached again and the trenches pushed forward on their
long-drawn zig-zag course towards the fort.

At midday something definite at last followed the discharge of the gun. There came a little avalanche of stone
down from the face of the wall, the first indication that

the gun was making an impression on the wall, twelve feet high and ten feet thick. Jorge rushed along to the sap head and stared at the wall. There was a little seam running up it now, like the trace of a water-course on the face of a cliff. At this distance of a hundred and fifty yards it was hard to be sure of details, but at any rate it was not now a smooth vertical ascent. There were at least projections and irregularities. A single man, active and unencumbered, might possibly climb it. That did not mean that an assault was possible in the face of a garrison a thousand strong, but it was at least a promise that a breach could be made sooner or later. And under the steady battering which went on during the rest of the day there were two or three further little avalanches. The wall was positively crumbling.

Jorge went back to the sap head to gaze at the wall again. It was dangerous work to show one's face there, for the garrison had lined the wall with musketeers, and at a hundred and fifty yards there was always a faint chance of a lucky shot—to say nothing of the fact that the besieged were always ready to pour in a torrent of grape if a fair enough target was offered.

Jorge came to the conclusion that another day's battering would pound ten feet of the wall into a practicable breach. He decided that that very night he must connect the advanced trenches with another parallel, a hundred yards or less from the ditch. And on the next night they would assault from there, with some chance of success. He left the men digging away at the sap head and proceeded back to the point on the road which a regular officer might have called 'headquarters', but which was actually only a convenient sort of rendezvous for everyone who had nothing special to do. His mind was busy with details; mentally he was allotting the various parts to be played that night by the different sections of the besiegers. Alvarez would have to take his men forward towards the wall as a covering party—irregulars were the best for that sort of night work. Princesa would, as usual, have to provide the four hundred men necessary for the digging; Elizalde would have to allot the task to whichever battalion he thought fit. In the second parallel and the first parallel there would be—Jorge was interrupted in his thoughts by a hand upon his arm. He turned and found one of the boys who composed the gun crew; he was out of breath with running after him and his lips trembled.

" The gun, señor ! " he said. " The gun ! "

" What about the gun? " demanded Jorge, with sudden fear at his heart.

The boy stammered and gesticulated, but he could not utter a word more of sense. With a curse Jorge turned away from him and began running heavily back to the battery, and what he found there was worse than he had anticipated. There were dead men there, but Jorge cared nothing for dead men. The gun, his beautiful big gun, was out of action. The carriage still stood, somehow, although half of one tall wheel was shattered. But the gun itself was tilted up at a grotesque elevation, and at the same time was twisted over on its side. One trunnion had been smashed clean off—the raw irregular surface of the broken metal was visible. The elevating gear and the training gear were now only represented by splinters of wood and distorted bars of metal. On the chase a wide area of the ornamental relief work had been ploughed off.

Jorge stood glaring at the ruin. He could not see how it happened. The explanation was brought home to him a second later. There was a howl like that of a thousand lost souls, and a wind that flung him back against the battery wall. A big cannon ball had entered by the embrasure as its predecessor must have done, but this one had gone clean across the battery from front to back without hitting anything. Jorge peered through the embrasure. On the top of the fortress wall, silhouetted against the evening sky, he saw a black hump close above the point where the breach was being made; it had not been there when he had looked half an hour before from the sap head. It was a big gun, foreshortened, pointing straight at him.

For all the anguish which afflicted him Jorge could picture what the French had been doing—he knew much about the handling of heavy artillery nowadays. Finding that no guns of theirs would bear so as to fire into the embrasure they must have set to work instantly building a ramp up the inside of the wall, with a platform at the upper end just below the top of the wall, and they had dragged one of their eighteen-pounders up the ramp to the platform. As soon as it reached there they had swung it round and begun firing into the battery. Now that Jorge looked closer he could see men's heads bobbing about round the gun as they reloaded it. Instinct caused him to pull down his head and crouch below the embrasure as the next shot was fired. There was a crash behind him, a ringing noise as though a great bell had been struck with a sledge hammer; a sizzling fragment of metal sang over his shoulder and buried itself in the battery wall close by his face. Jorge turned to see that the wreck of the gun was completed. The ball had hit the under side of the chase, making a great dent, and flinging down the gun from the wrecked carriage. Its breech had fallen on the ground and its muzzle perched up on the axle; the lettering round it in its old-fashioned Latin characters still said, "And our mouths shall show forth Thy praise."

CHAPTER XXIII

AT NIGHTFALL there was a good deal of activity among the besiegers of Salas. The gun would never fire again and the rumour of that had gone round the ranks, but they were in too high spirits still to be discouraged at the thought of that. Everyone could appreciate the desirability of capturing a fortress which completely commanded the whole line of communications of the enemy, and flesh and blood were to finish off the work the gun had begun. Salas was to be stormed that night. The men were to attack in the darkness, over a deep ditch, up a wall like a cliff. The wall was seamed by one tiny crack; besides that they had a dozen ladders taken from the farms nearby. Nevertheless the men had not the least doubt that they were going to succeed; their commanders naturally did not communicate their doubts on the subject to them.

In gloomy conference they had settled the details— Alvarez was to assail the breach, and Elizalde was to attack at one side and the rest of the Princesa Regiment at the other, while Jorge led the irregulars round in an attack upon the river face of the fortress. In the darkness they moved the columns of men up to the second parallel—that was difficult enough in itself—and some time after midnight they streamed out to the attack.

There is no need to dwell upon the details of that repulse. The French in Salas had given proof enough already of their activity and vigilance and courage. Only against a craven enemy, demoralized and unready, could the assault have succeeded. The summit of the wall blazed with the fire of the besieged as the Spaniards approached. Grape and canister from the guns mounted to sweep the foot of the walls tore the Spaniards to pieces. Tar barrels and bundles of oily rags, all aflame, were flung down from the walls and served to give sufficient illumination to the musketeers upon the wall. Live shells with short fuses, dropped down by hand, blew apart the little groups of Spaniards who reached the foot of the wall. Fanatical courage brought them up to the attack over and over again; until towards morning the courage suddenly evaporated, as it will do with undisciplined troops, and they broke and fled away from the walls in blind terror, leaving even the trenches deserted, and only the dead and wounded piled upon the glacis as proof of what they had dared before this panic overtook them.

In the grey morning Jorge came back from the wall where he had raged berserk but uselessly, and found Alvarez and the others at the roadside. He halted his men and bade them rest—the survivors of el Bilbanito's band, and O'Neill's band, and el Platero's band were very, very few now—while he went up to the conference. Alvarez' right arm was in a sling, and his clothes were in rags. Elizalde was in as bad a condition. Only Urquiola was as spruce and smart as ever, because his cavalry had taken no part in the assault.

"Delgado is dead," said Elizalde.

"Yes," said Jorge.

"So is Volpe."

"So are half my men," said Alvarez, "but I write no poems about it."

Jorge looked back at the fortress, at the low grey wall just visible over the rolling plain. Even at that distance he could see the speck which floated above it—the tricolour on its invisible staff.

Alvarez broke in upon the reverie into which Jorge was imperceptibly drifting.

"Holy Mary," said Alvarez. "Here comes a bird of ill omen."

They looked southward down the road as he pointed; a big man on a little white mule, his skirted legs trailing on each side so far down that his feet almost brushed the road, was riding up towards them. They saw the brownish grey habit, and the massive black beard. It was Brother Bernard.

No one wanted to listen to Brother Bernard at that moment. They moved restlessly under his reproaches when he heard the news, like lions beneath the lion-tamer's whip. They sulked and they snarled. They had done all that men —men without a gun—could do, and they resented bitterly his recriminations. They thought of the dead men along the foot of the wall, and Jorge thought of the gun, broken and grotesque, deserted in its battery.

"And the French will be here tomorrow from Valladolid," said Brother Bernard.

Alvarez looked up with a start.

'Who will be here?" he demanded.

Brother Bernard had not been idle, it appeared, while they had been pouring out their blood round the walls of Salas. He had seen the army of relief start out from Valla-

dolid. He had watched them all one day; he knew just how
the army was composed, and he had ridden hard all night
to bring the news. Every unit, every general in the French
army, was known to Brother Bernard. The names he let
fall were as well known to his listeners. They had all heard
of Kellermann and his dragoons—Urquiola had been
hunted by them times without number across the plains of
Castile which Kellermann ruled. And Dumoustier and the
Guard division; Dumoustier was a name Spanish women
used to frighten their children. Serras, too; small imagination was required to picture Dumoustier and Serras turned
loose to subjugate Leon. Twelve thousand infantry; three
thousand cavalry and a dozen guns; there would be fire
and rape and slaughter from here to the Cantabrian mountains.

And the connecting link which might have held the
army together in face of this danger was broken. The gun
was a gun no longer, and the courage and good spirits
which the gun had brought into existence had vanished
last night under the walls of Salas. Alvarez was thinking
about the charges Kellermann's dragoons could deliver here
on these naked plains.

"I shall take my men back to Navarre while the road is
still clear," he said. "I know the by-ways past Burgos.
Mina only gave me leave to help el Bilbanito for three
months, and the three months are ended."

The others looked at him, but he was quite brazen about
his motives.

"I risked my men in a forlorn hope last night," he said,
"but it would be worse than a forlorn hope to try and
defend Leon against Kellermann and Dumoustier. And

only the hope of seeing Navarre again speedily will keep
my men together. I shall march in an hour's time."

Urquiola looked automatically at his big silver watch.

"If Kellermann has left Castile," he said, "my place is
there. Our business is to be where the French are not. In
a week's time I shall be raiding up to the gates of Madrid."

"And what about Leon?" asked Brother Bernard.

Urquiola hesitated before he enunciated the heartless
truth.

"Leon must look after itself," he said.

The madness which underlay Brother Bernard's enthusiasm for the cause broke its bonds. He raised his clenched
hands above his head.

"Woe unto you," he said. "May God——"

Urquiola and Alvarez bore his curses as philosophically
as a resigned husband bears the scoldings of his wife, and
listened as heedlessly. The bonds of union had snapped
with the disabling of the gun; and moreover there were
sound military arguments in favour of a prompt dispersal
in face of the overwhelming force of the enemy.

And while Brother Bernard was calling down upon
Urquiola and Alvarez the enmity of God, Jorge slipped
unobtrusively away. It was not his duty, nor that of any
irregular, to stand a siege by a French army. Jorge was
determined not to be shut up in Leon or Saldaña or La
Merced to await inevitable death or captivity. He thought
of his native Cantabrian mountains. He had a horse still,
which was far more than he had had when he descended
from them. The relics of the guerillero bands would follow
him if he promised to lead them back home. The Princesa
Regiment—what was left of it—and the Leonese levies

could obey Brother Bernard if they wished. As for him, he
was off home. He had had his fill of commanding an army.

Over by the deserted trenches, foul with dead bodies, a
patrol from Salas climbed cautiously over into the battery.
They examined curiously the huge bronze gun which lay
wrecked upon the splintered flooring. A scholar among
them looked at the half defaced heraldic traceries upon it,
but he did not know which ducal house it was which bore
those arms. He was able to puzzle out the Latin of the
legend round the muzzle, and he translated it for his comrades, who were much amused. But, still, the gun had
played its part in history.

BOOK LIST FOR FURTHER READING

The Bombard by HENRY TREECE. Published by The
   Bodley Head. A simple story of early guns in the four-
   teenth century.
Captain of Foot by RONALD WELCH. Published by
   Oxford University Press. A very exciting story of action
   with Wellington in the Peninsula.
*_Death to the French_ by C. S. FORESTER. Published by
   The Bodley Head. A story of Rifleman Dodd, cut off
   behind the French lines at Torres Vedras.
The Adventures of Brigadier Gerard by ARTHUR
   CONAN DOYLE. Published by John Murray. A
   humorous account of the war from the French point
   of view.
Mr. Midshipman Hornblower and *Lieutenant Hornblower*
   by C. S. FORESTER. Published by Michael Joseph.
   School Editions published by Longmans in the Heritage
   of Literature Series. For stories of guns in action on land
   and sea.
*_For Whom the Bell Tolls_ by ERNEST HEMINGWAY.
   Published by Jonathan Cape. A story of Spain's suffer-
   ing in the Civil War (1936-39).
Corunna by CHRISTOPHER HIBBERT. Published by
   Batsford. A very exciting account of Moore's campaign.
Wellington by RICHARD ALDINGTON. Published by
   Heinemann. A very readable life of Wellington which
   includes a large section on the Peninsular Campaign.
†*The Years of Eudurance* 1793-1802, *Years of Victory*
   1802-1812 and *The Age of Elegance* 1812-1822 by
   ARTHUR BRYANT. Published by Collins. These three

volumes give a thorough background to the Spanish Campaign and the Napoleonic Wars.

Napoleon and his Marshals by A. G. MACDONALD. Published by Macmillan. This is a most entertaining account of the rise and fall of the great Marshals and Generals of the First French Empire.

English Battles and Sieges in the Peninsula by LT. GEN. WILLIAM NAPIER. Published by John Murray. Not a book to read at a sitting, but it was written by a soldier who was actually there. The details are not only authentic but fascinatingly alive.

Saturn: An Essay on Goya by ANDRÉ MALRAUX. Published by the Phaidon Press. This includes paintings and drawing from Goya's eye-witness collection of *Disasters of the War.*

The Wheelwright's Shop by GEORGE STURT. Published by Cambridge University Press. A detailed account of an ancient craft by a man who actually practised it.

The Gun Founders of England by C. J. FFOULKES. Published by Oxford University Press. A large and expensive book but well worth looking at in your library.

A *History of Firearms* by Y. C. CARMAN. Published by Routledge and Kegan Paul. A handy sized book but full of information and illustrations.

*Paper back edition published by Penguin
†Paper back edition published by Fontana

NOTES

CHAPTER 1

1 *Espinosa:* In the general rising which followed the French occupation of Spain, General Joachim Blake, against all advice, led his Army of Galicia against Ney at Durango on 31 October 1808. His ill-equipped troops were turned back at Bilbao. By 7 November, Napoleon himself was at Vitoria; on the 10th he struck at Blake near Espinosa and on the following day sent him hurtling back across the Cantabrian mountains.

Bourbon: The Royal House of Spain was a branch of the Bourbon family of which the French kings had been the head.

muskets: Smooth-bored and muzzle-loading firearms were still the standard infantry weapon for most of the armies of Europe.

regimental colours: These banners not only commemorated the regiment's battle honours but also served the more practical purpose of indicating on the smoke-hazed field of battle where battalion headquarters were to be found. This would be the rallying point and the place to go for orders.

2 *The typhus . . . pneumonia:* Under conditions of war an outbreak of these diseases is likely to spread fast.

French dragoons: Dragoons were originally mounted infantry, travelling by horse but fighting on foot.

Their name comes from the "dragon" or heavy musket carried in their early days.

2 *impedimenta:* Armies in the field must take with them all they need to maintain themselves as a fighting force. This was particularly true in Spain where there was little to be bought in village or town.

3 *traces:* The two side straps or chains whereby the horses pulled the gun limbers.

gunmetal: An alloy of copper 88%, tin 10%, zinc 2%. The metal was chosen because it could be melted at reasonable temperatures, could be poured into large single castings and, when cool, was hard without being brittle and could therefore be worked with tools and stand the shock of an explosive charge.

vent: The touch-hole through which the main charge was ignited by setting fire to loosely spilled powder.

liturgy of Nocturne: The night-office of matins deriving from the monastic watches of the night.

castle in the South: This must have been a Spanish Government arsenal or military establishment. No European government at that time would have permitted a siege gun to remain in the hands of a private individual.

4 *Baylen:* On 23-24 July 1808, just after the Madrid riots had been put down, General Castaños with his Andalusian army moving, typically, independently of all other Spanish forces, astonished everybody by forcing the surrender of Dupont and a French army of 18,000 at Baylen. This was the first time an Imperial French army had ever surrendered and the victory was disastrous for the Spanish cause,

for every other Spanish general tried, unsuccessfully, to repeat it and the British Government believed the Spanish regular forces to be in a much stronger state than they were.

4 *Gamonal:* Napoleon, after striking at Blake at Espinosa on 10 November, now turned a few miles south where the Conde de Belvedere and the army of Estramadura were making their stand at the village of Gamonal, north of Burgos. Napoleon all but destroyed the Estramadurans and went on to take Burgos.

Rio Seco: Marshal Bessières routed a Spanish Army in a pitched battle at Medina del Rio Seco.

Tudela: On 23 November, Castaños, the victor of Baylen, with Palafox had moved up to Tudela on the south bank of the Ebro and was defeated there by Napoleon's three-pronged drive toward Madrid.

Tuileries: The building was begun in 1564 by Philibert Delorme and it was used by the French kings as a palace. Under the Emperor Napoleon it became once more the centre of government.

Compiègne: The Chateau of Compiègne, 80 kilometres north of Paris, was built under Louis XV and was improved by the Emperor Napoleon.

Blake: Joachim Blake (1759-1827) was born Spanish but like the O'Neills was of Irish origin. He was one of the most stubborn of the Spanish generals. This made it impossible for him to get on with his allies or compatriots but also made him a dogged and determined enemy of the French. He and his devotedly brave Galicians took the full force of Napoleon's furious storming into Spain in 1808.

goad: A spiked stick for urging cattle along.

5 *limber:* A stout two-wheeled carriage to which the trail of the gun could be hooked and to which the horses could be harnessed.

three tons of bronze: This was very heavy for an eighteen-pounder, but as this was an ornamental gun of bronze it could have been massive in relation to the size of its bore.

CHAPTER 2

9 *alternating levers:* When one lever had lifted the gun as high as it could, a second lever, pivoting over a larger piece of rock, was used to take the weight of the gun and lift it still further.

11 *elevating screw and wedge:* A heavy wooden wedge was forced between the bed of the carriage and the breech of the gun, thus tilting the gun.

lock and lanyard: Muskets had various firing devices. The first was the matchlock which, on pulling the trigger, brought a burning match down on to the touch hole. The second was the wheel-lock, in which a wheel could be turned against the edge of a flint to send a stream of sparks on to the priming. Thirdly, there was the flintlock, in which the trigger lifted the priming-pan cover with an underside of roughened steel, which caused a flint to strike down it, so directing sparks on to the exposed powder. On a gun these mechanisms could be operated by pulling a long cord or lanyard from a safe distance.

laying and elevating: This is the process of bringing a gun to bear on its target. The gun is laid in the right direction by traversing the gun to one side or

the other. Elevating the muzzle of the gun affects
the range, causing the shot to follow a curved path
through the air so calculated that it will come to
earth exactly on the target.

11 *bore:* The diameter of the hollow chamber inside the barrel is the bore. The outside shape
of the gun shows that it is thicker at the
breech, to take the force of the explosion,
and thinner at the muzzle. The inside bore
is, of course, uniform throughout its length.

12 *commissaries:* It was customary to put troops
ashore on an enemy coast with little more
than their weapons and the uniforms they
wore. They were expected to live off the
country, foraging for food, fuel and shelter.
iron loop at the top of the trail: This loop
dropped over a spike on the back of the
limber so that the gun could be moved.

13 *to fight the French:* In 1793 Spain had joined
Britain, Prussia and Austria in the First
Coalition against France.

14 *wooden cheek pieces:* These were the four-
inch slabs of oak bolted vertically to the
sides of the gun carriage. Notches on top
held the trunnions of the gun, staples below
held the great axle. (See note to page 33.)

15 *Juggernaut:* At Puri in the province of Orissa
in India there is a temple sacred to the
Hindu God, Vishnu. Every year, devout
pilgrims take several days to pull the god in
his enormously heavy carriage, the Jug- *Rammer*
gernaut, through deep sands in the middle   *and*
of the rains, to his country house less than   *sponge*

one mile away. The pilgrims do not throw themselves under the wheels as legend would have us believe.

15 *Homerically*: In a manner fitting the great warrior heroes in Homer's epic poems *The Iliad and The Odyssey.*

16 *the Junta*: Improvised local governments of people influential in the area set up by the Spanish when Napoleon put his brother Joseph on the Spanish throne.

Moore: Sir John Moore was sent to Spain to help the Spanish armies in their resistance to the French. When Napoleon drove his three-pronged thrust into Spain, Moore knew that he could not hold back such an onslaught, but he sought to divert it by offering himself as the bait. Napoleon followed, but in appalling wintry weather in mountainous country he gave over the pursuit to Soult. Moore fought many delaying rearguard actions and at Corunna he made his stand and there pushed back and broke up the French forces. He was killed on the field of battle, but his victory enabled his troops to embark on waiting transports and to sail safely back to England.

17 *special example of priests*: Because they were the leaders of the little village groups, they had ideas of freedom and they fought for the faith the French had put aside. (See note on Father Prieto, page xv of Introduction.)

CHAPTER 3

18 *sierras*: A range of hills or mountains rising in peaks which suggest the teeth of a saw.

PAGE

18 *scarped:* With a steep face, cut away by the weather.

19 *ravines:* Deep and narrow hollows or gorges forming clefts in the mountains, troughs in the plains; usually worn away by a torrent.

cañons: Deep gorges or ravines with steep sides, at the bottom of which a river flows.

the guerillero leaders: They fought the French from 1808 to 1815, inflicted very heavy losses and kept forces tied up in garrisons which were needed desperately elsewhere.

20 *fieldworks:* Fortifications made in open country from whatever materials are available on the spot.

A *typical* fieldwork

23 *Bonnet:* General Bonnet went to Spain in 1808 as a Divisional Commander with Napoleon's Grand Army.

CHAPTER 4

31 *alcalde:* Mayor and justice of the peace in a town; in a village he would be the headman.

33 *relief:* The elaborate decoration on the barrel of the
    gun.

   trunnions: The projections on either side of the gun
    which take most of the weight, hold it firmly in the
    carriage but allow the barrel to pivot when the
    muzzle is raised.

   tall shears: A strong tripod made of three straight
    poles lashed firmly at the top and with the feet
    planted securely below.

   cabalistically: Using secret signs such as those used in
    the practice of black magic. Recording measurements
    by cutting thin and thick notches on a piece of wood
    was quite common up to this century.

34 *brazeros:* Iron baskets on legs; they burned charcoal
    and were used for cooking.

   cut out of its carriage: The iron hinges which held
    the trunnions in their wooden beds were rusted
    solid.

35 *in face of an eighteen-pounder:* El Bilbanito was quick
    to grasp the power the gun gave him. He could
    hit the garrisons at a range at which they could
    not hit back. Nor could they get away or avoid
    battle. Few French strongpoints would have eighteen-
    pounders.

   felloes: The rim of each wheel was made up of six
    wooden blocks or felloes. Two spokes joined each of
    the felloes to the hub, and an iron tyre, put on hot
    and shrunk by cooling, bound the whole assembly
    tightly. Ideally, the felloes were of beech or oak, the
    spokes of riven oak (here they were ash) and the hub
    of elm.

   axle pins: The axle pin was hammered into a slot at
    the extreme end of the axle where it protruded

through the hub, to prevent the wheel
working itself off.

37 *laying screw:* A screw adjustment which
would force the muzzle slightly to one
side, used in aiming. This was a considerable refinement which was not
introduced for most guns until about
1880.

the groove on the muzzle swell: Corres-
ponding to the foresight on a rifle.

250 varas: About 250 yards. An old countryman's measure: a *vara* means a staff
or rod.

Tyrolese rifle: A long-barrelled hunting
rifle. The Tyrol region was, and still is,
famous for its fine metalwork.

38 *slow match:* Loosely twisted rope of cot-
ton or hemp soaked in saltpetre. It
burned slowly without a flame and even
in rain would smoulder and not go out.

Linstock and
slow match

CHAPTER 5

43 *scotches:* Wedge-shaped wooden blocks to hold the
wheels from rolling back or down the slope.

45 *left his country:* Many Irish Catholics left their homeland to seek a better life in France or Spain,
especially when Protestant Britain attempted to
dominate their country and their faith by force.

I*

47 *a seventeen-hand grey:* The traditional way of measuring the height of a horse is from the ground to the point of the withers, the bump at the bottom of the horse's mane. A hand is now standardised at 4 inches and an average horse for riding would be 15 to 15½ hands.

CHAPTER 6

A *shako*

51 *The Princesa Regiment:* Part of the regular army of the deposed King Charles IV. Possibly part of the Spanish force which stood nobly with Moore at Corunna and covered the evacuation.

shakoes: Perhaps the commonest style of head-dress for the infantry soldier. It was a truncated cone and had a peak in front with the brass numeral or insignia of the regiment and a cockade or coloured pom-pom on top.

form square: Infantry marching along a road in long columns were vulnerable, not so much from opposing infantry as from cavalry who could charge through the column and break it up. The infantry's strength was in its massed firepower, but this could not be exploited if the column was separated into many groups. Hence the vital need to train them to move in perfect order from column to hollow square. The manoeuvre is a difficult one, as the four sides must come together exactly.

51 *Kellermann's dragoons:* General Kellermann commanded a cavalry division and his tremendous dash
on the battlefield had helped Napoleon to win the
battle of Marengo in 1800. These heavily armed
cavalry, who had faced the best soldiers in Europe,
could inflict terrible casualties on poorly disciplined
troops.

CHAPTER 7

56 *Ferrol:* The Spanish Junta for Galicia was at Ferrol.
It was well placed to organise resistance to the French
and to receive military aid by sea from the British.

57 *the great road:* This was the main supply-line between
France, Madrid, Portugal and the South. It ran from
Bayonne, San Sebastian, Vitoria, Burgos to Madrid
and thence to the South.

CHAPTER 8

61 *His Britannic Majesty's forty-gun frigate " Parnassus ":*
In many of Forester's " Hornblower " books he
stresses the versatility and the strength of British
seapower. A frigate was designed for a similar role
to that of the modern destroyer. It was fast but had
formidable fire-power. George III was on the throne.

62 *bo'sun's chair:* A knotted rope or a rope ladder were
the usual means of coming on board while at sea.
The bo'sun's chair was a cradle of rope and canvas
which would be swung over the side by a block on
the end of a yard-arm.

PAGE

62 *yard-arm:* The yards were the horizontal spars slung at right angles to the mast, to which the sails were bent. They provided a convenient place to sling a block and tackle to take on stores or to hang evil-doers.

64 *Fore to'ga'n masthead:* The fore topgallant mast-head; the highest point on the foremast. This was a normal punishment for cheeky or defaulting midship-men.

65 *carronade:* So called because they were made at Car-ron's foundry in Stirlingshire. They were also called "Smashers" as they were designed to hurl a heavy shot over shorter ranges (400-600 yards) than the main armament of twelve-pounders. They were located usually two in the bows and two in the stern. This was to enable the frigate to hit a heavy and unexpected blow while she was manoeuvring into a position to fire a broadside.

tompion: A wooden plug which fitted the bore of the gun and was used at sea to keep out the water.

67 *Tyrolese revolt, and the Lombard revolt:* Austria and Northern Italy had both been scenes of Napoleon's victories, but the Austrian people were far from defeated. This national feeling was expressed most strongly in the Tyrol. Among the leaders was Andreas Hofer, an inn-keeper with remarkable powers of body and mind. In their mountain strong-holds the Tyrolese were difficult to subdue, but it was equally difficult for their friends to carry help to them. After Wagram, in 1809, the Austrian government accepted a humiliating peace and the Tyrolese were overwhelmed by sheer numbers: Andreas Hofer was captured and shot at Mantua.

68 *not quite enough powder:* An 18-pound shot needed 6
 pounds of powder for a full charge.

 the four-pounder: A handy gun with a bore of 3¼
 inches, light enough to be manhandled and heavy
 enough to outshoot muskets.

 cutter: One of the ship's larger boats fitted for rowing
 or sailing. Its size may be gauged by the load of
 five tons which it was required to carry here in addition to its working crew.

 canister: See Introduction, p. xxvii.

Canister

69 *grape:* See Introduction, p. xxviii. The rounds used in
 the story were made up of thirty half-pound balls.

CHAPTER 9

71 *Wellington loose again in the South:* In 1809 Welling-
 ton had landed in Portugal and, defeating Soult at
 Oporto and Victor at Talavera, pressed into Spain.
 But, threatened by large French forces, he retired into
 Portugal behind the very strong defences of Torres
 Vedras. Masséna's vast army wasted its strength try-
 ing to find a way through, and in 1811 Wellington
 once more pushed forward into Spain.

72 *San Juan:* On 3 December 1808 Napoleon was at the
gates of Madrid and the Spanish Generals, Castel-
franco and Morla, came to terms with Napoleon,
allowing him to occupy vital parts of the city.
Spanish troops under Generals San Juan and Heredia
were ready to defend Madrid, entering from the other
side, but were kept out by their fellow Generals who
had, instead, opened their gates to the French.
General San Juan was unjustly murdered by his in-
furiated troops and on 4 December Napoleon entered
Madrid.

Colonel Berkely: All round the coast of Spain small
British Military Missions, supplied by sea, gave
advice and war material to the Spanish resistance
movement, working usually through the local
Juntas.

CHAPTER 10

75 *Major Jonquier was a Dutchman:* Napoleon was rely-
ing more and more on troops from his satellite
countries.

salle de police: The garrison prison cells.

77 *palisade:* A fence of wooden posts sloping outwards,
sometimes with sharpened tops. They were close
enough to prevent a man slipping through, but not so
close as to offer secure cover from the musket fire
from the ramparts.

78 *bastion:* A tower built out slightly farther at the
corner of the square building, so that fire could be
directed from it along the outer faces of two of the
convent walls.

*A plan of La Merced
to show the bastions*

78 *a six-pounder*: A common and handy size
   field gun. It was useful on the battlefield
   for giving weight to the firepower of the
   infantry regiments and light enough to
   be manhandled quickly to meet new tactical situations. At La Merced it suited
   the small space of the bastion and was
   adequate for normal defence; against the
   eighteen-pounder it was outclassed.
   linstocks: The linstock or slow match was
   used to light a more vigorous burning
   portfire or quick match and this was
   used to touch off the charge. (See note to
   page 38: *slow match*.)
80 *chicory substitute*: Not an important
   deprivation in itself, but an illustration
   of the many shortages which Napoleon's
   self-imposed blockade of the whole of
   Europe had brought about.

*Portfire
and holder*

81 *ladders up the slope:* The art of defence was to hold
the attacker at such a distance that he could not hit
the defenders but they could hit him. Thus an outer
palisade often surrounded the deep ditch, and the
earth taken from the ditch was used to make a steep
slope up the walls.

83 *fandango:* A lively Spanish dance. Jonquier seemed to
have no great love of Spain.

84 *breastwork:* A quickly made bank of earth literally
breast high.

    embrasure: A slit cut in the earthwork only just large
enough to let the muzzle of the gun show through.

86 *a devilish good gun:* The first shot from the 18-pounder
was six feet too low; the gunner corrected his aim and
the next was seven feet too high. Jonquier was impressed that the gun could be corrected so precisely
but a better demonstration was to follow when the
gun, having bracketed the target, now scored a direct
hit.

92 *red epaulets:* Shoulder straps, often decorated to show
the rank and regiment of the wearer.

93 *hit the ground six feet before the palisades:* Aiming
short on purpose, the gunner flung his grape shot at

Grape shot

the ground so that it would ricochet and beat up
stones and earth at the base of the wooden posts to
cut them down.

94 *one shot every four minutes:* Fifteen rounds an hour
was very good going, but Don Carlos O'Neill was an
artillery officer and doubtless had trained gunners
amongst his men.

95 *damage the gun:* By driving an ironspike into the
hole, smashing a trunnion with a hammer, or explod-
ing a double charge of powder in the barrel.

96 *Aim low:* There is always a danger of firing too high
when firing from above on targets beneath. Un-
seasoned troops in the heat of battle also tend to
snatch the trigger.

CHAPTER 11

98 *the Orbigo:* The river whose bridge La Merced was
planned to guard.

99 *redoubt:* A square fieldwork with the strongest parapet to the front. The breastwork described earlier is
the front of it. There would be smaller side walls and
probably an open back.

100 *dependent until the end of his days upon charity:* Few
nations rewarded their wounded sailors and soldiers
with a pension.

102 *Castilian lancers:* The cavalry rode in a wide crescent
in front to clear any small resistance or to spring any
ambush.

103 *minute gun:* A gun fired at minute intervals to mark
the time.

105 *remounts:* Fresh horses for the cavalry units.

106 *not for two long years*: Leon as the centre of a prosperous farming region had been heavily garrisoned by the French since their first invasion. It also protected the great road from any attack from the mountains of Galicia and Asturias.

CHAPTER 12

108 *Josefino*: The name for a collaborator.

109 *Franciscan friar*: The Franciscan Order was founded in 1209 by Saint Francis of Assisi. Brother Bernard burned with hatred for the French not only because he was a patriot but also because he fought for the Catholic faith against the atheistic French.

111 *Saragossa*: The siege of Saragossa is among the most heroic in the history of Europe. In 1808 when the French invaded Spain, the people of Saragossa under the leadership of General Palafox defied the attacks of the French Generals Lefebre and Verdier from June to August, when they were relieved by a Spanish force.

Marshal Bessières: Duke of Istria, Commander-in-Chief of the Army of the North of Spain and Military Governor. He had his headquarters at Valladolid.

115 *siege artillery*: Heavy artillery was not part of a normal military force but was only attached for a special purpose. A siege train contained guns too heavy and unwieldy to be used in a battle of movement. Mortars and howitzers were included, as they could lob their explosive and incendiary shells over the walls.

116 *wallpieces:* Firing a two-pound ball, they could out-range muskets and disperse concentrations of cavalry or infantry. They were useless against anything bigger.

117 *assault and escalade:* Terms from the art of siegecraft. The assault is the attack with infantry, and the escalade the climbing of the walls with hooked ladders. The technique was not yet out of date, for Wellington took Badajoz by this means.

CHAPTER 13

119 *garotte:* The standard Spanish method of execution. A screw within an iron band broke the condemned man's neck.

military citadel: A fortress designed and built according to the scientific principles of siege warfare, usually within the walls of the city but having a cleared area all round.

120 *breach the wall:* It was useless to attack with infantry until there was a wide gap in the walls. This was fairly simple at La Merced, but at Leon the outer walls were covered by inner walls and heavy artillery.

sally: The besieged forces left the protection of their fortifications to face the besiegers in open battle, or to do as much damage as possible to the siege equipment before returning to safety.

130 *porte cochère:* Carriage entrance; the narrow entrance through the thickness of the outer walls which would contain the guard room.

130 *white arsenic:* Arsenious oxide or white arsenic is, in
one form, white and opaque like flour, and it can
easily be so mistaken. Moreover, it has little taste and
no colour and is easily mixed with food for homicidal
purposes.

CHAPTER 14

131 *the one which Bessières had extinguished:* Marshal
Bessières entered Spain in 1808 with the innocent-
sounding "Corps of Observation of the Pyrénées".
When the Spanish rose to demand their proper king,
Bessières in the north put down the rising with great
severity.

132 *cortège:* A ceremonial escort.

133 *There is no Junta of Leon:* This gift for strong local improvised government was the core of the Spanish
resistance.

136 *Carlist wars:* The horrors of those days in Leon are
still remembered even when more recent suffering is
forgotten. Don Carlos (1788-1855), the younger
brother of Ferdinand VII, disputed the succession and
attracted some support. The civil wars which followed
(1833-1839) were bitterly contested. Don Carlos was
finally defeated and went into exile in France.

137 *Santa Eulalia; Mansilla; Saldaña; Carrion;* These were
all small garrisons guarding road and river crossings
between Leon and Burgos, Leon and Vallodolid.
sybaritic comfort of the English hulks: The Greek
colony of Sybaris was famed for its luxury. The
English hulks were old battleships, disarmed and un-
rigged, moored in the estuaries of the south of

England. They were used to house the increasing
numbers of French prisoners of war. Prisoners remained below decks in appalling conditions. Many
died of fever aggravated by near starvation. Sybaritic
is a slight exaggeration!

137 *Dartmoor:* The grim prison on the moor was built to
house French prisoners. It was a palace compared to
the hulks.

139 *Torres Vedras:* Very strong defensive lines built by
Wellington in the mountains which cross the
peninsula above Lisbon.
Albuera: General Sir William Beresford under Wellington's command met Marshal Soult at Albuera and
fought the bloodiest battle of the whole campaign.

CHAPTER 15

151 *snuffed:* Cut off the black charred end of the wick
to make a clearer, brighter flame.

CHAPTER 16

152 *acephalous:* Not having a head.

155 *Mina and Longa and el Marquesito:* There is many a
story still to be told of the exploits of these Spanish
guerillero leaders. El Empecinado and Temprano not
only raided the French but also helped the British in
a thousand ways, carrying messages, giving information, creating diversions, laying ambushes, and
rescuing British prisoners.

PAGE

157 *eighteen-pounders mounted on the wall:* This was a formidable defence as they could outshoot most guns likely to be brought against them. It also revealed that the walls were thick enough and strong enough to support the recoil of such heavy guns.

159 *the highly technical art of siegecraft:* Jorge made his plans from his own good sense, but they accord very nearly with all the expert thinking from the two previous centuries on siegecraft.

CHAPTER 17

162 '*covering party in skirmishing order:* Infantry free from heavy packs and equipment and lightly armed for night work.

parapet: Earth dug from the trench was piled in front of it to increase the effective cover.

164 *sap-head:* The end of the trench where digging continued.

165 *the French Guard:* The selection of these men and their training made them the élite of the French army. Famous for their discipline and endurance, they were Napoleon's greatest pride and he turned to them when most in difficulty or in danger. This was the Fourth Regiment of the Fusiliers of the Imperial Guard, the premier regiment of what was called the Young Guard.

*Jorge's engineer works at the siege of Salas. The scale of
the advance has been compressed in this diagram. The first
parallel was half a mile from the walls, the second a mere
200 yards.*

CHAPTER 18

171 *'the question'*: Skilled interrogation.

173 *the silver regimental eagle*: The French regimental standards were modelled on the eagles of the Roman Legions.

Wagram: 5 July 1809. The Emperor Napoleon with Marshals Masséna and Davout defeated an Austrian army under the Archduke Charles. At a critical point in the battle, Napoleon in the centre directed the concentrated fire of a hundred guns on the advancing Austrians and then smashed through with a column of 36,000 men.

Jena: 14 October 1806. At Jena Napoleon determined to break through the long precise lines of Prussian infantry by a direct frontal attack on a narrow front so that the opposing army would be broken before its strength had been fully engaged.

174 *Marengo*: 14 June 1800. Napoleon came over the Great St. Bernard pass into the plains of Lombardy and the Austrian army met him at Marengo. Napoleon had spread his forces in too wide an arc, and for a time the issue was in the balance. Then followed one of the most perfectly timed tactical operations of combined infantry, artillery and cavalry in the whole history of warfare.

Austerlitz: 2 December 1805. The Emperors of Russia and Austria lost on this day 30,000 men with all their artillery and stores: they were knocked out of the Third Coalition and Pitt in Britain gave up hope and died.

175 *his head from the drum*: The skins on the drum would magnify the sounds.

CHAPTER 19

178 *intelligent combination of the three arms:* Infantry can hold ground, artillery gives firepower, cavalry movement. Jorge uses all three in this way.

182 *skirmishers:* Skirmishers ran in front of the main columns and charged the enemy at random, so confusing his aim and taking his attention from the main attack.

183 *pas de charge:* Orders were given in battle by drumbeats.

voltigeurs: These were all short men, lightly armed, used to making forced marches quickly over long distances and to undertake military operations which bigger and more heavily armed men could not perform with the same nimbleness.

CHAPTER 20

188 *Almanac Imperial:* The Emperor Napoleon's Court Circular in which honours and promotions were published.

190 *Moniteur:* The Paris newspaper which had official backing and which gave detailed news of the latest exploits of the Marshals and Generals on the battlefield.

192 *foragers:* A working party out looking for food. The quest was endless.

193 *postern:* A door small enough to admit only one man at a time.

248 NOTES

CHAPTER 21CHAPTER 21

PAGEPAGE

194 *full uniform:* These beautiful uniforms were intended
to be worthy of the greatest Empire the world had
ever known. Younger men had to spend most of their
pay in keeping their uniforms correct to the latest
fashion.

the Imperial Staff: Moving and supplying thousands
of men on the roads of Europe needed careful plan-
ning. Napoleon's staff were chosen for their brains,
and many of his successes originated from their
paperwork.

astrakhan: The beautiful curly wool taken from newborn lambs.

195 *busby:* A tall fur cap with a flat top.

panache: A long plume of feathers of distinctive
colour.

196 *Chief of Staff:* General Darphin would act as second-
in-command to Bessières and see to the adminis-
trative, intelligence and operational work of the
headquarters.

198 *Tirailleurs:* Skirmishers. (See note to page 182.)

Fusiliers: Originally formed to escort and protect the
guns, they were given special flint-lock muskets, as
the old match-locks often dropped sparks which
sometimes fell in the open powder barrels. Later,
fusiliers were given the improved light musket and
used as high-grade infantry.

under orders to march south: The Gun and its followers had diverted three good divisions from reinforcing Masséna, who desperately needed them to use
against Wellington.

199 *Almeida:* Almeida and Ciudad Rodrigo were import-

ant fortresses guarding not only the roads into
Portugal but the roads back into Spain.

199 *Duke of Istria:* Bessières, the son of a surgeon.
Prince of Essling: Masséna, the son of a tanner and
soap-manufacturer.

CHAPTER 22

205 *Galician vaquero:* A herdsman or cowherd; here
possibly just a simple countryman.
sizzling end of the fuse: Shells were hollow iron
spheres packed with powder and with a long fuse to
the inside, trailing like a pig-tail.

A shell

214 *under side of the chase:* The chase of a gun is that part
between the muzzle and the trunnions.

CHAPTER 23

216 *glacis:* The steep slope from the bottom of the ditch
to the walls.

QUESTIONS

1. In what ways did Father Prieto show himself to be an unusual parish priest?
2. Why was el Bilbanito so successful as a guerillero leader and where did he fail when he had the gun?
3. What did el Bilbanito need to do before the gun in the quarry was ready to move into battle?
4. Compare the characters of Hugh and Carlos O'Neill and say why one was popular and the other was not.
5. "It was a blessing that Carlos had been able to move off at once in search of ammunition." Why was it a blessing and how did he accomplish his mission?
6. Describe the siege and capture of La Merced.
7. Was Major Jonquier in any way to blame for the fall of La Merced?
8. "Go up boldly against Leon . . . the hand of God is at work in Leon." Was this good advice which Brother Bernard gave to Carlos O'Neill?
9. Describe the events leading up to the death of Carlos O'Neill.
10. Write a paragraph on each of the following: El Platero; Alvarez; Don Cesar Urquiola.
11. How were a band of Spanish irregulars able to defeat a regiment of the French Imperial Guard?
12. What were Count Darphin's plans for the reconquest of Leon and how successful do you think they would be?

13. How did the gun change the character of Jorge?
14. "A talented engineer officer, set to besiege the fortress of Salas, would have acted just like Jorge." Write a report of Jorge's methods.
15. Write a short account of one of the following: British sea-power; Spanish priests; the French Imperial Staff.
16. What effect did the exploits of the Spanish irregulars, such as those described in this book, have on the major campaigns between Wellington and the French?
17. Write a brief account of the military value of the gun.
18. Is the story all the better for having no single hero whose life spans the book?
19. "A good way to learn history." Would you consider *The Gun* an adventure story, a military history, or both?
20. From reading this book, what have you learned of the nature of war and of the men who take part in wars?